Hush, Hush

G ABRIELLE   M ULLARKEY

TOWN
HOUSE
DUBLIN

First published in paperback in 1999
by

Town House and Country House Ltd
Trinity House, Charleston Rd
Ranelagh, Dublin 6

ISBN: 1-86059-103-5

Typeset by Typeform Repro, Dublin
Printed in Spain

Cover photo: Tony Stone Images
Cover design by Jason Ellams

Chapter One

'Who is it?' called Angela, teabag poised over cup. 'It's me!' yelled Rachel through the letterbox. 'When are you getting your doorbell fixed?'

Angela poked her head out of the kitchen and into the hallway. Rachel's pursed lips were framed on a canvas of blue air beyond the raised letterbox.

'Hang on, Rache, I'm coming. You're gusting in a freezing draught.'

Rachel hurried in, making exaggerated 'brrh!' noises. She was wearing a cream cashmere coat, a soft woollen scarf in rich baroque colours slung with casual care over both shoulders.

Since Robert's death, Angela had found Rachel's friendship both a tonic and a trial. Woman to woman, Rachel was sensitive to Angela's loss. But all her adult life, she herself had been resolutely single, with no discernible need for permanent male companionship.

Robert had only been gone a year and a bit. But one day soon, Angela half-feared, Rachel would launch a rearguard action, employing phrases like 'It's time to move on,' or even 'Mothball those widow's weeds, Ange! I know a bloke who's dying to meet you.'

They'd been friends since meeting at school, loosely united by the local mark of Cain – Catholicism – at

Wilmesbury girls' grammar, where black or Asian pupils were an exotic rarity, let alone Papists. Rachel's parents were posh, English Catholics, Angela's the despised Irish immigrant variety. Even among Rachel's family, Angela had felt like an interloper.

'How's it going?' asked Rachel in the kitchen, unwinding her scarf. 'Having a stick-your-head-in-the-oven sort of week, or a mustn't-grumble, could-be-worse sort of week?' She knew Angela well.

'Somewhere in between,' admitted Angela. 'Mum's been on at me to smarten up my act and go back to work.'

'Well,' began Rachel carefully, 'why don't you? I'm not suggesting you brave the fleshpots of London just yet. But how about temping locally?'

Angela slurped her tea. 'The old keyboard skills are a bit rusty after four years out of the rat race.'

'You never forget. It's like riding a bike. Or sex.'

Hastily, Angela changed the subject. 'I was hoping you'd come round to requisition me for mini-market duties. I could make a few quiches or wotnot.'

Each March, the church held a fete-cum-rummage-sale in the playground of the RC primary school, to raise money for CAFOD. Rachel had long been a stalwart stall-runner, organising a second-hand clothes stall with the same ease and dedication she applied to her job as an occupational therapist at Wilmesbury General Hospital.

Angela's mini-market role had always been peripheral. She guessed cake weights and bought bric-à-brac in the belief it was as blessed to spend as to get stuck in. Buying stuff at Rachel's stall was always a genuine pleasure. Many of the cast-offs came from Rachel's own wardrobe, which was infinitely superior to Angela's.

'Hands-on help is always appreciated,' smiled Rachel noncommittally. 'Don't slog your guts out making quiches, Ange. After the year you've had, no one expects…'

'…the Spanish Inquisition,' muttered Angela, slumping inwardly. She was thinking of her mother – again. She couldn't help it.

Mother and daughter were still recovering from the ordeal of Christmas Day, spent at Sadie's. Angela had cried a lot. It was her first Christmas without Robert. Sadie had been alternately soothing and helpless. During Angela's worst blubfest, post-sherry and pre-Queen's speech, Sadie had worn the look of a rabbit trapped in car headlights, albeit a rabbit wearing a star-spangled paper crown.

'Anyway, I'm off,' announced Rachel, draining the last of her tea. 'I only popped in on my way to the ossie. There's a job going there, you know. Secretary to three of the consultants. Can I tempt madam?'

Angela gulped. 'To be honest, I've already made moves on the job front,' she lied feebly.

'Ooh!' Rachel looked up eagerly. 'Anything doing?'

Angela tried to look mysterious and thoughtful. 'I've applied for a couple of jobs I saw in *The Guardian* this week. Thought I'd give the old sub-editing in London another try. The money's better than temping.'

'Good for you!' grinned Rachel. 'I know you hate London, but you might be right to get out of Wilmesbury on a day-to-day basis. I knew you could do it, Ange!'

Her encouraging shoulder-squeeze made Angela feel mortally depressed. She hadn't even bought *The Guardian*. Now she'd have to invent at least one interview and endure Rachel's sympathy when nothing came of it.

Rachel didn't know exactly why Angela hated London. Angela hadn't worked for the past four years. Not since the 'incident' on the Underground – at Tufnell Park on the Northern Line, to be precise. As assistant manager of

Hartley's, the travel agency in the High Street, Robert had earned enough to keep both of them in non-luxurious comfort.

Despite his playfully rotund features, Robert hadn't been an obvious heart attack candidate. He'd walked briskly to and from work. He'd been spared the early-morning scrum over the footbridge at Wilmesbury station for the half-hour train journey to Victoria that had normally taken Angela an hour.

After giving up work, she'd found it surprisingly easy to fill her days. She'd cooked meals for the first time in their marriage – proper meals instead of frozen blocks slung in the microwave. She wasn't much of a cook, but Robert had appreciated the gesture of real mashed potato and pan-fried cutlets after a hard day selling budget breaks to the plebs.

Angela had also done some GCSE English tuition, helping out a couple of kids as a favour to their parents. They'd waved away her protestations that she wasn't a teacher. She'd had a job checking the English on a women's magazine, hadn't she? That was good enough.

She and Robert had been so lucky that, in retrospect, it couldn't have lasted.

With Rachel finally on her way to work, Angela sat down on her saggy green sofa and cried.

It wasn't as if she had nothing to do. The saggy green suite needed replacing. But she didn't have the money to replace things willy-nilly.

Robert had died suddenly, nine years and six months into his latest job, without qualifying for the company's ten-year pension plan. As a couple, they'd never squirrelled away for rainy days. It wasn't that they'd thought themselves invincible. It was simply that time seemed infinite and money better spent when you were a late-thirties couple with no children and no intention of having any.

Drying her eyes, Angela looked around the room. The whole place was a bit tatty. On the far wall, the white undercoat glimmered through a thinning top layer of buttercream. The tacky painting over the fireplace gazed back at her, the Spanish urchin's fat crocodile tear glistening on his cheek like a crystalline wart. Robert had snapped it up at a house clearance. Angela had always hated it.

Maybe Sadie could give her a few pennywise redecorating tips. Sadie was always discovering stuff in skips. Only this month, she'd rescued a claw-footed chair and reupholstered it in rose-striped silk. 'What do you think?' she'd asked Angela, unveiling the chair on a recent visit.

'Lovely. Chippendale is it?' Angela couldn't refrain from asking.

Sadie had given her A Look. 'It's not for sitting on, mind. It couldn't take your weight.' This was more to do with woodworm than Angela's dimensions. She was a skinny creature anyway, just like her mother.

Angela decided to make a sandwich, but found the breadbin empty. She blew her nose self-pityingly. She had nothing to do all day, and still couldn't keep the breadbin stocked.

The kitchen cupboards yielded a stock cube and a tin of curried beans. She emptied the tin into a saucepan and sniffed suspiciously. Curry powder and baked beans seemed an unnecessarily explosive combination. 'Ingredients,' she read out loud on the back of the tin, 'starch, emulsifier, added sugar.'

Her mother's daughter, she tsked disapprovingly. Sugar was the preservative, no doubt. Sadie would've recommended straining out the sauce altogether, wherein lurked the dreaded sugar. But that was not Angela's way. In fact, she now felt determined to mop up every last drop of sauce with – the stock cube? Damn. She'd forgotten she had no bread. Memory like a sieve, she recalled belatedly. I don't have a sieve, either.

Sadie had those artful ways of mending and making do – boiling up soup out of chicken bones, stitching old bra cups into her bathing costume to make it last longer when the Lycra sagged – that were beyond Angela, child of the throwaway society. Sadie was proud of the fact that back in rural County Clare in the thirties, family members wasted not and wanted not by sharing each other's dentures, spectacles and bath water. When Angela's father died, Sadie had appropriated his reading glasses. Angela found this ghoulish.

Sadie rang while Angela was eating her congealed beans.

'Hello, Ma,' said Angela cautiously.

Angela loved Sadie. But it was a gift of love wrapped up in a thorny package of resentful childhood memories and dishonourable teenhood defeats. Added to this was guilt. Guilt that any half-decent daughter should love her mother unreservedly. Guilt that Sadie, the strong one for so long, was growing frail, and Angela was trying not to notice. Anyway, it wasn't fair. As a healthy, hearty, over-strict mother, Sadie had held the whip-hand. She wasn't getting the upper hand again, by virtue of an age and frailty that warranted respect and making allowances.

'Now then, Angela,' began Sadie. She had a low, growly, radio voice, lent added attractiveness by an Irish burr. 'Rachel told me you've got a job.'

'Bloody hell, that didn't take long!' exploded Angela – and not from curried beans. 'Talk about Chinese whispers. Rache only left here five minutes ago. That was fast work, even for you two.'

'Rachel was passing the bus-stop and gave me a lift home,' replied Sadie mildly. 'So have you got a job or not? Why tell her you had if you haven't?'

'I didn't! I said I was putting out feelers.'

Sadie waited.

'About sub-editing back on a women's mag in London,' growled Angela. 'And actually – you might as well know – I got an offer this morning. I didn't tell Rachel or even you, because I was weighing up the pros and cons.'

Sadie's bottom teeth did a little castanet dance of excitement. 'What's to weigh up, lovey? It'll do you the world of good to go back to work. Help take your mind off the last terrible year, and the money's a bonus, of course.'

In her house on the other side of Wilmesbury, Sadie grimaced at herself in the hallway mirror. She usually got foot-in-mouth disease talking to Angela. She sensed Angela's tense expectation of being insulted, however obliquely, and her responding nervousness usually obliged.

'Which magazine is it?' asked Sadie humbly.

'Er – well – oh God, my saucepan is boiling over, Mum. I'll have to go.'

'I'll wait while you turn it down.'

Angela clattered the receiver onto the telephone table and glared at it. Bloody hell, now what? She had to think fast.

She picked up the phone again. 'It's a new launch,' she said weakly. 'So everything's hush-hush. I can't even tell you the title until the first issue hits the stands. I haven't got an exact start date, either.'

'OK, lovey.' If Sadie smelt a rat, she was playing it deadpan. 'How about meeting up in town tomorrow for lunch? My treat, to celebrate your new job. I'm so proud of you! After all the ups and downs since Robert.' She honked emotionally into a hanky. 'Would you like that, Ange?'

'Er – great,' said Angela, feeling sick. 'I'll meet you outside Baggio's at one. Gotta go now. See ya.'

'Wait! And after lunch, I thought we'd look in the sale at World of Leather. Now don't argue, Angela. You need a new suite, and now you're earning... earning properly again, I mean... look, I know it's horrible throwing out stuff you chose together as a couple. Kind of a reminder you're moving on without him. Everything's tough, I know, when you're not long widowed.'

Practically chewing the phone cord in her desire to escape, Angela tensed. She translated 'not long widowed' as 'not able to cope.' Was Sadie implying that she'd never catch up with her in the coping with widowhood stakes? Well, Sadie had a five-year head start. Also, she'd been widowed at sixty-two when, reflected Angela, you were psychologically prepared, however subconsciously, for the sudden cull of your life partner.

'Interior design has been low on my list of priorities,' sniffed Angela. 'But I am prepared to refocus on the petty trivia of life. Suede or mock suede? That is the question. Whether 'tis nobler in the wallet to go for a colour that hides stains or just buy bigger cushions.'

'Don't be sarky, Ange.' Angela could hear real hurt in Sadie's voice. Straightforward abuse she understood. Sarcasm she did not.

'Sorry, Ma,' said Angela sincerely. 'I'd genuinely appreciate you casting a critical eye over the stuff in World of Leather. See you tomorrow.'

They hung up, mutually frustrated by the conversation.

Angela scoured her bean-studded saucepan, wishing she could wipe out her lie about the job just as thoroughly. Somehow, Sadie had forced her into it – ringing up, all agog, practically demanding that she'd got herself a job!

Oh hell, thought Angela, wringing her scouring pad instead of her hands. That won't wash. It's my fault. Mum asked me a perfectly direct question and I fluffed it.

She put the clean saucepan back in the cupboard and sat down in the darkening kitchen. She liked to sit in the dark a lot. Night was the perfect cover for minute self-analysis. Basically, where Sadie was concerned, Angela was a really thick lab rat. No matter how many times she reached the heart of the maze, she never made the connection between the electric shock and reaching for the cheese.

Sadie filled a bowl with cat food and dropped it on the kitchen floor. She didn't trust herself to bend from the waist. She might stick there, like those petrified people from Pompeii. Consequently, when the bowl fell to the floor, it wobbled like a tired whipping top and dark chunks of tuna-with-rabbit hopped onto the tiles.

Binky slunk in and nosed the escaped morsels fastidiously. He looked up at Sadie, awarding *nul points* for presentation.

'You know, she's getting back on track,' Sadie told him. 'She did enough crying on Christmas Day to irrigate Africa, but they say you have to cry it out before you work it out.' Sadie paused, unwilling to relive her own bereavement. 'Anyway, point is, she's turned the corner. Now, if she could find a nice man to look after her. I know, I know,' she muttered guiltily, as Binky looked at her again. She'd learnt to invest Binky's single expression with all the nuances pertinent to his role as devil's advocate. 'Robert's only a year dead. But if she waits too long, she'll be forty before she knows it. And I read somewhere, a woman can forget it after forty. Even men who are out there second time around have been snapped up. Still, she might meet someone in this new job.'

It was unusually secretive of Angela to apply for a job without a hint of her intentions. Maybe all those tears on Christmas Day had bucked her into a new year's resolution to start over. Good for her!

Sadie herself had felt pretty tearful on Christmas Day. Fenton wasn't there to make familiar jokes about her lumpy gravy, while Owen rang briefly on a scratchy line from Canada and sounded indecently happy not to be in Wilmesbury. She'd grieved for Robert because Angela was breaking her heart over him. She'd always thought Robert a nice, unremarkable man.

But even on their wedding day, a sneaky little serpent had bedded down in Sadie's bosom, hissing its certainty that Angela could've done better. Now, of course, Robert was beatified by untimely death. But the serpent went on hissing softly, no louder than waves brushing shingle. His death gave her a second chance.

Angela stood in front of the bathroom mirror, checking for lumps. Robert had liked this task, though his thoroughness couldn't be trusted. After cupping a handful, his eyes would grow hazy and lambent, his intentions clear.

Angela shut her eyes, probing for pea-shaped hardness.

Her hands slid down from her breastbone to the V of her knickers. She stroked her rough pubic hair, then she slid inside herself, finding her way with deft, piano-tuner fingers. Usually, she waited until she was alone in bed, in the dark, thinking of Robert. But she needed a DIY orgasm now, to blot out the great lie. Oh God, oh God! she groaned with longing and self-loathing, sweat running between her breasts. Why had she said it? Who in their right minds would employ a woman who'd been out of the workforce for four years? You're useless, oh come,

come, you useless slut, breathed Angela between gritted teeth.

But she was not totally useless, she reminded herself, as the heat of self-loathing subsided on a wave of self-gratification. She had managed to keep body and soul together in the previous year. If Rachel and Sadie thought her capable of landing a decent job, maybe she should start thinking the same.

The summer after A levels – the summer she met Robert – was also the summer that gave Angela her lifelong hang-up about seeking, and finding, a job.

She trailed home after her last exam, swinging her satchel in a heat haze, inhaling the sharp scent of mown grass and the mellower bouquet of freedom. As she meandered through the kitchen door, Sadie, thumping pastry on a worktop, looked up and said, 'Lal Doherty's got you into the frozen food place for six weeks. You start the day after you break up.'

'What? No way, Ma!' Jolted out of her reverie, Angela collapsed into a chair.

'Now don't let me down, love,' pounded Sadie. Her pastry-pounding was unnerving. She had a pugilist's blunt intent. 'Lal's pulled strings to get you into the wages office instead of the factory floor. Told them you were a bright girl, probably going to university, so they've taken you on without an interview. It's only making up pay packets and sorting out the canteen money for the bank.'

Angela slumped deeper into her chair, not even thinking of enlisting her dad. Sadie's word was law.

'You might've asked, Mum! I'm crap at maths – grade D remember? You know what'll happen. The first time I make a mistake, all these left-school-at-sixteen types will go, "I thought you had A levels" and, "So much for education, if you can't do a bit of long division in your head." Bloody, hell!'

'Oh now, don't be gutless, lovey,' cooed Sadie, letting the bad language go. 'I can't let Lal down.' That had always been the way with Sadie. She pretended (or believed) that it was she, not Angela, who would face the direst consequences of foiled plans laid on Angela's behalf.

It had taken Angela another couple of years to recognise this as emotional blackmail. She should've said, 'Stuff Lal Doherty. I never asked him to do me a favour, and this is my last summer before I have to go to work for ever, so I want to enjoy it.'

She'd already decided not to go to university. She'd pre-empted her decision by putting far-flung choices on her UCCA form. She'd had two offers, from Aberdeen and Lampeter (somewhere in Wales) and had no interest in going to either.

But instead of two-fingering Lal Doherty, Angela cowered inside her school blazer, nibbled a knob of raw pastry and knew she was beaten. The murphia had struck again.

The local murphia was a loose-knit but cohesive cabal of Wilmesbury-based Irish who scratched each other's backs whenever possible, county feuds carried over from home permitting. The murphia influence was vital in working-class jobs because anything vaguely middle-class and professional was quickly sewn up by the Order of Nicodemus, the Catholic church's answer to the Freemasons. In Wilmesbury, the order were also anti-Irish, ranged against the superstitious peasantry who gave restrained, royalist Catholicism a bad name. Rachel's father, a wealthy solicitor, had turned down an invitation to join the Order of Nicodemus. He was a member of the anti-Nazi league instead.

Lal Doherty's string-pulling for Angela was now ratified

and official. Moreover, if she welshed on the deal, a Nicodemite's daughter might sneak into the frozen food factory's wages office instead. Non-manual summer jobs were at a premium for students and school-leavers.

Angela's brother Owen (who was at university) worked each summer as porter at Wilmesbury Hospital. The previous summer, a nutter had stabbed him in the hand with a syringe. But frankly, Angela would've traded Owen a swivel-chair number at the frozen food factory for the casual violence of the NHS any day.

She started at the factory a week later.

She chafed against life's unfairness as she piled up verdigris'd coins under the baleful eye of Mags, the chief cashier, then popped them into polythene bags and finally into a blue cloth bag for Neville, the factory gofer, to take to the bank.

At the end of that first week, Mags and her colleagues, Joan and Florrie, made up the pay packets in silence, testimony to the solemn responsibility of their vocation.

Angela had her own little pile to do. After making up and sealing twenty-two pay packets, she noticed a fiver left over on her desk. Heat and a dull sense of terror surged through her abdomen, a terror not felt since she'd turned over an exam paper in the fifth year and realised she couldn't answer a single question.

'Oh my gawd,' said Mags, eagle eye alighting on the fiver, 'she's gorn and left some money out of a packet.'

'For fuck's sake,' puffed Joan. 'Ain't ye got the brains ye woz born wiv?'

Angela despised Joan. She despised stupid people who went through life stupendously ignorant of their own stupidity, and got chances to put down people like Angela, who spoke grammatically, recycled their empties and agonised now and then about the global distribution of wealth. Angela started to cry, without warning and without really caring.

'Oh there now, lovey, it's not the end of the world,' tutted Florrie, the oldest and kindest person in the office. Angela liked her. Florrie's husband was called Monty, and Florrie was able to keep a straight face while saying things like, 'My Monty's a martyr to his corns.'

'We'll have to undo those twenty-two packets and see who's a fiver short,' sighed Mags with the disdainful ennui of a bomb disposal team leader. 'It would be the end of the world, Florrie, if even one of those maggots on the floor came up so much as a penny short. Gimme those packets over here.'

Angela carried over the slippery little pile. This was even worse than her first-day fiasco of printing three hundred and twenty clock-cards upside down on the clock-card printing machine. 'D'ye think cardboard grows on trees?' Joan had shouted.

'I'm leaving,' announced Angela, depositing the pay packets and wheeling round to face the room.

The silence was not very stunned. 'Bout right 'n' all,' snorted Joan.

'You wasn't really cut out for it here,' nodded Mags, a shade kinder now that Angela had done her dirty work for her. 'We've years of experience between us,' she added even more gently, acknowledging that youth could be callow as well as thick.

Angela got her coat and left at once, the weight merely slipping from one shoulder to the other. There were now Sadie, Lal Doherty and the family honour to consider.

'Bye,' she said carelessly, closing the office door behind her.

'Take care, lovey,' called Florrie.

'Thick as pig shit,' observed Joan.

Angela walked home slowly in the wavery heat, kicking

stones. She'd made the discovery, long-suspected, that she didn't like working in an all-woman environment. This posed a problem, as office work beckoned in one form or another. Her only practical skills beyond anticipated A levels were stage two typing and eighty words a minute shorthand.

Sadie did her nut. There was much reference to ingratitude, failure to stick at things, and even (last resort stuff) offering up a horrible job for the souls in purgatory.

Angela sat on the settee, pretending to listen, but peeking at Tabby the cat, who was standing behind Sadie, four white socks neatly aligned, peeking back coquettishly through the arched window of Sadie's bow legs. '...find yourself something else to do, so I can let on to Lal that you got a better offer,' finished Sadie with a deflating sigh, like the air going out a Lilo.

'Fine. Rachel Cockburn's invited me to a wedding afters,' remembered Angela. 'She said I can stay with her for a few days as well. She hasn't got a poxy summer job cos her mum and dad want her to enjoy her last summer as a free woman,' she added daringly.

'The Cockburns! They're made of money,' retorted Sadie. It was shorthand for 'not our sort'.

'Well,' said Angela, edging out of the room before she delivered her final thrust, 'in that case, I'll warn them about standing too close to naked flames.'

She took a sleeping bag and her week's wages from the factory to Rachel's house on the posh side of Wilmesbury. Angela and Rachel had spent their school years sussing each other out. There'd been plenty of rows, imagined slights — Angela was particularly sensitive to the notion that she might be a project, a Harriet Smith to Rachel's sophisticated Emma — and shortlived break-ups followed by effusive returns to best friendship. It was only in the years since school that they'd become friends on more equal terms.

The wedding afters, held in a local hotel, was memorable for two key incidents. First, Angela got locked in a toilet cubicle in the Ladies at the pounding height of the evening disco. After rattling the bolt back and forth, it broke off in her hand. She shouted for ages above the steady throb of a distant drumbeat, before footsteps tapped her way.

'Help, I'm stuck!' she squeaked. 'The bolt thingy has come right off and I've cut my finger.'

'Hang on,' said a male voice. 'Stand back and I'll kick the door in.'

Angela cowered by the toilet bowl, thrilled.

Her rescuer kicked the door viciously and groaned. 'Must be made of solid titanium,' he growled in a face-saving mutter.

'Try again,' encouraged Angela, who knew the door was flimsy plywood. 'You nearly had it then.'

This time, when he kicked, his foot came right through the wood and waved about helplessly, trapped between jagged splinters.

'Stop kicking and I'll disentangle your foot,' ordered Angela and, grasping the polished black shoe, she shoved him outwards. She heard him collapse in a noisy heap on the other side. 'OK?' she called.

'Oh yeah, never better. I've just missed cracking my head on a sink.'

'Well, excuse me, but I'm still trapped in here,' snapped Angela. She was usually tongue-tied with boys, but it helped when you couldn't see them. It did occur to her that she might be making a fool out of a hunk. 'Actually,' she went on, eyeing the hole in the door, 'I can wriggle out through this gap. I'm pretty limber and my dress has no ruffly bits to get snagged. Here I come!'

She thrust her arms through the hole and began to clamber out, then twitched in surprise as white-cuffed hands encircled her waist. As he pulled her towards him, the continuing shock of his touch made her arms go limp and her legs unhelpfully stiffen. 'Jesus,' he puffed manfully, 'heavier than a sack of spuds.'

She gathered herself off the freezing floor tiles and wiggled her spaghetti-strap dress back over her hips. 'I'm actually quite small-boned and underweight for my height, not a sack of millet.'

Then she risked looking at him. Not a hunk – way too short for a start, and wearing an awful lilac-coloured cummerbund around trousers with mummy's boy creases. He explained later that the cummerbund was standard issue for the ushers, a job he'd been corralled into as a friend of the groom's.

But even at that first encounter, Angela had been mesmerised by his eyes. Deep brown eyes with chocolate-dark irises, fringed by girly lashes. They gave his ordinary face a soulfulness, a depth that she subsequently never tired of falling into.

His brown eyes met and held her prosaic grey-blue ones.

'Oi!' said a hotel person, stomping onto the scene and surveying the wrecked door. 'You'll have to pay for that. That's wilful destruction of property.'

'Huh, we should sue you for faulty door locks,' said Robert, standing up for both of them and using the magical 'we' pronoun. 'This lady's cut her finger badly. I assume you have a first aid box at reception?'

He successfully took command of the situation. That was the moment Angela fell in love with him.

A week later, Angela got a jiffy bag in the post, containing a limited edition tin of mints to celebrate the frozen food factory's centenary. It was clear from her scrawl on the compliments slip that Florrie had gone to courageous lengths: 'These mints were earmarked for you by management who didn't realise you'd left and I don't see why you shouldn't still get them even though the others wanted to keep them with the biscuits for elevenses.'

Angela had been saddened to see an obit for Monty in *The Wilmesbury Herald* a couple of years later.

Sitting up in bed, Angela flicked to the media section of her week-old copy of *The Guardian*. She still bought it now and then to check out jobs she didn't have the nerve to apply for.

She paused to agitate over an ad that she'd already ringed in half-hearted biro strokes.

Everybody loves *Goss!*
It's what makes the world go round.
Wanna be a part of our world?
***Goss!* is looking for a super sub who**
can spot a litiral at 50 paces, write
sassy heads and captions, keep to tight
deadlines and maintain a tip-top sense
of humour at all times.
Think you fit the bill?

Goss! was a downmarket women's weekly, big on makeovers, diets that let you eat chips, and tips on how to stuff cushions and lag pipes with rolled-up pairs of old tights. They were obviously desperate. Angela could tell from the sense of humour reference, though surprisingly, there was no mention of 'team member'.

Team-member was ad-speak for, 'must be prepared to be humiliated and crapped on by people who've been there longer than you, so they can get a bad mood out of their system.'

Angela was skilled at pretending to be a team member, though. It meant sloughing off every semblance of your individuality, like a snakeskin, the minute you revolved through that office door, and enduring the slings and arrows of some PMT-raddled cow (invariably your boss) without letting her see that you cared or that you fantasised about killing her.

Angela had actually worked for a male boss once. God, what a treat that had been, like the Elephant Man living it up on a colony for the blind. Lazlo, chief sub at *Woman Today*, had been gentle and patronising, compensating fitfully for his sexism by promoting Angela beyond her carefully concealed abilities.

He was nice to her and to his other female subordinates, because he didn't see women as his equals, and therefore wasn't threatened by them. Angela reckoned that all women were born equal in each other's eyes and would cheerfully slit each other's throats for the key to the stationery cupboard.

Oh Jesus, she thought, flopping back on her pillow, I have become paranoid in these last few years. I have allowed incidents from the past to grow out of all proportion. I shouldn't be so down on my own sex, the oppressed sisterhood. I should apply to the desperate people at *Goss!*, even having the nerve to spot their 'litiral' at fifty paces. I need a job, I need the money, I need to appease Rache and Mum in different ways.

Tomorrow, she'd dust off her CV. Tomorrow, she'd pen a letter that repaid the ad-speak with equally coded gimme-a-job-speak. The day after, she'd probably get the job by some freak of nature – first choice candidate killed by a dangerously swung cat or something. If that happened – if she got a job back in dreaded London – would it then be too late to stop the world and get off?

Chapter Two

The nice people at *Goss!* were desperate enough to call Angela for an interview. She didn't expect to get the job – didn't really want any job – but she'd go for the interview experience. She'd only applied to *Goss!* because its office was within walking distance of Victoria station. No Tube trains would be involved. She hoped.

There was always an outside chance that a suspect package would close Victoria on D-day. Then she might be re-routed to somewhere out of the way, like London Bridge and, as she'd never braved a London bus, that would leave the Tubes.

Angela tried not to panic unduly. On the one hand, it was stupid to worry about factors beyond her control. On the other hand, it was better to clench her buttocks in anticipatory readiness. It was like going to the dentist. If you dreaded a root canal and updated your will beforehand, you always got off with a scrape and a polish.

Of course, over lunch in Baggio's, Sadie was keen for more particulars of her new job.

'What's the hold-up with your start date?' she waded in over starters.

'No hold-up, Mum. It'll definitely be within the next couple of weeks.' By which time she'd have a convincing lie for the job's disappearance. The hush-hush new mag would come a cropper before the first fence. But why? She quite fancied citing a spectacular row between the editor and the publisher over launching the first issue with an exposé of the late Princess Di's allegedly kinky sex practices.

Sadie prodded a spring onion under her dentures. 'Will you be able to cope with the commuting to London? Remember, you gave it up four years ago because it stressed you out.'

'Needs must,' shrugged Angela uneasily. 'I daren't fail, with you and Rache nagging me to rejoin the rat race.'

Angela had never told Sadie about the Tufnell Park incident. Sadie believed that Angela had given up work because the stress and spiralling cost of commuting had outweighed her modest salary. And because Robert hadn't encouraged her to stick at it. 'Let's have no more talk of failure and nagging, lovey. You'll put yourself under pressure before the off. I agree with Rachel that temping locally might've been a gentler baptism.'

'So you've talked about me,' muttered Angela.

'We both care about you. You've become a bit of a recluse in that house. It's not healthy.' Sadie waved a salad-laden fork. 'Look at me. I felt like giving up after Dad died. But I got on with it, took that job at the newsagent's, readjusted. Of course...' she met Angela's hostile stare, '...it takes time. Nobody expects you to jump into a power suit and start running ICI.'

'That's a relief.'

'I think you should start this job with a "so what?" attitude. So what if it doesn't work out? With the initial experience under your belt, you'll gain the confidence to pick and choose applying for other jobs.'

'The mocha mousse looks nice,' said Angela.

Sadie gnashed her irritation into a lettuce leaf. 'Call me an interfering old biddy,' she hazarded.

'As if, Ma.'

'But I know the score, Ange. Sit and fester over what might've been, and you get out of bed one day and find a couple of years have whizzed past unnoticed.'

'Caused by a rift in the time-space continuum?'

'I'm only trying to help.'

'I know.' Angela banged the menu shut. 'For some reason, the more you and Rache try and help me, the more I resent the pair of you. I'm just an awkward customer at the moment. Please try and forgive me.'

Back home, Angela wrote out a small cheque for Sadie's favourite charity. She agreed with Sadie on one thing. There were always people worse off than you, and if they couldn't benefit from your days of smug contentment (when you forgot their existence), it behoved you to remember them when personal misery came to call.

She caught the nine-fifty to Victoria. The commuter rush had passed and there was a leisurely day-tripping atmosphere among the backpackers and ladies who lunched. Angela sat carefully upright in her suit. It had seen better days.

She was tall, long-boned and sallow, not suited to lilac. But at least the suit was clean and pressed and, what was more important, went with her only pair of dressy shoes.

They were cream, square-heeled court shoes, bought six years ago for Rachel's wedding-that-never-was. After Rachel had changed her mind at the eleventh hour and given Kevin the boot, Angela had mothballed the shoes. She wasn't sure why. She did think Rachel mad to dump Dr Kevin Whitaker. Tall and dark with a killer smile, he was the archetypal hero of the hospital romance he'd kindled with Rachel.

Rachel could be hard on men, thought Angela, tucking

one cream shoe over the other. Kind men eventually bored her, handsome men were too much competition (in Angela's silently held opinion), rough trade no more than a temporary distraction. But then, Rachel wasn't looking for Mr Right and roses round the lintel. She was hooked on variety, the spice of life – and that tended to jade the palate quickly.

Angela fidgeted on her seat. It seemed ages since she'd visited London by train. Now and then, she and Robert had driven up to take in a show. But his heart was never in it. He hated the traffic and fell asleep before intervals. *Les Misérables* made so little impression on him that, by the following week, he was convinced it was *Cats* that they'd seen. They'd argued pointlessly until Angela dug out the programme.

Angela had sold the car after his death. It cost too much for a non-driver to tax and insure.

She flattened her forehead against the window as the train slid into Victoria station, shrieking brakes startling a flock of pigeons out of the rafters. Angela's heart quickened. The immensity of London, reflected in the boastful masonry of its Victorian railway stations, oppressed her once more.

On the concourse, a respectable-looking man, using Sadie's index for such things, was kicking a chocolate dispenser. Builders mooched atop the inevitable scaffolding. Scurrying dots converged at the Underground sign, occasionally colliding and twirling in a brief dance of platform rage.

Angela hurried, head down, out of the station. London flowed past her and soared above her. The air was pungent with an over-succulent potpourri of chip fat, exhaust fumes and roasting coffee.

She reached the rambling gothic façade of Marchbank Publishing – in days of yore an alms house – with inflamed nerve-ends, but its carpeted foyer and smiling receptionist soothed her. That was, until the receptionist buzzed *Goss!* and announced, 'Mizz Carmody's here for her eleven-fifteen.'

'Carbery,' mouthed Angela.

The receptionist put down the phone. 'Take the lift to the second floor, Mizz Carmody, and somebody called Marla will meet you there.'

Marla Symonds was chief sub-editor of *Goss!*

Angela practised her death's-head grin in the lift mirror. Who would stick their hand out first for the handshake? If she did it simultaneously with Marla, there might be an embarrassing collision of fingers, like warring stick insects.

Just as the lift doors opened, Angela noticed that one half of her blouse collar was poking over her jacket lapel. She prodded it back into place and found Marla's hand swooping down to shake hers. 'Hello, I'm Marla! Thanks ever so for coming in to see us.'

Wasn't that the brush-off speech at the end of the interview?

'Thanks for having me,' mumbled Angela and cringed.

Marla didn't seem to notice. Her sensible shoes tapped efficiently down a narrow corridor, Angela following in her wake because there wasn't room for two abreast. This meant that Marla had to toss smalltalk over her shoulder and Angela had to field it back deftly. 'Smooth journey getting in?'

'Oh yes, very smooth.'

'That new rail link thingy makes all the difference.'

'Absolutely.'

'Well, here we are. Tea or coffee?'

'Neither, thanks,' beamed Angela, dry lips cracking. Cups of tea and coffee, like squishy chairs, were best avoided. Too much scope for slopping and flailing. She was four years out of this game, but she wasn't a complete greenhorn.

In Marla's tiny, chaotic office, the large and horsy Marla pored over Angela's CV, apparently reading it for the first time. She looked up and smiled invitingly. 'Tell me a bit about yourself.'

For pete's sake, screeched Angela's desperado inner voice, all about myself is on my CV, you silly bint!

'Well,' she began, folding her hands on her lap, 'as you can see, I was widowed fairly recently. I gave up my sub-editing job four years ago to, um, assist my husband in his car dealership business, but before that, I had a lot of varied experience in the magazine industry. I love subbing,' she lied, with solemnly sincere eye-contact.

Marla nodded. 'So, you were helping hubby with the books and admin, that sort of thing?'

Angela nodded modestly. 'It was a small-time operation, but it kept us ticking over. I had to wind things up after Robert died.'

This lie was strictly functional. No prospective employer would be impressed by the Tufnell Park incident. Thankfully, Lazlo had waved her off four years ago with a glowing reference and a kindly-meant plea to 'get some therapy.'

'You're very brave,' said Marla, eyes pools of professional sympathy. 'It's not easy re-entering the fray after a lay-off. I took a year out after my baby, and found it hell on wheels getting back into the old routine. You wouldn't mind if we give you a little subbing test? Sorry the photocopy's not the best quality but any probs, give me a shout.'

Alone in Marla's office, Angela studied the photocopied article she was required to edit for length, sense, grammar and spelling. The photocopy was so dim in parts that she

had to guess the end of paragraphs. Maybe it was also an
initiative test.

Her tights were scratchy with heat on her inner thighs
and she wanted to leave that second, but Marla's office
was glass on two sides and even her body language might
be under scrutiny. She straightened her shoulders, picked
up her blue marker and began.

Angela liked an interview to be followed up by a letter.
Phone calls threw her. When Marla rang two days after
the interview, Angela was about to poke a knife into her
toaster in search of a slice that had never popped out.

'Angela, it's Marla Symonds. Listen, we'd like you to
join the team, if you'd still like to join us.
Congratulations!'

'Er – wow – thanks.'

'I assume you're available for an immediate start? We
should've discussed it at the interview, but it's all hands
to the pumps, and we could do with an experienced sub
a.s.a.p. Does the day after tomorrow suit?'

'Yes – I mean no! Oh boy, Marla, you've caught me
out with such a swift comeback. You see, I booked a
holiday a few weeks back, you know, before I saw the ad
for the job. I'm going – tomorrow – for two weeks.
Sorry.'

A tiny pause lasted an eternity. Marla was pissed off.
Marla was withdrawing her offer. 'Fine!' said Marla,
perhaps too chirpily. '*Nil problemo* at all. You'll be
refreshed after your break and we can work you like a
slave. Hah! Only joking. Going anywhere nice?'

'Canaries,' supplied Angela crisply. Good choice. She'd
have been caught out with a destination that closed down
for the winter.

'Right, I'm just readjusting my diary,' murmured

Marla, flapping pages her end. 'See you on Monday the sixth then, nine thirty. Don't do anything I wouldn't do!'

'Sure won't, Marla!'

God, why did people say that? She couldn't imagine doing anything that Marla, with her robust, loose-limbed horsiness, wouldn't do in a flash.

Angela sat down on the stairs, heart thumping. She'd lied out of panic (again!), as soon as she'd heard the word 'team'. She'd never expected to get the poxy job, and now she'd have to leave herself in reception every morning, and grin with new-girl eagerness to please, at least for the first few weeks.

But with two weeks' grace, why not go on holiday? A week would do. Ian Bradley, manager of Hartley's, had begged her at Robert's wake to pop in any time and avail of an under-the-counter bargain.

No time like the present, she decided, with a spurt of adrenaline. After all, somebody wanted to employ her! She did a little dance of self-importance. She could afford to bask in the moment, before reality kicked in and forced her to consider rail ticket prices, wildcat strikes, leaves on the line, unpaid overtime and being called no fun at the Christmas party.

Angela pushed open the door of Hartley's. It would always give her a wrench to come in here. Magdalena looked up from Robert's desk and smiled. Angela's heart froze. Magdalena had a degree in leisure and tourism, woefully under-used booking fly-drives to Florida and booze-ups to Ibiza. She also had great dark, soulful eyes, courtesy of an Italian mother, and an air of obdurate humility that got Angela's goat. Since Robert's death, Magdalena had been promoted to his job.

Now, as Magdalena's liquid eyes settled on Angela, they brimmed à la Spanish urchin over the fireplace. 'Mrs

Carbery – Angela – what a lovely surprise! How can I help you?'

Angela took a deep breath. 'Actually, Magdalena, I came to see Ian. Nothing personal,' she lied.

Ian Bradley bobbed out of his back office. 'I'll deal with Mrs Carbery, Magdalena. Pull up a chair, Angela. What can we do for you? You're looking splendid, considering all you've been through.'

Ian was a man with the right word for every occasion. Robert had made fun of him, but Angela liked to give him the benefit of the doubt. He was plump and shiny, like a sausage about to burst its skin. A forty-something bachelor, he lived with his mother, wore slightly outré ties and called women of a certain age, susceptible to flattery, 'bonny hens'.

'I need a cheap week somewhere hot, at short notice,' explained Angela.

'Let's see.' He spread brochures over his desk. 'Lanzagrotty? Not your scene. I see you somewhere more – sophisticated.' He sat back and narrowed his eyes to visualise Angela in this context.

She fidgeted. 'I don't think budget bookers can afford to be sophisticated. I'm afraid it's straw donkeys and sangria by the funnel over yachts cruising the Aegean.'

'OK. Morocco. It's up and coming, but not too pricey. And the lager louts find it too foreign.' He pushed a brochure towards Angela. As she studied a picture of Agadir, his plump finger slid against her wrist.

Angela drew back as if scalded. 'Fancy it?' grinned Ian.

'Pardon?'

'The Hotel Maroc, Agadir. I can wangle a week at short notice, with no single supplement.' He paused. 'Maybe we could discuss it over a late lunch.'

'I can't. Is that the time?' She leapt up shakily. 'I'm meeting my mother for lunch. I'll take the hotel wotsit, leaving whenever. I'll ring you when I get home to go over the details. Thanks so much for your help, Ian.'

Outside, Angela drew a deep breath. She hadn't imagined that fat finger. He was Robert's boss, for pete's sake! While she was obviously carrion for every circling vulture. Bloody hell! No longer giving Ian Bradley the benefit of the doubt, Angela stomped towards Boots in search of suntan lotion.

Climbing out of the pool, she reached for her large beach towel. The Hotel Maroc in the sun-kissed resort of Agadir was a low-key, three-star place, its poolside patrolled interchangeably by lugubrious waiters and cats, on the respective lookout for tips and scraps. Angela preferred the cats.

Encased in her towel, she scurried to her room to prepare for that afternoon's half-day excursion to a Berber village in the mountains.

It was brilliant being so far away from the richly imagined team at *Goss!* But she was missing Robert with a physical pain.

At a rational level, she'd known how difficult this would be – her first holiday alone, after a year spent pottering no further than the town centre.

She was thrilled that she'd reached Morocco at all without a major panic attack at the airport. It was the thought of Sadie's likely reaction to any *volte face* decision – disappointment hardening to impatience – that had buoyed her up.

But now, actually on holiday, the vibrancy of the place struck a forceful reminder that Robert wasn't there to feel the sun on his back and rub factor thirty into hers. She'd already found nicknames for the other hotel regulars, a favourite game of theirs on holiday.

'That's Cat-shooer,' she told Robert now, leaning on

her balcony and pointing down to the bodies arranged
under the fringed spheres of poolside umbrellas. 'He shoos
away every poor kitty who comes looking for food.
Though one day, he tried to fob one off with a chip
dipped in ketchup! There's Big Boobs with her Danielle
Steel. She's been wearing the same tight top since she got
here, just in case anyone's failed to notice what eye-
pokers her bazookers are.'

She broke off her bitchy litany to ponder a sobering
thought. What did the other holidaymakers call her?
Stand-offish Woman? Pubic Hair Eruption? Every time she
thought her bikini line was under control, she'd emerge
from the pool with long, dark stragglers stuck to her
thigh. Maybe couples talked about her, lying in bed at
night with the balcony doors open to the heat, giggling,
'Have you seen that funny old trout on her own who
treads water in the shallow end? Old man bolted, d'you
reckon?'

Angela sat down on the room's single rattan chair, and
had a brief, cathartic cry. Deep down, though, she felt
proud of herself.

She'd chatted to people in the bar most nights, she'd
even got up and danced with a curly dagger strapped to
her waist at the 'Moroccan dinner under canvas' in the
hotel garden. She'd resisted the urge to court pity and
admiration by confiding her widowhood to casual
acquaintances like Renee and Norm from Bromsgrove,
who'd clocked her wedding ring but made no comment
on it.

I am a presentable thirty-eight, thought Angela firmly,
blowing her nose and stirring herself to put on trousers.
She remained too white and goosepimply to risk her single
pair of shorts.

At least on excursions (this was her third), she could
sit at the back of the coach and draw Robert's attention

to the tree-climbing goats and the village women in biblical blue, balancing pots on their heads.

She waited outside the hotel for the coach, checking the pile of coins in her battered leather purse. Wherever you went as a foreigner, you were accosted as a matter of routine by old, apologetic men, young, impatient men, excited children and breast-feeding mothers, all with hands outstretched for alms. Angela was happy to oblige. She felt she was giving something back, however small, in return for exploiting their country in the fatuous pursuit of picturesque palms, teeming souks and Technicolor sunsets.

The tour coach was late. Eventually, a battered Land Rover drew up and a huge man swung his brown legs out of the driver's seat. 'Car Berry?' he asked in mellifluous foreign tones, and Angela's heart sank.

'I'm Angela Carbery. Where's the rest of the tour?' she squeaked.

'You're the only one,' he smiled kindly, 'so we go by car instead. We can go further up the mountains in car. You see more.'

So, this personalised service at no extra cost was Angela's treat.

She slid about in the back of the Land Rover, an unlashed cargo of arms and legs, while big, brown Habib careered round mountain hairpins and kept his eyes fixed on her, delivering an informative commentary on tribal conflict, flowering desert and average rainfall. 'To your left, you see a typical rock formation,' he shouted above the engine rev. 'No Mr Car Berry then?'

God, she'd wondered when he'd get to this. 'Didn't come with me,' she yelled back evasively. Handsome nosy git!

By the time Habib had led her round a souk and blocked a road with the Land Rover so she could

photograph a donkey with a determined glint in its eye
that reminded her of Sadie, Angela was thawing out a bit
towards him. He was direct, not nosy. And she was too
hard on Arab men. They were probably no bigger sexists
than Lazlo.

Habib bought her sweet black coffee in a cafe
overlooking date-palmed gorges, before the return trip to
the hotel. He told her, casually, that he was looking for a
western wife. 'Why? Easier to browbeat?' probed Angela
controversially.

Habib smiled his man-sized smile. 'Because they live
their own lives. I don't want to have to make all the
money.'

'Maybe you could just marry it.'

'Oh, if only I could.' His smile grew wider, and
Angela realised that he was teasing her as much as she was
teasing him. She relaxed. 'So it's not economically viable
to follow Muslim tradition and have four wives?'

'Only for the rich,' grimaced Habib. 'And just think,
four mothers-in-law! Not a problem for your husband, I
think.'

'He's dead, actually. I'm a widow, but not a rich one.
I have to work.'

Habib's face expressed regret, understanding and
admiration, in the correct sequence. 'But you are young
enough to marry again.'

'That's what my mother reckons.'

'Your parents live?'

'Only Mum. She's a widow too, but it's not such a big
social gaff at her age. People react as if I must've killed
off Robert by nagging or working him to death.'

'And now you live with your mother?'

Angela's cup trembled its way onto her saucer. She
hadn't anticipated the question. 'Not bloody likely!
Anyway, she wouldn't live with me. We'd be at each

other's throats inside three days. She does her own thing, still works part-time, and she'd never leave her house to move in with me. She's lived there forty-three years and knows every ruck in the lino. My brother and I were even born at home.'

'What does your brother do?'

Relieved at the change of subject, Angela flopped back in her canvas chair. 'He's a bit of a case, to be honest. He emigrated to Canada when he was twenty-one, married a Canadian, and took her name, if you don't mind. Dad said nothing, so we knew he was hurt. Owen asked Mum if she minded, but she said, "Do what you like, I only borrowed the name by marriage. I still regard myself as Sadie Dignan." We don't know the ins and outs because we're not there in Canada, but it seems his wife got him to ditch his Irish surname. It's Feeney, you see. Doesn't go with black tie dos and charity lunches at the yacht club, where his wife's a member.'

She sneaked a look to see if Habib had nodded off.

His big smile was back in place, as wide and gleaming as the vista before them. He'd probably only half-followed her ramblings, but he was her favourite kind of therapist. A stranger whose approximate grasp of English shortened his attention span, filtering out juicier indiscretions. 'I drive a different way back to show you sunset,' he said.

'OK,' smiled Angela, feeling shriven and reckless. He could now hurtle off a hairpin bend into the blue oblivion if he wanted. She felt like she'd just made her last confession, and if he did sheer off a precipice, there'd surely be time for a gabbled act of contrition before the airborne Land Rover bit the dust.

Habib delivered her safely back to the hotel, though later that evening, as she eased her aching bottom into a restaurant chair, she drew disapproving looks from the Zimmerframe brigade. Some of them had probably seen her take off with Habib for the afternoon and speculated, when the canasta and gin-rummy palled, that she'd hired him for a private rogering session. Let them think what they liked. Truth was, big men had big private parts (allegedly), and Angela was scared of big privates. Too much like squeezing the Titanic through the Panama Canal for her liking.

That night, as the sun set over her balcony, she wrote her postcards.

'You were right about me being a recluse,' she conceded on Sadie's, a picture of a donkey. 'I hope to return a new woman.'

Rachel got a fat, moustached water-seller in national costume. 'Don't fancy yours much, Rache. Nobody's pinched my bum yet, but can't decide if that's good news or bad.'

That Saturday, she bagged a window seat on the flight home. She kept her head down, reading about snowboarding in Aspen in the in-flight mag. She had an absolute belter of a headache malleting the side of her nose. She shut her eyes and turned in to the window, wedging her poor, sore nose against the glass. Someone came and sat next to her. She cared not. The stewardess asked for her attention during the safety demo. Angela withheld it.

When the in-flight meal arrived, steamed up redly under its plastic cover, Angela discovered that she could be hungry if she put her mind to it. She peeled back the cover, prodded and sniffed.

'Breast of chicken in tarragon sauce with pasta underneath,' said the man next to her, reporting expertly on his first mouthful. 'Not bad, if you've had nothing to eat in the last ten hours but a Rich Tea biscuit.'

'Would you like mine then?' asked Angela timidly. 'I don't care for meat much.'

'You could eat the pasta underneath,' said the man, his soft burr obscured by chicken. Was he Cornish? Scottish?

'The pasta will taste of chicken,' sniffed Angela.

'My, my, aren't we fussy?' snorted her companion. 'Don't mind if I do.' He pounced on her meal.

Angela turned to glare at him. What a Neanderthal! He was a scruffy brute of a man, unshaven, and shovelling in pasta like a mechanical digger. He also whiffed of something indefinable, but definitely not aftershave.

He saw her wrinkling nose. 'My jumper smells of fish,' he said with his mouth full. 'Spent the last twelve hours on a smack so I could get to Agadir airport in time for this flight. It won't be putting you off, as you're not eating.'

'You're Irish,' she realised.

'Guilty as charged. Irish, ugly and smelling of fish.' He grinned and pasta-smeared white teeth glimmered out of his nut-brown face. 'Not exactly holiday romance material. Do you want that unidentifiable dessert? I think custard may be a key component.'

'Be my guest.' He wasn't ugly, actually. Just blunt and covered in travel-dust. And very hungry.

Pain lanced through Angela's head. 'Jesus,' she whispered and slumped forward over Fish-Jumper's second meal.

'Jesus, Mary and Joseph,' he expanded. 'You OK? You having a turn or something? Shall I call a stewardess?'

'My lens!' Angela tipped her head back and blinked. She blinked again at Fish-Jumper and shook her head. He was still a complete blur. 'I've lost a contact lens!' she panicked. 'I think just now, when I leant over the tray. It's in your food!'

Fish-Jumper picked up a plastic fork and began trawling

through soggy pasta. 'Not like that! You'll shred it!' wailed Angela.

'Very bloody sorry, Missus.' He put down the fork and glowered.

'Oh my God, I'm not insured and they're only six months old. Why did it have to happen to me?'

'The great philosophical question of our times,' observed Fish-Jumper, folding his arms. 'Got a pair of glasses to put on?'

'Don't be stupid!' snapped Angela. 'You can't see through glasses when you've still got a contact lens in.'

'I stand corrected. Why bother, anyway? They're so fiddly. They fall down the U-bend, get hoovered up, slip round the back of the eye and rot there. What's the point?'

'To look good!' goggled Angela, looking anything but good (she knew) as her lensless eye wavered and wept. A hundred quid's worth of wafer-thin plexiglass was currently basting in tarragon sauce that no amount of fizzy build-up tablets would remove. 'And they can't go round the back of your eye. Especially not mine, because they're soft, and when you bung them in, they just float around until they find where they're meant to be and settle there.'

'And take out a mortgage, I suppose.'

'You're no help!' snarled Angela, wincing as she touched her forehead.

'Yeah, you're right,' acknowledged Fish-Jumper after a pause. 'If you need help at the other end, I can put you on a bus or call a taxi for you or whatever.'

'Mind your own business!'

'OK, OK, keep your hair on,' he retorted, in a much milder tone. 'I can see you're tired and emotional. Look, I'll go through this tray very carefully. I've already found a rogue hair.' He lapsed into a concentrating silence. She was vaguely aware of his index finger excavating the chicken and pasta with patient thoroughness.

Her heart choked her at the spectacle she'd reduced herself to. 'There's no need, really,' she sighed, flaunting her desperately recovered equilibrium. 'Look, I'm sorry I was so rude and snappy. The lens is gone for good, and I'm calling off the search. These things happen.'

'Especially to you, right?'

She bridled. Was he goading her, laughing at her or just sneering at her?

When the plane landed, he grappled down her luggage from the overhead locker and deposited it on her foot in the aisle. 'Can you manage?' he asked ungraciously.

She just growled, grabbed her suitcase handle and trundled away.

At the carousel, they took up positions at opposite ends. Typically, Angela found herself furthest away from the point of luggage disgorgement.

She seized her navy holdall off the belt and threw it on to a trolley with a casual toss that nearly dislocated her arm. Then she made her exit towards the pick-up point where Rachel was meeting her. Her dignified exit was spoilt a bit by the trolley's wonky wheel. She found the only way to reach 'nothing to declare' was to point the trolley towards the gents' toilet. And she still had a headache.

Chapter Three

'But the main thing is, you enjoyed yourself,' said Rachel. Angela sighed. 'I've been going on, haven't I? You must be dying to get home to your own bed.'

'Not yet, Ange. I'm intrigued by this bloke you met on the plane.'

'Oh, Fish-Jumper. What's so intriguing about him?'

Rachel had come in after driving Angela home. Now, as they lingered over late-night coffees laced with brandy, Angela still chafed inwardly over her lost contact lens. The lone survivor was safely potted in the bathroom.

'Fish-Jumper,' she recalled, 'hoovered up two in-flight meals like an industrial nozzle, and my lens with them.'

'Yes, but why was he on holiday alone? Why did he need a lift to the airport on a fishing smack?'

'I dunno. Probably smuggling hashish in his turn-ups and reckoned customs at Heathrow would leave him alone if he whiffed of the EU mackerel quota.'

'There's got to be more to it.' Rachel's gaze settled on the middle distance with a matchmaking gleam that Angela knew and dreaded.

Rachel, currently between admirers, sat with casual elegance on Angela's unravelling wicker chair, one golden leg folded beneath the other. Her body boasted a pre-Christmas tan from Jamaica. Though it was winter and

Rachel went without tights, she never sported plucked-chicken legs, and wicker splinters knew better than to sink into that peach-glow skin.

'Look, Rache, I'm just like you,' pretended Angela desperately. 'I don't need a man to look after me. I am coping. I start a new job on Monday, remember.'

'I'm sorry, Ange, but I'm with your ma on this one. You do need a man's protective custody. You're not weak or anything, you're just – a lot more yourself in a couple.'

'I could be very insulted by that.'

'Don't be. You know something? I wish I wanted a soulmate. I get tired of flitting from flame to flame, getting my wings singed.'

'At least you're an exotic sort of moth,' grumbled Angela. 'Even if I was a butterfly, I'd be a cabbage white.'

It was Sunday morning. Examining a shaving nick in his bathroom mirror, Conor McGinlay thought about the daffy woman on the plane.

Daffy or not, he'd been rude and ungracious. He was out of practice, talking to women socially.

'You getting up?' he yelled into the space behind him. 'I'm only offering once! If you want a cooked breakfast, speak now or forever hold your peace.'

He cocked his ear for the usual assenting grunt. He heard nothing.

The house wasn't too much of a tip, considering his two-week absence. Mrs Turner had polished his hardwood floors and maple doors with zeal. The house was her pride and joy, too.

Blood dripped into the sink. He blotted his chin roughly with toilet paper. God, he wasn't exactly an oil painting before adding lacerations. His best feature, according to Kate, was his expression. A brooding animal

expression. Big deal. An expression was hardly likely to
see you into old age, the way a mellowing, even sagging
collection of half-decent features would.

Right now, his animal expression was knackered
bloodhound. He'd worked nights as well as days on the
logistics of the Hotel Paradise Beach. The contractor had
a mass market vision of paradise: five hundred and ten
rooms, a vast restaurant bisected by an artificial waterfall
and a lobby bigger than Agadir airport. The waterfall was
the real nightmare. Still, work kept his mind off other
things.

He padded out of his *en suite* bathroom and down the
gleaming staircase, enjoying, as he did every morning, the
simple elegance and spacious modernity of his dream
home. His hand caressed the banister rail, as cool and
silkily curved as the hollow of a woman's spine. 'Sausages,
fried bread and fried mushrooms coming up!' he yelled in
a town crier voice. 'This really is your last call,
lazybones!'

At the foot of the stairs, he frowned. His luggage lay
piled untidily in the hallway. On the top was a small case
he didn't recognise.

The phone eventually woke Angela. She opened one eye,
panicking. Was it Monday morning already? She squinted
at the clock radio, her other eye refusing to open. Her
lids were gummed together with weepy stuff. The phone
went on ringing.

Angela half-tumbled down the stairs, cursing her
blurred vision and lack of a phone extension. Wearily, she
lifted the receiver.

'You're back then,' accused Sadie. 'I thought you'd
ring last night when you got in.'

'Wasn't up to it, Mum.' She recounted the lens saga.

'And the eye it fell out of is still giving me gyp like you wouldn't believe.'

'You'd better see an optician first thing in the morning.'

'I can't. I've got *Goss!* tomorrow.' She hardly wanted reminding first thing on Sunday morning. She'd planned to start getting depressed about four in the afternoon.

'I'll come round and make you lunch,' decided Sadie. 'See you at oneish.'

'That's only an hour from now! There's no need.' The line went dead.

Angela stared at the phone furiously. She'd never got a chance to go to plan B – pretending that she wanted her afternoon free to visit the cemetery, alone.

Actually, she had to be in an upbeat mood to go anywhere near the cemetery. If she went along feeling the least bit cynical, all that dripping stone Victoriana and the desolate cries of crows (buzzards?) wheeling overhead plunged her into an ultimately fruitless search for reasons to believe in an afterlife.

Catholics were buried at the far end of Wilmesbury cemetery, a good half-mile walk through an avenue of sombre yews. And when she reached the Catholic section, she was forced to indulge two griefs for the price as one, as Robert was buried only two rows behind her father.

She'd stand with head bowed, her bitterness at their comparative ages wrestling the demon guilt. A stranger wouldn't have read Fenton's headstone (Fenton Feeney, 1919–1991, 'Taken from us too soon') without remarking on his good innings compared to that bloke two rows back (Robert Anthony Carbery, 1958–1996, 'Dust has its sweetness too,' whatever the hell that meant. Pressed to supply a headstone soliloquy at short notice, a shell-shocked Angela had simply stuck a pin in the undertaker's Patience Strong almanac. In retrospect, she'd have preferred, 'Snuffed out before his time. Thanks a lot, God.')

Angela tottered back upstairs, her gummed-up eye as stubborn as a clam.

She ran cold water into the bathroom basin, and plunged downwards. When she came up for air, gasping, her eye finally popped open. It stared back at her from the mirror above the sink, threaded with veins, but mysteriously well in focus. Then she realised why.

Beyond the blue rim of her iris shone the silvery rim of her contact lens. It had been there all the time; the cold water had floated it back into position! It had popped off on a detour, despite all she'd said to Fish-Jumper.

Scrabbling it out and into her lens bottle, she didn't know whether to feel relief or anxiety that she'd slept a good twelve hours with a foreign body rattling round her orbital socket.

'For God's sake, try to stop worrying,' murmured Robert inside her head.

She sat down on the toilet lid, suddenly weepy with nostalgia. On Sunday mornings, he'd always got up first and made rounds of toasted cheese. Straining her ears, she could even hear the grill pan tinkle downstairs.

Slowly, she rose and went to get dressed.

She'd kept him in the living room for the week before the funeral, in a closed casket. She'd asked Sadie to stay for the week, partly for the company and partly to keep Robert's mother at bay, farming her out to a sympathetic neighbour. Robert's mother, who'd made the journey from Wales, didn't approve of bodies in the house and other Catholic mumbo-jumbo.

On the night of his homecoming, Angela had a vivid dream of Robert climbing out of the casket to come upstairs and sleep in his bed where he belonged. She'd woken suddenly in the wee hours, already damp with sweat, alerted by creaks on the stairs.

She'd stared at the door handle a long time, panic clawing with hope, but the creaks fell silent, the door handle stayed unturned. She'd never told Sadie. Sadie had a robust impatience with ghosts.

Once dressed, Angela wandered downstairs. She stared at the grill pan, then foraged in the cupboard for cereal. Sadie had stocked up in her absence. The cupboards now bulged with siege supplies of rice, tinned vegetables and even powdered milk. No cereal, though. Angela fancied nothing less at this juncture than a Cadbury's Flake crumbled over a bowl of Rice Krispies.

She was finishing her second cup of coffee and her third chocolate wafer from a six-pack, when knuckles rapped loudly on her front door. She jumped guiltily, brushing crumbs off her lap. Sadie was here already! 'Coming!' she called, running a hand through uncombed hair *en route* to the door.

She flung it open.

'Your doorbell's knackered,' grimaced Conor McGinlay.

Angela gaped. He looked vaguely familiar. Fish-Jumper! Only he'd smartened himself up, an open-necked shirt visible beneath his unzipped ski jacket. He was shaven too, a plaster clinging raggedly to the sheer cliff of his chin. 'Well, can I come in?' he grunted. 'I've come all this way to reunite you with your luggage.'

'What luggage?'

'You mean, you haven't even missed it?' He stepped into the hallway, brandishing a small holdall. 'I haven't looked inside it, but I assumed you'd be going bonkers, reporting it as lost to the airline.'

'Oh.' Angela glanced guiltily at her unopened baggage behind the door. The only thing she'd unpacked the previous night was her toilet bag. 'How did you end up with it?'

'You must've left the plane at warp speed without checking you had everything. I would've assumed anything left was mine.'

'Blimey. Well, thanks for bringing it round.' That was a lucky stroke, attaching an address tag. She didn't usually bother for hand luggage. One of Robert's little habits that died hard with her. 'Did you have far to come?' she asked belatedly.

'Loxton,' he grunted. 'Fifteen minutes in the jalopy.' He jabbed a thumb over his shoulder. 'I couldn't ring first, as you wrote the address on the luggage tag, but omitted your name.'

'Oh. Wouldn't have mattered. We're – I'm – ex-directory.'

He grunted again. 'It's bloody precious having a phone and not listing the number.'

Angela took a deep breath. 'Cup of tea?' she offered half-heartedly.

'No thanks. Things to do.'

'Angela? Who's your friend?'

Angela groaned as Sadie trotted up to the door, right on cue. 'We haven't been introduced,' she said breathlessly to Fish-Jumper. 'I'm Angela's mother.'

He allowed his large brown hand to be pumped up and down, glowering at Angela from under thick, rust-coloured brows. 'Oh, sorry Mum, this is... er... it'll come to me in a second.'

'Conor McGinlay,' he snapped. 'And remind me again. You are...?'

'Angela Carbery,' supplied Sadie. 'You mean, I've doorstepped you two on your first meeting? I'm so sorry to intrude.'

'Angela and I met yesterday,' drawled Conor with a

momentary gleam in his eye. 'She failed to recognise me with my clothes on.'

Angela threw him a furious look.

But Sadie actually laughed. 'I like a man with a sense of humour! So you two met in Morocco?'

'Angela chatted me up on the plane coming home,' hissed Conor McGinlay intimately, and dug Sadie in the ribs. 'Now I see where she gets her spark from!'

Sadie pinkened coyly. 'Get away with you, flatterer! Now, I mustn't hold you two up, if you're going out to lunch. You might have said on the phone, Ange.'

Angela glared. 'But I – we – there's no…'

'Get along, the pair of you!' Suddenly, Sadie was in the hallway and Angela out on the porch with Conor. 'You don't want an old biddy cluttering up your first date after your holiday! I'll crack on with the unpacking while you're gone, love, load up the washing machine. Don't suppose you'll bother otherwise!' She waved merrily and shut the door in their faces.

Conor wiggled a mobile brow at Angela. 'Forceful little thing, isn't she?'

'You were a big help, with your sexual innuendo.'

'Ach, she was tickled pink that her spinster daughter might have been up to naughties abroad.'

'I'm a widow, not a spinster!' She held up her finger in an unintentionally rude gesture, flourishing the band of gold topped by a solitaire engagement ring.

'Sorry!' Conor McGinlay's brown face flushed a shade deeper to match his wiry, rust-coloured mop of hair. 'I'm not known for my subtlety. You hungry?'

'Not really. I've just had breakfast.'

'I've just had a big fry-up. Tell you what, we'll go for a spin to keep your mother happy. She'll never let you into your own house again until she sees proof of you making an effort.'

'I can't see anything! My lenses – remember?'

Conor eyed the front door. 'I can't see your mum letting you back in with that excuse.'

Angela raised the letterbox flap and squinted into the hallway. 'Ma! Open the door. I can't go out, cos I'm blind as a bat. Ma? You listening?'

Sadie's aproned midriff shuffled into view. She opened the door a crack and thrust out a dusty glasses case. Then the door shut again.

Angela opened the case and winced. She'd forgotten what Deirdre-from-*Coronation-Street* dinner-plates they were, complete with pale pink plastic frames. 'I can't be seen dead in these,' she announced, snapping the case shut.

Conor McGinlay proffered a guiding arm with slow and deliberate flamboyance for the benefit of her narrowed gaze.

'I need a coat to go anywhere,' she stalled. 'It's brass monkeys.'

He peeled off his ski jacket.

Before he could hand it to her, and score even more points for gentlemanly conduct, Angela shoved on the glasses and hurried down the path ahead of him, looking into the grass verge as she went. Already, she'd reverted to her pre-lens stance of hair over face and face bent over a minute examination of pavement cracks.

Conor McGinlay, jacket over one wrist, whistled as he unlocked his car.

They ended up with coffees in a drive-thru McDonald's. 'Not like you to forgo a nosh-up,' observed Angela, falling back on the one characteristic she remembered about him. 'By the way, you drive like a maniac.'

He stirred his coffee aggressively. 'I do not! I'm merely assertive.'

Angela made patterns in spilt sugar with her fingertip. She bet he was assertive in every situation – including bed. Hands as big as shovels gripped his coffee. He was stocky rather than huge, weather-beaten but not haggard. His mouth was a fine, rather sensitive specimen and his eyes a deep jade green. A bristly stubble matched his thatch of luxuriant, wavy, collar-length hair. Rachel would've called him 'moreish'.

'Giving me marks out of ten, are you?' he muttered.

Angela looked down at the table. She must've been staring.

That gave Conor McGinlay his chance to look at her. Second impressions: tall, thin, no boobs to speak of, marvellous skin (courtesy of the Irish blood, no doubt). Dead straight, shiny brown hair with a centre parting. The glasses magnified eyes of a pale, translucent blue. Not a raving beauty, but then, neither was he. She was restful to look at. Like a water-colour you wouldn't mind hanging over the fireplace. Christ, I'm a sexist, he realised, and grimaced.

'Lousy coffee,' he said to Angela, who caught him in mid-grimace.

'How come you were holidaying alone?' she asked abruptly. Might as well get the answers to Rachel's key questions.

'I wasn't on holiday. I go around the world helping to build hotels. I'm a civil engineer. How come you haven't got a tan?'

'Oh.' Blood rushed to her pale face. 'I just go red and peel. My husband was the same.'

'Er – how long ago did he –?'

'Over a year,' she replied quickly. 'Heart attack. We'd been married sixteen years. No kids or pets.'

'You did better than me. My wife left me.'

Angela's tongue stuck to the roof of her mouth. She

hadn't expected that. He was big and bluff – maybe he'd hit his wife?

'It was a civilised parting,' he shrugged dejectedly. 'I was always gallivanting off to build hotels, and she got sick of being stuck at home with Shane, our son. She warned me often enough before she took off. Can't say I blame her for calling my bluff. Shane lives with me. Kate lives in New York. She wanted a clean break. She's very creative, a graphic designer. They were keen to snap her up over there and make her feel appreciated again.'

'So, you have a son?' echoed Angela feebly. 'H-how old?'

'Fourteen now,' grunted Conor. 'Stroppy adolescent runs rings round me. Course, I'm battling the guilt of absent father syndrome half the time. My cleaning lady, Mrs Turner, moves in for the duration when I'm away. She loves being there and she keeps a gimlet eye on Shane. It's not ideal, but I have to work.'

'Well – yes, of course. Don't we all?'

'What do you do?'

'Sub-editor,' muttered Angela shyly. 'Women's mag. Boring old desk job. Start a new one tomorrow.'

Conor nodded absently. He was fidgeting now, eager to be gone from this set-up. He hadn't fooled himself. He couldn't small-talk a woman any more.

'You're Irish,' she reminded him shyly, apparently seeking confirmation.

'Yeah. Both your parents or just your ma?'

'Both. Dad's dead now. My husband, Robert, was half-Irish and half-Welsh.'

'A Celtic conspiracy,' he nodded. 'Kate was as English as flapjacks. Her dad was a fire and brimstone, slightly to the right of Attila the Hun low-churcher who threw a wobbly when she married a bog-trotter. I didn't realise it at the time, but my racial inferiority was my main attraction. One in the eye for Der Führer.'

Angela got up, sensing his restlessness. 'Are you and Kate divorced?' she asked nosily, information-gathering for Rachel (she told herself).

'Yes,' he replied, and sadness leapt out of his mobile face. 'Paperwork came through five months ago. Her dad was right about us for the wrong reasons. A crying shame we ever got married. And I say that with her best interests at heart.'

She made Conor McGinlay drop her off at the bottom of her road. His car was a big, four-wheel drive thing. She couldn't put a name to it, though Sadie and Rachel would want to know.

'Well, I enjoyed that,' he said in a tone that implied the opposite.

Angela squirmed out of the passenger seat, overcome with nerves and shyness. Was she supposed to say, 'Me too'?

'We must do it again some time,' grunted Conor at the dashboard.

'Pardon?'

'You, me, go out,' he repeated, in Tarzan-like staccato. 'If I'm not stepping on toes. I mean – your husband. Got a phone number?'

As she turned away, she was ninety-nine per cent certain that she was going to feign deafness. But the stray one per cent – curiosity? a lifetime habit of responding politely to strangers' requests? – got the better of her.

'Eight four two six six three,' she gabbled at high speed, as Conor crunched his gears, preparing to depart.

'Come again?' he shouted above a tortured gear-box.

Angela turned and fled.

In Angela's rarely used dining room, Sadie ladled out her famous fish pie. Angela poured two glasses of full-bodied Moroccan wine. 'McDonald's!' chided Sadie. 'You could've steered him towards a Harvester at least.'

Angela bridled. 'Why would I want to steer him anywhere?'

'And fancy meeting him on a plane like that!'

'Someone had to sit next to me.'

'Your sarky gene is surfacing, lovey! Cheers.'

Sadie tipped a stream of wine under her unreliable dentures. 'And he came round with your luggage and asked you for a date? Well done, Ange! I wouldn't have thought you capable of such subtlety. You were always a what-you-see-is-what-you-get kind of girl.' Sadie pondered, then qualified this. 'You're honest.'

Angela decoded. 'You think I left my bag behind to give him an excuse to look me up? A variation on the dropped hanky? I'm afraid you were spot-on with your original analysis. I'd never be that "subtle", or sad, as I prefer to call it.'

'I liked him,' prevaricated Sadie. 'I liked him a lot.'

'He's a divorced Irish Catholic with a teenage son and an ex-wife who fled to New York to get away from him. How can you like him? Robert led a life of blameless morality in comparison and all you did was berate him for being a half-Prod Welshman with a suspected interest in ferrets.'

'Angela!' Sadie looked genuinely shocked. 'I wish you wouldn't talk like that, twisting the facts.'

Angela found solace in her wine glass. 'Be honest, Ma. You're giving Conor McGinlay the benefit of very large doubts because he's one of your own.'

'I just think...' Sadie hesitated.

'Yes. Yes?'

'If he rings, you should hear him out. A social life beyond gossiping with Rachel wouldn't go amiss, Ange.'

'I don't see Rachel doing that badly in her successful, single life.'

'Rachel is...' Sadie eased off her shoes under the table and sought for words that skittered away as wine seeped into her brain. 'Rachel is a lovely girl, but she's too cynical about men. I bet she still cries into her cocoa over letting that nice doctor slip through her net.'

'She plucked him out of her net and threw him back in the sea, where other fish are said to be plentiful.'

'My point, is, she's scared of commitment. You've already proved suited to it.'

'I don't know, Ma.' This was sounding all too plausible.

Sadie chewed fish pie carefully. 'Make an effort on your next date with Conor. Looking the part is so important, and your glad rags are mostly rags these days. Will you let me buy you something nice?'

'No, Mum!' Angela shoved her plate to one side and stomped out to the kitchen. She plunged her spoon into an M&S tiramisu, briefly wishing it was Sadie.

In her teens, Angela had tried to keep her dates a secret from Sadie. But once Sadie weevilled out the truth, the advice was the same: 'Shoulders back, chest out, tummy in. A man hates a girl who droops. Don't wear a skirt with a slit up the back in case he thinks you're easy.' (Sadie pronounced it 'azey'.) 'Always have your nails trimmed because a man notices bitten nails. Always carry a hanky, spare tights and enough change to call for a taxi and tip the driver. You should never, ever go on a date without a handbag of essentials.'

Angela used to pause on her way out the front door to tick off a checklist of handbag contents, adding loudly, 'compass, map, spirit level, Kendal mint cake, cuddly toy...' until a goaded Sadie would fly out of the sitting room and shoo her on her way.

Sadie had turned every first date of Angela's into an interview for a dream job that would never be offered again. To rebel, Angela had probably gone too far the other way, turning up for dates in scuffed shoes and trailing hem-lines, round-shouldered and peering at her feet, even after the duckling-to-swan transformation afforded by contact lenses. It had been sheer chance that she'd met Robert at a wedding, when she'd been competing with Rachel to look her best.

She carried the wobbly mounds of tiramisu back into the dining room. 'It's too soon after Robert to start dating. And now I've got this new job to cope with.'

'Wouldn't Conor be a pleasant distraction?' hazarded Sadie, with an answer and a new question for everything.

Gloomily, Angela shoved her glasses up her nose, leaving a cream-smeared fingerprint on the plastic lens. Her verbal parrying was not at its best in glasses. She bent her head to avoid Sadie's beady eye, studying formations raised by her spoon on the stippled texture of beige mousse.

Conor drove uphill in fourth gear for a whole minute before he even noticed. He changed down with a growl to match the protesting gearbox. As unmitigated disasters went, he gave his meeting with Angela Carbery a healthy nine out of ten. Despite a retentive, incisive memory, he had only the vaguest recollection of the phone number she'd tossed over her shoulder. She'd surrendered it unwillingly, perhaps made it up on the spot. The question was, should he bother talking things any further?

He pulled into the next service station and topped up with petrol. As he stood in the queue to pay, he noticed that the young woman behind the till had a beautiful smile, flashed indiscriminately at every customer.

Conor decided that that was the problem with women, or rather, *his* problem with women. Since becoming single again, he couldn't read between the lines of a beautiful smile to distinguish between women who felt sorry for him, women who liked him as a friend and women who fancied him.

He'd taken a chance on Rosie. He'd only gone into her shoe shop to buy a pair of brown nubuck shoes. But he hadn't seen anything he liked, apart from Rosie. At the door, he'd taken advantage of the fact that they were alone in the shop and turned to blurt out, 'Fancy coming out some time?'

He'd taken affirmative action. It had worked – and ended in disaster.

'Twenty pounds,' the woman behind the till said to him, and ladled out her smile as if it came free with petrol tokens.

He peeled a twenty off the back of a tenner. He saw the woman's wedding ring on her finger and thought of Angela. The ball was firmly in his court. If he wanted to see her again, he'd have to take affirmative action again. It was a watershed moment. Should he or shouldn't he?

Back in the car, he thumped the dashboard in frustration. Goddamit, there came a time to stop worrying about the impression he made on the opposite sex, and just go for it on the assumption that he had as much to offer as they had to give. Angela Carbery wasn't going to be scouring the phone book for his number, was she? It wasn't the done thing. He'd have to make the next move.

Chapter Four

'And this,' said Val, ending her guided tour, 'is the sacred stationery cupboard of popular legend. Mandy in admin sleeps with the key under her pillow. You have to fill out a form in triplicate for a paper-clip, so if I were you, I'd label my stapler, dictionary and anything that isn't nailed down.' Val's voice dropped an octave. 'People here are so possessive. Petty, I know.'

Angela nodded sagely. It was her first day, and office politics were thickening before her once again. Could she even trust clear-eyed, blonde-rinsed Val, a mother of three with thick ankles and guileless charm? 'Love many, trust few, always paddle your own canoe,' as Sadie had it. Caution dictated that a serpent nestled in the bosom of the one you felt most inclined to trust. Val was therefore a prime suspect. She understood so well.

'I understand just how you feel, coming back to work after a few years off,' she said, leading Angela back to the subs' end of the open-plan office. 'I took five years out having Ricky and the twins, and Marla's had a year off with Barnaby.' She dropped her voice again to add, 'Marla's a bit two-faced. All over you one minute, criticising your time-keeping the next. Just be aware of it. She's under strain at home. I know people shouldn't bring their private lives to work, but Marla's husband is unemployed and resents her success as a woman. He spends all her earnings to highlight his disaffection.'

'Right,' said Angela, dropping into her swivel chair. She made frantic mental notes. Marla, keep on right side of. She clicked her mouse, calling up the page they were easing her in with, and smiled at her fellow-sub, Pauline, across the desk. Pauline stared back.

Angela's PC said 'Oops!' loudly. The machines were all equipped with irritating noises that advertised your every mistake, your movement to a new document or your opening of an e-mail.

'Fuck, it's crashed,' panicked Angela, hammering the space bar with one finger.

'Let me.' Pauline sprang forward like a darting eel and pressed the restart button on Angela's keyboard.

'Thanks,' smiled Angela. Officious cow! She'd been about to press the restart button herself.

'It's never a good idea to bash one key like that,' said Pauline, still staring. Then she twisted round to accost Marla, who was frowning over folio sheets spread on top of a metal cabinet. 'Marla, d'you think we should send Angela on a Mac refresher course?'

Do you think Angela would like to be asked, muttered Angela silently.

Marla looked up, still frowning. 'I understood Angela was conversant with Macs and the software we use.'

'Angela is,' said Angela, with a humble, ingratiating smile, the one she'd have to wear for at least a month until she could safely mothball it and reserve it for the elite who had to be humoured on a permanent basis. Butt out and stop showing me up, she silently addressed Pauline's chestnut cowlick.

Peering at the words onscreen, Angela surreptitiously enlarged them. Her Deirdre glasses were crap. Her ailing contact lenses had refused to go in at a quarter to seven

that morning, so she was saving them for a midweek
entrée to the office.

At eleven o'clock, she decided to risk a coffee.
'Anyone for a drink?' she asked brightly, knowing that the
quickest route to ingratiation was to volunteer for active
service on beverage and snack runs. A chorus of 'Ooh, yes
please,' went up, and team *Goss!* offered up their dirty
mugs for her to rinse and replenish.

The kitchenette was full of fag hags. Angela thought it
disgusting that they were allowed to smoke in the food
area. Five women lounging round the fridge broke off a
heated discussion as Angela clattered in with her cups. 'So
I said,' resumed one puffer, 'say that again to me, you
dirt bird, and I'll knock your fucking molars through the
back of your turkey-veined neck.'

'I'd have said the same,' nodded a fellow-hag.

'Excuse me,' said a third, as Angela burrowed in the
fridge for milk. 'You are going to use your own
departmental milk, aren't you?'

'That's the idea,' grinned Angela, extracting a carton
that lacked possessive markings of any kind. Fuck knew
which department owned it. Silently, the fetid five
watched her splash microscopic amounts of milk into each
mug. Angela tensed, waiting to be physically assaulted,
trussed up and cast out into corporate darkness, via a lift-
shaft.

'Anyway,' resumed fag hag number one, 'I told lover-
boy he was welcome to her, told him I wouldn't touch
her cunt with a ten-foot willy dipped in Dettol.'

Angela staggered out with her tray of mugs. What a
place! A woman had said cunt! She obviously just wasn't
ballsy enough for a world that had coarsened so noticeably
in her four-year absence. Should she hand in her notice
today or wait till the end of the week?

'Verdict on your first day?' asked Val kindly, as they travelled down in the lift together at five-thirty.

The urge to blab was too much. 'I don't know if I'll hack it,' blabbed Angela. 'I read somewhere that it takes up to six months to settle into a job, longer if you'vè been out of circulation.' This was an appeal to Val to confirm her long-term prospects if she didn't cut the mustard within a week. She was slow on the PC, she knew that. Painfully slow. She kept apologising to Marla when Pauline was away from her desk, and Marla kept conjuring a smile out of her perpetual careworn frown, and saying she'd get the hang of it, and no one expected miracles on her first day. But what about her second?

'You've nothing to worry about,' Val assured her, hurrying with her to Victoria station. 'We've had complete dorks in freelancing while they advertised your job, and none of them got the push.'

This was only vaguely comforting.

'One thing though,' said Val, turning to her at the station entrance, 'tread carefully with Pauline. You may have noticed, she's a bit intense.'

Angela nodded eagerly. She wanted the full low-down on Pauline, but realised she'd have to make do with a whetted appetite, as Val had a train to catch. 'Just watch your back,' advised Val, poised to rush. 'She's one of those people who takes for or against you, five seconds after meeting. No second chances given. She's been here for aeons, so doesn't suffer fools gladly and can't remember what new job nerves are like.'

'Oh God!' panicked Angela. 'She's been throwing me killer looks all day. What shall I...?'

'Not to worry,' sang Val, taking off for platform three. 'See you at the coal-face tomorrow. Byee!'

Angela reached home, exhausted. It was half seven and she'd been up since half six. She'd have time to eat, bathe, catch the headlines on *News at Ten*, and fall into bed comatose, before rejoining the treadmill for day two of the rest of her life.

The morning and evening commuter rush were as scary as she remembered. It had been almost surreal, hurrying across the footbridge that morning in a silent phalanx of train-catchers, their uniform the belted mac, their shields the broadsheets they raised defensively once sitting or standing on the train.

The only saving grace was working so close to Victoria. As long as she left work dead on five-thirty, it looked as if she'd bag a seat on the five-fifty-three to Wilmesbury, without having to run all the way to Victoria and get a stitch.

The first thing Angela did when she got home was unplug the phone. She couldn't cope with Sadie or Rachel ringing for news of her first day.

It was Sadie she really feared. She'd end up blabbing about Pauline and the fag hags and crashing the machine — all negative things, rooted in worry about her fitness for the job — and Sadie would make things worse by observing, 'You're so paranoid, lovey. It's perfectly simple. If you're nice to people, they're nice to you. Any other outcome involves contributory negligence on your part.'

Sadie put the phone down. It was ringing at Angela's end, but she must've unplugged it for the night.

Halfway up the stairs, on her way to run a bath, Sadie paused to regain her strength. She gazed up at the remaining treads. She could swear her staircase was actively steepening, rising millimetre by millimetre, week by week, with the incremental stealth of a suspension bridge.

She loved her narrow, high-ceilinged, terraced house,

but it offered an increasingly cold shoulder. Doorknobs slithered away from her grasp. The kitchen units were creeping higher up the wall to join elusive cobwebs.

Rationally, she knew the problem was her arthritis. It forced her to concentrate on reaching, grasping and retaining wall and door projections that had once rushed to fit snugly in her hand.

Loneliness compounded the bothersome onset of infirmity. She had Binky of course, but he was a pensioner in his own right, with joints and a temper that stiffened in the damp. When Binky went to the great litter tray in the sky, Sadie doubted she'd have the heart to start over with a new, frisky incumbent.

Perched on the edge of the bath, leaning in to check water temperature, a flame of hot arthritic pain (she called them twinges) shot up her leg and into her pelvis. Moodily, she stared into the swirling water, waiting for the pain to pass, like a labour contraction. Arthritis was a bugger. It crept up on an otherwise healthy body, crabbing and twisting it into blasted tree formation, while inside, your perfectly spry mind cried out not to be judged on appearances.

Sadie had tried copper bracelets and heat pads on her wrists and insteps. She'd given up ambitious gardening (anything that involved bending or hunkering) and now passed desultory days hoeing weeds from a great height. Her rose arbour and vegetable patch had reverted to a boring hanky of manageable lawn, attracting sympathetic comment from spryer neighbours over both bordering fences. The local consensus was, 'Poor old gel isn't up to it any more.' Which was why Sadie still made such an effort to keep the grass mown and the weeds hemmed back to the edge of the trellis, sulkily intent on encroachment but not yet daring to try.

She also sensed that her tip-foraging days were

numbered. Even her part-time job at the newsagent's (which she loved) was becoming a strain; all that scrabbling change out of the till and clawing penny chews out of bottomless jars.

Naturally, being Sadie, she'd hidden the true extent of her pain from Angela.

But since Robert's death and especially since Christmas Day, Sadie had dared to think the unthinkable. Should the widows cranky live together? Would Angela cope better if she, Sadie, was on the spot?

Though frankly, Sadie had felt worse than inadequate on Christmas Day, rocking Angela in her arms, aware of Angela's embarrassment battling with her desolation. Even as a child, Angela had never been cuddly. If Sadie had picked her up and tried to cuddle her, she'd squirmed away like an impatient cat.

So Angela wept in Sadie's arms on Christmas Day, but hated herself for it, and resented Sadie for seeing her like that. Words of comfort had stuck in Sadie's throat like a boiled sweet swallowed too soon. What could she say? She'd too often damned the living Robert with faint praise.

He'd been scared of her forthrightness, for which she'd despised and bullied him a bit, using humour as her cover. She'd poked gentle but relentless fun at his golf jumpers, spare tyre, and his dun-coloured hair brushed so carefully away from a side parting. He'd taken such pride in his ordinariness, it had irked her.

'I can't suggest living together now,' she reasoned with Binky, who'd strolled into the bathroom. 'Supposing this Conor bloke has real potential? A live-in mother-in-law might scare him away. Remember all those Les Dawson jokes?'

She nodded sagely at Binky, mindful of where duty and

sacrifice lay. 'Anyway, which house would we settle on? Angela wouldn't want to live back here.'

Sadie's terraced home, humble as it was, still had the cachet of being larger and more valuable than Angela's semi-detached hut. Sadie's house was turn-of-the-century stolid redbrick, built before boxy dimensions and cheek-by-jowl living became the suburban norm. But Angela's hut was centrally heated, closer to town and easier to get around. The stairs were less steep, for a start.

'It's all academic,' she told Binky, rising carefully from the side of the bath. 'I have to wait and see how things develop with Conor. And if all goes well on that front, an old battle-axe like me can't be putting obstacles in the way.'

In her lover's studio flat, Pauline sat on the edge of the bed, closing her bra at the front before twisting the cups round from the back. 'The new woman started today. A fairly timid thing, watery eyes behind glasses, bit of a weeping widow, I'd say. There's a hint of steel beneath the weeds, though. I wouldn't like to push her too far. Seen my other shoe?'

Her lover raised himself up on one elbow with ineffable weariness and twisted his other arm under the narrow bed to locate Pauline's suede pump.

She chucked her clothes everywhere, partly because time was short and partly, he reckoned, because she equated random discarding with wild abandonment.

But she didn't have to live here. He was much tidier. After all, it was only a studio flat. Walking to the shower in the mornings, he often trod on a lone Pauline earring. She wore small, sharp-edged ones that dented bare feet, awakening a sleep-fuzzed brain much more rudely than a perked cup of coffee. Surely by now, her earring collection rivalled the average man's sock collection?

For these and other reasons (she could witter for England; she wittered on about work, global politics, her goldfish having mange), he had decided to end the affair.

'God, I'd better rush,' said Pauline, glancing at her watch.

She bent backwards and kissed him from a supple and imaginative angle. Then she stood up and smoothed her bright chestnut hair under its Alice band. 'I'll ring if I hear about tickets for Eddie Izzard. Otherwise, same time next week?'

It was more a rhetorical than an open-ended question. She was already halfway to the door before he'd stirred himself to reply. The door had shut by the time he'd framed the first of his impressively dispassionate reasons for not seeing her next week or any subsequent week.

Quickly, Conor McGinlay shut his wardrobe door. He'd been beaten back by an onslaught of hairy tweed and mildewed mothballs. Scratching an itchy armpit, he strode into the bathroom and dived without preamble into the linen basket.

It was Shane's turn to load the washing machine, which explained why the basket was still full.

Conor emerged clutching a pale apricot cotton shirt. He sniffed it from a distance and then bravely snuffled the armpit. Next came the wrinkle inspection.

Shane loped into the bathroom, wearing his Walkman. He eyed the shirt.

'Looks a bit past it.'

Conor lowered the shirt. 'Looks can be deceptive. It was your turn this week to load the machine, chuck in a couple of detergent scoops and turn the knob. Not too much to ask, is it? Mrs T still does the tricky bits — unloading, sorting, ironing and magically redistributing.'

'Didn't know it was my turn,' shrugged Shane.

'Ignorance is no defence,' frowned Conor.

'Ye wot?' Shane lengthened his jaw for that village idiot look that irritated (and didn't fool) Conor.

'D'you think I need to iron this shirt?' he asked, going for manly solidarity.

'Don't even try, Dad. You could burn your ear if the phone rings.'

'Is that a Dad joke or an Irish joke?' asked Conor dangerously.

'It's an old joke,' replied Shane sweetly, and staggered out of the bathroom.

He wasn't drunk or stoned, as Conor had first feared when he'd noticed how much staggering about Shane did. Uncoordinated lurching, exaggerated by army-sized backpacks of schoolbooks, was the perambulatory norm for Shane and his peers.

Conor decided the shirt would do. For some unfathomable reason, he felt guilty about what he was embarking on – or at least, planning to embark on.

He almost felt as if he was cheating on his son. A ridiculous notion, given Shane's supreme indifference to his comings and goings for work. But then again – what did he expect? He came and went so often that both he and Shane would be wrecks by now if his son was at all needy and clingy by nature.

He was not a skilled father. Guilt made him over-compensate for his absences with lavishly indiscriminate amounts of pocket money and gifts (bribes, Kate called them). Still, Kate paid her own blood money and spoilt Shane with his latest heart's desire. Thank God he wasn't a scheming child, playing them off against each other. Shane would return home from Kate's New York loft, laden with trainers (soon forgotten about), softball racquets (never used) and fleece-lined jackets (lost within a week). He wasn't overly acquisitive. He accepted parental largesse with a certain amount of well-bred embarrassment.

Returning to his bedroom, Conor hung the shirt on the back of his wardrobe door. It smelt OK. If in doubt later, he could slosh a bit of aftershave over key areas. He wondered, with a brief flicker of panic, if he'd become a total barbarian since Kate left, a raging troglodyte in matters of etiquette, cleanliness and civility. Sometimes, he caught Mrs Turner looking at him in astonishment as he polished off a KFC chicken bucket after living on nettle soup up some godforsaken mountain for a week. And Angela Carbery had thought him a pig on the flight from Morocco.

At such times, Conor had the grace to blush. But he was a man – a man who had to shave twice a day to look human – and as such, he had to grunt his way out of embarrassment, dismissing and deflecting all put-downs. If there was a more civilised approach to life, he longed to find it, or find someone who'd point him in the right direction.

It was Friday. At the end of Angela's first week, she was still doing the eleven-o'clock beverage run. But she didn't really mind. She could escape from her desk and daydream by the kettle for a few minutes. She tried hard not to wonder about Conor McGinlay. Maybe, if she'd been nicer to him, sparkled with a bit of feminine gratitude for taking up his time… if she'd made an effort to give him her phone number properly.

Luckily, she'd been too whacked to see Sadie in person during the week. By tactical skill, she'd kept Sadie's midweek phone call within the parameters of her first week at *Goss!*

Braving the office kitchen no longer fazed her. The kitchen fag hags had crystallised into individuals, one of whom was Mandy of admin fame. Angela now realised they were far less threatening than she'd first thought. They were simply bored women having a raucous laugh.

Cradling her noon mug of coffee (she'd already done the group beverage run), she tip-toed back to her desk. She didn't look at Pauline, in case she blushed at being caught with a unilateral beverage.

Val looked up from a proof and gazed past Angela, puffing down her nose like a horse on a frosty morning. 'Who,' she whinnied, 'is that?'

Angela and Pauline turned.

Angela's heart squeezed into a ball that hurt her chest.

Conor McGinlay was ambling through the open-plan office like a bull in search of a thirty-two-piece dinner set. His thick hair gleamed a foxy red under the strip lights. He wore a surprisingly attractive dark linen suit. He was clutching a small bunch of freesias to a crumpled orange shirt-front. Aware of being gawped at, his expression was one of pained fury.

Finally spotting Angela, he cantered over like a mettlesome charger. 'I've had to donate a kidney at reception to get into this place,' he announced, thrusting the freesias towards her nose.

Angela fought back tickly petals and took a deep breath. 'How did you know I worked here?'

He shrugged. 'Rang a few publishing outfits and asked to speak to you. Came up trumps fourth time lucky.'

Angela blushed with wild joy at his persistence.

'Angela?' Marla bore down. 'Perhaps your friend could wait down in the lobby for you? It's not policy to let civilians roam at large in the corridors of power.' She beamed at Conor, a smile infused with authoritarian good humour.

Conor grunted. 'Can you come to lunch now then, Angela? I'm parked on double yellow.'

Angela looked quickly at Marla.

'Yes, yes!' shooed Marla. 'Off you go, the pair of you.'

Watchful eyes followed them to the lift. Angela studied the carpet, the freesias carried upright in one sweaty hand, like a talisman. He said nothing to her. She felt perturbed that he'd spilt her life so publicly all over the workplace. She was also thrilled that he'd bothered.

In the lift, she realised they were about the same height. Well, she was tall for a woman, and he was stocky.

'I like your shoulder bag,' he said. 'It's very − you.'

Angela clutched her bag protectively. A twenty-first birthday present from Rachel, its faded orange cotton was decorated with tap-dancing frogs. Hardly a byword for sophistication. 'Thanks for the flowers. I should've left them on my desk. They'll get droopy now.'

'We'll stick them in the back of the car.' His voice sounded thick, and he sprang out of the lift the minute the doors opened. If she hadn't seen at first hand how growly and forceful he was, Angela would almost have thought him shy.

His four-wheel drive was in the process of being ticketed. 'Errand of mercy,' he told the grizzled traffic warden, and smiled a smile that would've stopped invading Barbarians in their tracks. Angela was trapped by chance in its ray of blazing tenderness. How could such a macho face smile like that − like a mother looking into a crib?

'Not my problem, mate,' snapped the unappeased male traffic warden, tearing the ticket off his pad. 'I don't care if your girlfriend was having triplets under the dashboard.'

Using some internal re-set button, Conor's face reverted to pre-growl mode. As he drove away, he balled the ticket and shoved it in the ash-tray.

'Where are we going?' ventured Angela. 'I've only got an hour for lunch.'

'I'm in a rush, too. Thought we'd picnic *al fresco* in a little park I know not far from Oxford Street. An oasis of calm amid the madding crowds.'

'Won't traffic be a killer?'

'Not with a madman at the wheel.' He grinned sardonically, crumpling his brown face into all sorts of interesting planes. 'Not to worry. I intend to show that I'm a perfectly safe driver. The sort who escorts hedgehogs across the road.'

He reached his destination quickly, and without incident. He even managed to park legally.

'Told you there'd be no problem,' he smiled triumphantly. It was yet another smile from his wide repertoire. 'I've got some sanbos and a rug to spread on a bench. I made cheese and ham separately, in case you're a veggie.'

'You've gone to a lot of trouble,' said Angela, surprised and touched.

But then she realised that was the wrong thing to say. The back of his neck flared red as he stomped away towards a pair of wrought-iron gates, swinging a carrier bag, the car rug slung over one shoulder like a clan tartan.

'Sorry!' she panted, scampering after him. 'I wasn't accusing you of – going to a lot of trouble. I mean, not in a chasing me up sort of way. You know what I mean?'

She looked around, stopped in her tracks by the miniature prettiness of the park. On all four sides, ugly buildings glowered over plane trees shrivelled by noxious fumes. But within the magic circle of drooping branches lay springy grass and tangle-free bushes, stacked and polished like museum-piece tumbleweeds.

Conor spread the rug on a bench between two etiolated silver birches, delved into the carrier and thrust two packets at her, wrapped in greaseproof paper. 'Ham's the one on the right. Eat.'

While she nibbled a cheese sandwich, he unscrewed the top of a flask and poured her a cup of hot, black coffee. 'Forgot milk,' he grunted. 'Do you mind?'

'I prefer it black,' she lied, taking the cup. No one had ever taken her on a picnic in the heart of London before, and she wasn't going to split hairs.

The drone of inner-city traffic barely penetrated the greenery, heavy with dewy dampness. Sparrows hopped hopefully out of the underbrush, and she began throwing crumbs. 'I'm enjoying this!' she enthused, turning to him with a smile. 'It was a lovely idea. Thanks.'

'You're welcome.' For once, he too looked almost relaxed, his legs stretched in front of him. He tackled a ham sandwich with wolfish delicacy, then thought better of it and laid it carefully back in the greaseproof paper. 'I come here to think,' he revealed. 'Few people bother coming in because they think it'll be full of druggies and dossers. It's one of London's many well-kept secrets.'

Angela nodded dreamily, nibbling a crust.

'How's the first week in the new job going?'

'Not too bad,' she laughed. 'A few ups and downs along the way, but no one's given me my marching orders yet.'

He hadn't seen her laugh before. It sent an electric spark to those blue eyes, magnified by her glasses.

Angela looked down at the crumbs round her shoes. 'I wish I was wearing my lenses,' she muttered, 'but they're not always up to a full day's work on a VDU screen.'

'I like your glasses. They suit you.'

'Pull the other one!'

'All right, God's honest truth – I don't notice them one way or the other. Kate wore reading glasses as thick as Coke bottles.' He stopped and pounced on the rest of his sandwich.

'Why – you know – did you track me down, Conor?' She'd never said his name before. Its aftershock lingered on her tongue.

He launched into a response with pre-prepared overtones. 'Because I'd like to get to know you. Meeting you on the plane struck a chord with me. You're a plain speaker, like myself. If we didn't get on, neither of us would bother pretending otherwise. Right?'

'I suppose.'

He coughed into a brown fist. 'Maybe I'm being previous, though. After all, you've just lost your husband.'

'My mum says you can't expect opportunities in life to crop up at convenient times. Or, in my case, after a decently elapsed time of mourning.'

'Is that what we've got ourselves here? An opportunity?'

Now it was Angela's turn to blush. It spread like rose wildfire across her alabaster complexion. Again, most attractive, Conor thought.

'I don't know what we've got ourselves. Except – I wouldn't be much cop as a surrogate mother.'

His eyebrows shot up into his matching hairline. 'Oh, I see. You think I'm after a baby-sitter for when I'm working abroad? Not on my agenda, Mrs Carbery. My son and I have managed perfectly well for two years, without me duping some impressionable woman into glorified housekeeping duties. I can and do employ a functionary in that capacity.'

'All right, keep your hair on! I wasn't impugning your squeaky-clean character. I was just letting you know that a woman isn't automatically *au fait* with the domestic scene because she is a woman.'

'I do know that. I was married to Kate.'

'I mean, Robert thought women were born with an ironing gene.'

Conor glanced down at his shirt. 'Ironing's a doddle for today's reconstructed man. Another sanbo?'

Angela was chafing to hear more about Kate. But she'd already strayed into dangerous territory, offering that disloyal titbit about Robert. She wasn't prepared to get a handle on Kate by trading indiscretions. Anyway, caution ruled with prudence. A man whose wife had seen fit to leave him had to be approached with open-eyed cynicism.

They sat in thoughtful silence for some time. He poured himself a coffee without wiping the mug first — endearing himself to Angela. She didn't like fussy germ-busters.

'Jesus, is that the time!' After a couple of sips, he suddenly threw the coffee onto the grass and leapt up. He seemed to twitch in all directions, folding up the rug, stuffing leftovers into the carrier bag. 'Sorry, but we've gotta go like the clappers. I've a meeting back at company HQ in five mins, on the other side of London.' He paused belatedly. 'Having too stimulating a time to notice it ticking by.'

Angela said nothing. Compliments made her shy. Especially from someone as scratchy and complicated as Conor McGinlay. Why had he bothered chasing her up? One undiscussed possibility loomed large. Sex. Maybe he wasn't getting it, and thought a recently widowed woman must be desperate. Well, he'd be right if he assumed that. She did miss sex, like vinegar on chips. But sex with her husband.

As for Conor McGinlay, she couldn't imagine him going without by choice.

If he was on the prowl, it must be down to the fact that he spent long spells trapped in remote locations with other blunt, stocky civil engineers. But there were plenty of female civil engineers these days.

Her negative thoughts accompanied her back to his car.

'Hop in,' he said urgently. 'Now I'm afraid I may drive like a madman.'

A few minutes later, he screeched to a halt in front of traffic lights. 'This is where we part company, I'm afraid. Angela?' He rested a fan of fingers on her skirted knee. 'Can I ask for your phone number again? Write it down on the back of this.'

He unballed the parking ticket and scrabbled about for a biro in the glove compartment. His urgency gave her no time for coy reflection. She scribbled down her number.

'Thank you, I'll ring soon,' he said, with such fervent humility that, as he sped away and left her on the pavement, it took her a few seconds to register her situation. He'd dropped her off near Regent's Park Tube station.

Angela peered into the station's dark maw, jostled by impatient travellers at the top of the entrance steps. She gazed wistfully at Conor McGinlay's receding tail-lights. And she'd left the freesias in the back of the car. 'Excuse me!' huffed an angry woman, clattering Angela with shopping bags. 'Of all the places to stand!'

Angela shifted guiltily. She'd been blocking the stairs, just like a meandering tourist. She looked around for a taxi. But it would cost a fortune in lunch-hour traffic from here to Victoria. And she only had a tenner.

The heat of anger penetrated the frozen top layer of terror. It was Conor McGinlay's fault – dragging her across London and then dumping her, leaving her barely enough time to get back within her lunch-hour, even if she did take the Tube.

And facts were facts. She'd have to take the Tube.

She moved, trance-like, down the steps, Persephone descending to the underworld, leaving behind light and air (such as they were in London).

She wasn't going near the automated ticket machine, which claimed, in theory, to change twenty-pound notes. Instead, she joined the fractious queue at the window. She bought, without incident, a single to Victoria, and turned to do battle with an automated turnstile.

It sucked in her ticket and drew back a metal arm, beckoning her into the station proper. Or was it bluffing? Would it wait until she was halfway through and shoot out its retractable arm to snap her in half?

Angela ran through and the turnstile spewed out her ticket on the other side.

She was sweating. This was bigger stuff than dodging the three-headed dog on the shores of the river Styx before you haggled with the ferryman.

At the foot of the escalator, she scanned a wall-map, working out her route: one stop on the Bakerloo Line to Oxford Circus, then straight down to Victoria on the Victoria line. It couldn't have been easier, even for a Tube-phobic like her.

The platform was filling up. The tunnel mouths at either end emitted faint rumbles. Travellers peered expectantly down the platform, as if waiting for something to roar out of a tunnel and claim a virgin sacrifice.

Angela concentrated on Conor's probable reaction to this silly hang-up of hers. He'd be gobsmacked at first — then impatient, and finally, derisive. Wouldn't he? After all, she hadn't dared tell her own mother, or Rachel.

A train roared into the station, nearly tearing off her earlobes. She'd forgotten that visceral roar, loud with the hunger and ruthlessness of life in the urban rat-maze.

She prayed she'd be standing in front of a door when the train stopped. She was unlucky. The door she'd been banking on slid along the platform and a grim crowd set off in pursuit. Angela followed half-heartedly.

Then she got a lucky break. A man disembarking tangled with an over-eager punter pushing his way on, and a Tube tantrum broke out. Angela wriggled unnoticed between them and dived for an overhead strap.

Only one stop till I change, she told herself, as the train slid off. I'll have to do it all again in a minute.

After an uneventful minute, the train lurched to a stop in no-man's land between stations. Time lengthened ominously. People in seats shifted wearily. A man in tight jeans opened his legs out even further and gave his balls a good airing. Angela tutted with silent disapproval, glad that Robert had never been that sort. She couldn't imagine Conor exhibiting his bits like a hothouse plum either. Though really, she reasoned guiltily, it was a sign of an unhealthy mind to even ponder Conor's endowments.

Tight-Jeans caught her eye and winked.

Angela blushed furiously.

The Tannoy system crackled. A voice wavered through static like Neil Armstrong faintly asking Houston if they copied. '...defective signal... inconvenience... should be moving in... minutes... thank you.'

Nobody bothered to seek an interpreter.

Angela's head buzzed. Stale air gusted through an open window, wafting in a bouquet of diesel and garlic with a topnote of Brylcreem. From nowhere, a sea of whiteness rose up to engulf her.

'Oh my God!' were the last words she heard before she crumpled to the floor, face down on a pair of lace-ups. Amazing, really, that there'd been enough room to faint into.

When she came to, she was on the seat gallantly vacated by the plum exhibitor. She could see his denim legs in front of her, but little else. Her head was wedged firmly between her own legs. She tried to sit up, but a hand shoved her back down. 'It's too soon. Wait a bit longer!'

'Poor old gel, she's still green,' said plum exhibitor and Angela decided nothing worse could befall her.

The train was moving and could've been for some time. She jerked her head up in panic. Had she missed her stop? 'Haven't reached the next station yet,' said the woman who'd shoved her down. 'There was no point pulling the emergency cord when you blacked out cos we were stuck anyway. You OK now? Claustrophobia, is it?'

'How wouldn't it be on these trains?' snorted a man swinging happily off Angela's strap. 'Those people who picket veal lorries should take a look at our travelling conditions.'

'And no proper explanations when you're stuck,' nodded plum exhibitor. 'Never mind there could be someone in your carriage having a baby or an epileptic fit.'

Angela understood from this that she'd constituted an unreasonable burden to her fellow veal calves. She sat up, stricken with embarrassment and irrational rage at Conor McGinlay.

She staggered off the Tube at Oxford Circus, and clung to the pissy tiles of the platform wall until the surge of humanity had eased off.

As she found the platform for Victoria, a Tube train was pulling in.

Angela prepared to hop on, relieved to see that both platform and arriving train were relatively empty. Her lungs swelled briefly with elation, just as giddy as her recent panic. She was going to make it! A whole Tube journey by herself, without hysterics or throwing up!

Then she glanced down the platform and saw Pauline

standing at the far end. Something in Pauline's stance sent icicles up Angela's spine.

Pauline's toes hugged the edge of the platform. Her arms were rising slowly, her calves bunching purposefully through the clingy cotton of a long ethnic skirt. She was aping the graceful trajectory of a pearl-diver, poised to take flight with an angelic leap of blind faith. And she was waiting — waiting for the onrushing train to come her way.

'Pauline, no!' Angela had thought her cry would emerge as a bat-squeak. Instead, she heard her desperate roar bounce off the echoing roar of the Tube train.

Pauline looked up in astonishment. Just for a second, she teetered dangerously, arms flapping. Oh my God, thought Angela. She is going to fall in front of the train. And all because I yelled at her.

Pauline stepped back from the edge. She waited calmly as the Tube doors slid open, then boarded.

Further down the platform, Angela boarded, heart hammering. She had made a spur-of-the-moment incursion into Pauline's life, prompted by instinct. But what of the consequences? Pauline, who'd probably been daydreaming, would think she was mad, hate her, make work a misery.

At Victoria, Angela hung back in the exodus from the station, keeping Pauline within her sights. Pauline strode ahead, not a chestnut hair out of place beneath her velvet Alice band.

Angela scampered towards the sanctuary of Marchbank Publishing. Eyes down, she almost tripped over Pauline, who'd stopped to look at a display of pipes and pipe-racks in a shop window.

'H-hello,' nodded Angela, continuing to walk.

Pauline left her vantage point and fell into step beside her. Her silence drove Angela to gabble. 'Sorry about that — shouting at you on the platform.'

'You thought I was going to chuck myself under the train,' said Pauline as a cool statement of fact.

'Course not!'

'I sometimes think about playing chicken on Tube platforms,' confessed Pauline dreamily. 'I enjoy facing my fear and inciting other people's. I like to stand too close to the edge, and look up to see terror on the Tube-driver's face. Isn't that wicked?'

'Dunno.' Angela felt Pauline's habitual stare and shrank deeper within herself.

'Was that your boyfriend, the bloke who came in with the flowers?' asked Pauline.

'No. Yes. Sort of. We only met the other day.'

'He's a looker.'

Angela said nothing. Agreeing would sound big-headed and demurring like false modesty.

'They're all shits,' said Pauline suddenly. 'I can't stand women who'd rather tolerate a shit than be on their own.'

Was that a challenge or an accusation? 'Yeah, well,' said Angela nervously. 'I'm wary myself. There's a lot in that old saying, never trust a man with testicles.'

Pauline laughed. A great snorting laugh of vented agitation. Beneath its sharp edge lay the faint belltone of unhappiness. Some man had treated Pauline like a shit. Recently. Angela toyed with the idea of confiding the Tufnell Park incident.

But then the revolving doors of work loomed before them, and Pauline disappeared inside. She didn't hold the lift for Angela.

Back at her desk, Val was waiting. 'Angela! You kept quiet about him. Red-haired, Irish, bringer of flowers and springer of surprise lunch dates. He's gorgeous.'

'Is he?' Angela curdled with embarrassment as Marla

looked up as well. 'I haven't known him long. You don't think he's a bit – rugged?'

'If you can't see he's gorgeous, you need bifocals,' sniffed Val.

Pauline said nothing. Now and then, throughout the afternoon, Angela felt the heat of Pauline's stare on the side of her neck. But this time, it had a different intensity, a subtler pitch. It was a thoughtful, not a hostile stare.

She walked to the station that night with a light tread. She had picnicked with a man who was interesting and interested in her. She had made a Tube journey. And she had forged an unspoken alliance with Pauline, without trying to, and without knowing why. 'You're no longer scared of her,' she could hear Sadie murmuring. 'You've glimpsed her vulnerability. If fear is the beginning of wisdom, understanding is the beginning of friendship.' As usual, Sadie was getting carried away. She read too many self-help books.

Chapter Five

'Tell me again why I have to be here when she comes,' demanded Shane.

Conor drew out the grill pan and sniffed the fish fingers.

'Try poking them with a fork,' advised Shane. 'If it goes through, they're done.'

'Right pair of master-chefs, aren't we? Anyway, you don't have to be here. You happen to live here, and if I invite someone to Saturday lunch, why shouldn't you be eating your lunch here at the same time?'

'Because it's not someone, it's a woman. And most blokes in your size twelves pay the kid the going rate to sod off for the afternoon.'

'Nice try, but that's not me.' Conor rammed the pan back under the grill. 'And will you kindly moderate the "sod offs" and "friggin' hells" when Angela is here?'

'Friggin' hell! What am I, Little Lord Fauntleroy?'

'You will be if you don't behave. I'll make you wear velvet pantaloons, talk with a lisp and answer to the name of Crispin for the afternoon.'

Shane gurgled with adolescent laughter. He was exceedingly fond of Conor's empty, unenforceable threats. 'But seriously, Dad, won't you scare this woman off if you introduce the offspring, like, too soon? Or are you letting her see the worst from day one, so she can't accuse you of springing a nasty surprise six months down the line?'

'I've told you, Shane. If I invite a – woman to lunch, I want to behave naturally. That means, neither hiding you under the floorboards nor parading you as the only-begotten, OK? It's no big deal.'

He turned away to fuss with the dinner plates, so their eyes wouldn't meet.

Shane was left to snort in silent contempt. No big deal! This was a blatant attempt to reverse the Rosie fiasco.

Shane still had vividly unpleasant memories of Rosie. Conor had kept her under wraps until it was too late for civilised introductions, allegedly out of deference to Shane's allegiance to Kate.

So, instead of being forewarned and forearmed, Shane had stumbled upon Rosie in the bathroom one morning. God, what a sight! Brassy red hair in shoddy imitation of his mum's *au naturel* tresses. Big bosoms slung inside Conor's dressing gown, fat arms and legs. Dad was slumming it and then some! She'd been a cheapie, pay-by-the-hour lookalike of Kate Stanton McGinlay. Their eyes had met in the bathroom mirror with mutual antipathy.

Rosie had played a stormer in the following weeks, though, pretending to be an earth-mother in front of Conor, ruffling Shane's hair, squeezing his kneecaps, buying him presents and looking downcast and wounded when she didn't get a kissy-huggy response.

Shane was conducting a phoney war – and losing – until the day he caught Rosie in the act.

He came upon her one morning, while Conor was downstairs making breakfast, rifling through the wardrobe in his parents' master bedroom – still occupied by his father, but never by his father and Rosie. When she stayed the night, they did the business (as far as Shane could tell) in the motel-like anonymity of the spare room.

Rosie had already appropriated a small pile of Kate's things on the dressing table – two négligés, an unopened three-pack of white M&S pants, a Cellophane-wrapped box of Chanel No 5.

Rosie was busy stuffing the pants into her handbag when she turned and caught Shane smiling at her. 'I won't tell if you sod off for good,' was the deal he offered.

She'd shoved the stolen goodies back onto the wardrobe shelf. 'Get stuffed, small-fry! Who's going to believe you, anyway?'

'I am,' said Conor, surprising them both. He'd come looking for them to announce breakfast. He stood behind Shane with folded arms, thunder darkening his face.

Rosie recovered. 'Suits me,' she'd snorted, pointing a melodramatic finger at Shane. 'There's no future in a relationship with a man who has to drag a little shit like you around wherever he goes.'

Shane had fought the urge to frisk her on the way out, in case the family silver (two crested teaspoons, to be precise) nestled in her undergarments. A week later, there was still no sign of her, but Shane had needed to make sure and feel safe.

'Rosie gone for good, Dad?' he felt driven to ask unsubtly one evening.

Conor had shrugged laconically. 'As far as I'm concerned. Sorry to put you through that, son. There must've been something off-beam about her all along.'

It had been on the tip of Shane's vinegar-soaked tongue to replace 'off-beam' with 'crazier than a shit-house rat', the meaning of which still eluded him but the tone of which sounded just right. But something in Conor's demeanour had stopped him. The sunken chin, the TV remote control dangling limply from one hand. He might take it personally.

'Did you – you know – pick her cos she looked like Mum?'

Conor's chin tightened as it sat on his chest. 'I never noticed a likeness.'

'What about the red hair?'

Conor jumped up suddenly. 'I'm going to get a beer. Thousands of women have red hair, including your auntie Grainne. That doesn't mean I grew up fancying my sister, and latched onto Mum cos she looked like Auntie Grainne.'

'Thought never crossed my mind.'

'Good. And no, you can't have a beer with me.'

Ever since, Shane had lived in mortal dread of Rosie mark two hoving into view. Because, when it came to women, it had to be said, Conor specialised in women with problems.

Even Shane's protective love of his mother was tempered with this unpalatable truth. Shane adored Kate but he was often confused by her behaviour and sometimes downright scared of her outbursts, though he never let on. The last time he'd been in New York, Kate had tried to tuck him in one night, then burst into tears and smashed a couple of ornaments when he pointed out (very gently) that he was way past that stage. He supposed the drinking didn't help, though it wasn't her fault she'd had a nervous breakdown before she left Loxton. It wasn't Conor's fault, either. It was, according to Granny Margaret in Dublin, One of Those Things.

And now, this Angela one coming to lunch. As far as Shane could see, the old man wasn't up to it. Even Kate had taken the bloke for a ride, dumping the kid on him and doing a flit.

Shane had only recently decided that the old man's

quest for female companionship must have something to do with his alleged good looks. These had first been alleged at the school gates by a couple of giggling girls when Conor had collected Shane after football one night. Secretly flattered on the old man's behalf, Shane had taken to comparing their features in shop windows and car doors when they were out together. The results were not encouraging.

Conor doled out burnt fish fingers, spuds and over-steamed peas.

'You should let me cook, Dad. I came top in cookery last year. This is a pretty sad effort.'

'But you've got other, more cerebral homework,' fretted Conor, shoving the grill pan in an overflowing sink. 'I'll do pasta with tuna tomorrow. I can't burn that.'

They ate in silence for a bit. Conor held his elbows at tense angles, sawing through an overcooked roast potato of the frozen rather than the peeled variety. If only he could persuade Mrs Turner to live in permanently and become a well-paid domestic slave. Hell, she'd been widowed for eight years and lived on a tough estate, visited sporadically by her foul-mouthed daughter-in-law. She might go for live-in servitude, sleeping in the converted loft.

Shane gave up the ghost and dropped a potato from his mouth onto his plate, still steaming and whole.

'Shane!'

'It's frigging thermonuclear!'

'I hope you'll be on your best behaviour for lunch with Angela.'

'Aw, Dad, do I really have to? Isn't one ugly McGinlay enough at a time?'

'But she's looking forward to it!' lied Conor. Angela had sounded terrified at the prospect over the phone.

'She's a widow, right?'

Sadie had gone for granite, which looked weather-beaten in the space of a year. Robert's black marble headstone still gleamed, rain or shine, the white lettering picked out with the sharp definition of bones on a Hallowe'en skeleton suit.

Angela wiped her hands on her coat and stood back to admire her handiwork. The budded tulips pointed upwards, tiny praying hands.

Instinctively, Angela felt guilty. She was trying to appease Robert, buying him off with a votive offering, so he'd leave her alone to get to know Conor. It was two weeks since the London picnic. Tomorrow, she was going to Conor's for lunch.

'Hey!' called Sadie. 'You're standing on an Eva Shanley's grave.'

'Am I? Sorry,' said Angela to the unknown Eva Shanley. She joined Rachel on the bench, treading carefully. 'Mum, what was Owen like at fourteen?'

Sadie looked thoughtful. 'Much as he is now, middle-aged and serious. He never gave me and your dad a moment's trouble, which was worrying in itself. I should've realised he was just biding his time to skip off and reinvent himself. Is this about Conor's son?'

'Yes,' admitted Angela frankly. 'Should I bring him a present? Or should it be a general thanks-for-having-me-to-lunch gift, like a bottle of wine?'

Sadie pondered. 'You could always slip the lad a fiver as you're leaving. He probably gets cards full of fivers from his aunties and puts them towards things you'd never dream of buying for him.'

'Good idea,' brightened Angela. 'And a bottle of Blue Nun for politeness.'

'A shame the kid'll be there at all, cramping both your styles,' murmured Rachel, slinging a cat among the pigeons. 'I mean, there you'll be, in his house, with a master bedroom going begging upstairs, wine sloshing round your pleasantly numbed faculties and limbs, the Catholic guilt on temporary hold.'

'Sssh!' Throwing a look at Sadie, Angela slid down next to her and hissed, 'No references to physical contact, if you please. Um – you don't think that's why he's invited me to lunch *en famille*, do you? In case I pounce on him across the salad bowl?'

Rachel laughed smuttily. 'You – pounce? I know he hasn't known you long, Ange, but he must have the measure of you as far as pouncing goes.'

'What's that supposed to mean?' muttered Angela, knowing exactly what it meant. Her womanly wiles, such as they'd ever been, hadn't exactly been honed by sixteen years of comfortable marriage to a man who'd still fancied her in winter flannel nighties.

'I think the son's presence is significant,' backtracked Rachel. 'It's like being invited to tea to meet your beau's parents.'

'But he's not my beau!' spluttered Angela. 'And he dropped it too casually into the invitation – oh, by the way, you'll probably get to meet the child prodigy – in fact, the more I think of it, the more it comes across as a way of keeping me at arm's length.'

Sadie puffed up to join them, suspicious of the muttering. 'Now, if I were you, Angela, I'd find out a bit more about the wife.'

'Ex-wife.'

'Has she gone for good?' mused Sadie. 'Is she likely to reappear on the scene? '

'Why she did a runner,' prompted Rachel. 'And has he got a cellarful of ex-wives, like Bluebeard?'

'Enough already! How am I supposed to subtly extract all this key info?'

'Who said anything about subtlety?' snorted Rachel,

snipping stalks with gusto. 'Just ask him straight out what happened to his marriage. It's not as if you've anything to hide. Your spouse didn't leave by choice.'

Angela stood up. 'I find these – unwholesome wonderings distasteful in this setting.'

'Just remember' – and here Rachel wagged a finger – 'don't do anything daft, like really fall for him, until you know about the wife.'

'Ex-wife!' snapped Angela.

'I still can't help liking him, for a divorced man,' revealed Sadie, apropos of nothing. 'Though God knows where you'd marry. The church can't give its blessing.'

'Slow down, Ma! You can't help liking him because he's shown an interest in me, without being a multiple bigamist or on the run from Broadmoor. As far as we know. Isn't that the bottom line?'

Sadie turned away, twisting the J-cloth through shaking fingers. 'Lowest form of wit, Angela.'

'Sorry!' winced Angela, assailed by a rush of guilt, filial tenderness and roaring resentment of her mother. The joints of Sadie's fingers looked swollen, and not just from the cold. It was the arthritis kicking in, Angela knew. But when she'd offered to clean Fenton's headstone, Sadie had feigned deafness and scrubbed at the granite with renewed zeal. She was determined to play the martyr.

'Let me take your coat,' said Conor as she stepped over the threshold.

'Th-thanks.' Angela twisted out of it, an idiot smile clamped to her face. 'Ooh, your house is lovely!'

Despite the cringe-making note of cliché, it was true. Angela was awe-struck. 23 Pacelli Close, Loxton, had looked an imposing detached house from the outside, flanked by other four-bedroomed detached houses, and surrounded by luxuriant but pruned trees, always a sign of middle-class affluence.

But the inside was something else. A gleaming wooden floor, carefully littered with pastel rugs, swept up to a spiralling wooden staircase. Through a door to the left, she glimpsed a cream velvet sofa cradling gold-tasselled cushions, and beyond that, a pair of french windows, hung with amazing, ruched curtains. The sort you had to unswag every five seconds and dust – or so she suspected. It was like something out of *Homes & Interiors*. No wonder his 'daily' was often a live-in 'weekly'.

'This is Shane,' announced Conor, while she gawped.

She turned a few degrees, with a smile not so much clamped in place as held by invisible fixative. A figure shuffled down the stairs, extending a hand.

'How do you do?' mumbled Shane.

Angela gawped again, before muttering, 'Pleased to meet you!' and pumping his hand over-enthusiastically.

He wasn't what she'd expected. Conor's son was a skinny stick-insect of a child with a prominent Adam's apple, sticking-up mousy hair and a pair of pebbly glasses. He had nothing – not an iota – of his father's stocky masculinity, red hair or green eyes – nor any discernible prospect of succeeding to such attributes. Angela could only presume that Shane had been hit with the ugly stick via Kate's genetic input. She was ashamed to find this suspicion comforting.

'Goodness!' said Angela lamely. 'You don't look like your dad. I mean, you're clearly going to be – taller.'

Shane shrugged and tugged up a sock that couldn't get a purchase on his skinny leg. He's probably a nice, sensitive, introverted kid, thought Angela, ashamed of judging by appearances. He probably collects insects in jam-jars – and empties them down the back of his father's fancy-women's necks, a cynical inner voice surmised. Could it have been Robert's?

'Lunch is all ready,' announced Conor, guiding them both across the polished floor. 'Easy journey here, Angela?'

'Oh yes. Ten minutes on the train, like you predicted.'

'I'd have been more than happy to pick you up at the station.'

'Oh, but I enjoyed the walk. Loxton is blessed with such leafy – boulevards.'

She was perspiring as they reached the kitchen. He seemed very eager to stuff lunch down her neck, without the preliminaries of an aperitif or a guided tour. Already, she and Conor were playing mannered roles. Here in his home, where he should've been at his most natural, he'd become a hostly automaton. She missed the little she knew of him so far – his grunting, scratchy inability to chat her up or ooze slick patter.

The kitchen made her gawp again.

Utensils gleamed from hooks on a terracotta-tiled wall. A pine dresser heaved with – presumably original – Delft. The huge pine table in the centre was set with pale blue plates, matching linen napkins, and a blue plumbago trailing from a blue-and-white marbled vase. 'Gosh, how colour-coordinated,' she gasped, seeing Conor in yet another new light. He didn't exactly need a woman's touch about the place. Unless.

'Did your cleaning lady set the table?' she asked with innocent bluntness.

His mouth curled good-humouredly. 'Shane's touch, mostly. He's also been slaving away over a hot oven, preparing a vegetarian chilli for you. Not too hot, of course. Wine before you eat?'

'Oh, I brought some.' Angela thrust a paper-wrapped bottle at him, relieved that she'd plumped for a respectable Chilean red instead of the Blue Nun. She should've guessed from the four-wheel drive that Conor was worth a bob or two. Not that it made any difference to her – or to him, she guessed. He clearly didn't go in for designer togs, *haute cuisine* or name-dropping at the golf club. Today, he wore a navy T-shirt over baggy chinos. His brown arms were sprinkled with a fine down of red-gold hair, like the fuzz on a newly-hatched chick.

She realised she was gazing at it when Shane touched her elbow and pointed to a chair. 'That's your seat, Mrs Carbery.'

'Call me Angela.'

She unfolded her napkin, peering at its fringed edges as if it held clues to buried treasure. Sounds filled the kitchen. Conor uncorking and pouring wine. Shane rattling the oven door. Everything except the easy flow of conversation.

The chilli looked and smelt delicious. Angela smiled up at Shane as he placed a black earthenware pot on top of her pale blue plate. 'I'm looking forward to this! I'm not totally vegetarian, but I draw the line at white meat, breast of chicken, that sort of thing.' She remembered the rejected in-flight meal from Morocco. 'Even then, I'm a fussy eater.'

'Dad likes veal,' mumbled Shane.

'Er – only now and then, when it's served at wedding receptions and the like,' grunted Conor, slapping two plates of pasta down on the table. 'You can trust Shane to ensure that all my warts get the full glare of publicity.'

'Never mind his warts,' said Shane. 'You should see his bikini-line rash.'

Angela expected Conor to explode, but he didn't turn a hair.

She took an eager mouthful of chilli – and nearly exploded herself.

God, it was laced with gunpowder – all detonating on the roof of her hapless mouth! Eyes and nose streaming, Angela plunged them both into her wine glass.

'You OK?' frowned Conor, cocking an eyebrow at Shane as he spoke. 'Chilli's not too full of chillies, I hope?'

'Blimey!' Angela extracted herself, gasping, from her glass, and ran to the sink. There was no time for the niceties of introducing a glass under the tap. She stuck her head under the tap and gaped like a blind fledgling in search of worms. She gulped, dribbled, and finally groaned into her napkin, produced at her side by Conor.

'I might've accidentally made it a teensy bit hot,' said Shane contritely. Conor missed Shane's evil smirk as he turned back to the table. But Angela didn't.

'What's for afters – *bombe surprise?*'

'Lemon sorbet,' said Conor, in a soothing tone that was new to her. 'A nice mouth coolant. Here, leave the hot stuff and tuck into some pasta. Shane will dispose of your tex-mex – without involving next-door's cat,' he added warningly. 'The last thing the neighbourhood needs is an exploding cat.' He sighed at Angela. 'Shane sent a West Highland terrier into orbit last month with a strategically placed biryani in the outside wheelie bin.'

'That'll teach the varmints to forage!' said Shane triumphantly.

Angela sat down gingerly at the table. 'But I'm not a varmint,' she grumbled directly at her tormentor. 'I'm a blameless member of a higher species.'

'Honest, it was an accident, Mrs Carbery!'

'Call me Angela,' repeated Angela heroically, touching her burning inner mouth with her tongue. She wouldn't give up just yet. One more practical joke, though, like a firecracker leaping out of her lemon sorbet, and she'd wring his scrawny neck.

She was surprised that he was such a horror. Conor had all the makings of a firm disciplinarian. But then, he was away a lot. The kid must run riot. Spare the rod and all that. Hang on, Angela chided herself, taking a careful mouthful of pasta. She'd been a victim of Sadie's strong-arm parenting. Sadie was a big fan of corporal punishment for the under-twelves. Angela had grown used to offering the back of her legs for a good smacking before Sadie's hand even descended.

No, thumping the physically weaker was not the answer.

'You've got spaghetti sauce on your front,' said Shane helpfully.

Angela looked down and blushed. She'd chosen her blue dress for the visit. She'd bought it in Morocco, a soft shift dress in swirling sea and peacock blue, set off with a pale blue bolero cardigan. The only advantage of her lack of curves was that she looked good in angular, tube-like dresses that flattered her fashionably boyish slimness. But there was nothing fashionable about the threadworms of orangey pasta stuck to her front. She dabbed sadly.

Conor said in a tone of desperation, 'Tell Angela about that project you're doing at school, Shane. The rain forest one.'

Shane threw his father one of those dagger-drawn looks that only pass between child and parent. 'It's dead boring, there's nothing to tell,' he snapped.

'Let us be the judges!' roared Conor suddenly, making Angela jump as well.

Shane turned to her reluctantly. 'Like, we each have to represent a different aspect of the rain forest, so I'm doing parrots and bird life and stuff. Then we stick it on this big mural thing and the idea is, it's put in the foyer of the local library, so people can see what a rain forest is like.'

'And which bird is your favourite?' asked Angela, clutching at a straw of potential conversation.

'None really. Matty Hyde, like, got to do monkeys and stuff. Female monkeys have periods.'

'Wearing your contact lenses these days?' Conor asked Angela firmly.

'Yes, they're enjoying a new lease of life.' She batted her lashes experimentally, only to find that Conor's jade eyes were looking deeply into her own.

'Sorry your husband's dead,' said Shane at her elbow.

'Shane!'

'No, no, that's OK,' twittered Angela. 'Um, thanks for your condolences.'

'We were doing marriage in RE,' began Shane.

'RE?' interrupted Conor. 'I thought it was called sociology or general studies now, with a bit of sex education thrown in.'

'It's still RE at my school,' said Shane pompously.

'Ach, well.' Conor raised a coppery eyebrow at Angela. 'Apparently, there are still some advantages in sending your kid to an RC comprehensive.'

'We were doing marriage,' repeated Shane doggedly. 'And Sister Imelda was saying that you're still married to someone even if they die.'

Angela sucked in her teeth. 'That's kind of true, I suppose. I still wear my ring.'

'Like, circumstances beyond your control forced you apart,' rumbled Shane. 'You'd still be married to Mr Carbery if he hadn't snuffed it.'

'That's enough RE, thank you, Shane,' thundered Conor. 'Dish up dessert and put a sock in it.'

Three spoons scraped blue bowls in tense silence. Angela began to feel wibbly. The whole situation was unreal. Eating lunch in a designer pad with a barely-known man and his nakedly hostile son. And the kid was right in his own unsubtle, hands-off-my-dad-you-gold-digging-harridan way. She was still married to Robert. Betrayal was unthinkable.

To her horror, her eyes filled up.

'Just going to powder my nose,' she announced, looking into her bowl as she rose.

'Upstairs, first on the right,' grunted Conor, who'd apparently also chucked in the towel and let his son win.

She scuttled towards the stairs, followed by Shane's loud whisper, 'She's gone to have a snoop!'

'Load the bleeding dishwasher,' came the non-whispered reply.

In the tastefully appointed bathroom, Angela sat down on the aquamarine toilet lid and cried into several yards of quilted toilet paper, before stuffing the reams into her cardigan pocket, causing an unsightly bulge in her streamlined blueness. Her slimline shoulder-bag — sans tap-dancing frogs and equipped with essentials — was downstairs.

At last she rose, examining her puffy eyes in the mirror. Given her pale complexion, she had those slightly piggy-pink eyelids that went bright red at the first hint of a tear duct cranking into gear. She splashed her face with cold water and descended the staircase with what dignity she could muster.

She snatched her bag off the phone table, preparing to sneak out. It was better to end things this way.

'Angela!' She turned to see Conor lounging on the cream sofa. 'I've poured you a coffee. The brat is cleaning the kitchen with a toothbrush, and then I'm hiring him out to clean the chimneys at Battersea Power station. There's a lot to be said for exploitative child labour.'

Angela smiled wanly, and stepped into the lush sitting-room.

'Shut the door – please,' begged Conor with gruff humility.

She obeyed. Avoiding a close look at the framed photos covering polished surfaces, she sat down on the edge of the sofa. Conor passed her a cup of coffee and offered an Amoretti biscuit. She shook her head palely.

He kicked off his olive-green loafers to reveal holey socks and stretched out with a sigh.

Angela concentrated on his big toe escaping from a sock. There was something poignant in the sight.

'Angela?' He'd said her name like a whispered incantation.

She glanced up in alarm and found him leaning towards her, big brown palms cupped under his chin. Solemn green eyes lasered into her own.

'What can I say? Except that he is fairly human under the outer layer of monster.'

'Oh. You mean Shane? He was fine.'

'It's a tricky one. Do I get to know a woman properly and then introduce her to him? Or is that overplaying the issue, making a meal out of the whole single father thing, instead of letting things find their natural level?'

'I don't know, Conor. I'm no expert in the field.' How many women did he make a habit of introducing? No wonder Shane was wary and hostile – not to mention downright mischievous at being given the Nero-like power to deliver the thumbs-up or down.

'Angela – don't look like that.'

'Like what?' she snapped, sipping coffee to cover her confusion.

She looked on, mesmerised, as he took the cup from her hands, sturdy knuckles brushing her own. Then he took her hands, enveloping her in a tent of warmth.

'Please relax,' he half-grunted, half-implored.

She raised narrowed eyes, and was too late to deflect

the descent of his mouth on hers. It rippled hotly against
her quivering fieldmouse of a mouth. A chaste yet lustful
kiss, burning intent mingled with brotherly respect. A kiss
waiting for her response before it decided which way to
jump. But oh, it was delicious. Too delicious.

Closing her eyes involuntarily, she pressed back.

He moved closer. She swayed back onto over-stuffed
cushions and he fell next to her, his dislodged lips now
clasping barnacle-like to the hollow of her neck. But the
pressure was like a butterfly grazing. Little flurries of
kisses swooped up her neck and nudged her jawline. His
weight lay across her, but finely judged, careful not to
crush. Her right shoulder began to feel pins and needles,
pressed into the cushion, but she was afraid to break the
spell and scare him off. She realised, with surprise, that it
wouldn't take much to shatter his confidence. He wasn't
an assertive seducer at all.

The sitting-room door flew open. 'I've tidied up,'
announced Shane icily. 'All right if I go round to Matty's?'

'So you found out nothing!' accused Rachel, shifting on
the splintered wicker chair.

'I found out the son hates me.'

'All fourteen-year-old boys are rampant misogynists.
Conor won't let that put him off and neither should you.'

'I glimpsed the mother in a photo on the window-sill
but couldn't get a proper butcher's. I did clock that she's
stunning.'

'So? What are you, the Elephant Man's kid sister?'

'Easy for you to talk, Rache. You also happen to be
stunning.'

'Oh fiddlesticks, Angela. He wants you, doesn't he? He
tracked you down, rang you up, might've even kissed you
and ravished you senseless if the child of the damned

hadn't interrupted proceedings. And you'd have enjoyed it.'

Angela sipped tea warily. She'd given Rachel and Sadie a very potted history of events, by-passing Conor's successful kissing attempt, hinting only at its suggestion in his attentive manner and careful manoeuvring of cushions.

'So when are you seeing him again?' probed Rachel.

'The twelfth of never, I reckon.'

'Oh come on, Ange. But if you're going to play silly beggars, allow me to break the news about my new man.'

'Rache!' Angela thwacked down her cup with a mixture of relief and genuine excitement. 'You old dark horse, you! Will this one be another interlude or something more permanent?'

'Early days,' replied Rachel smoothly. 'You know me. The interlude's usually more attractive than settling down for the main programme.'

Shane banged the front door loudly, signalling that he was back from Matty Hyde's, and prepared for a showdown.

Conor was leafing through technical specs on the kitchen table.

'Walked her to the station, did you?' Shane got the ball rolling.

'Who? Oh, my lunch-guest. The extremely nice woman you poisoned, insulted and drove upstairs to weep in the bathroom.' Conor shuffled papers. 'Yes, she's gone. And no, we didn't take things further than a kiss on the sofa. Another one bites the dust.'

Shane hovered. Conor's alternative to sound and fury was often scarier. He oozed with disappointment in his son. And Shane, competitive by nature, hated to be labelled a disappointment. 'You seeing her again?' he muttered.

'Is it worth it?'

Shane looked askance at his father. 'How should I know? You're the one who fancies her.'

'I mean – is it worth it, if you're going to chuck a giant spanner in the works every opportunity you get? What is it with you, anyway – lack of love and attention? Are you punishing me for screwing up your childhood by screwing up my marriage?'

'I can't follow that logic, Dad.'

Conor's green eyes snapped. 'Look. I'll make a deal with you. When you get to thirty-five, you can turn round and say, "It's all your fault," like most kids do when they hit early middle-age and need a scapegoat for their ordinary lives and ordinary failures. But lay off me for the intervening years. Let me get a life, however pathetic and wrong you think it is. I won't stop putting you first. Haven't I always put you first?'

Shane scuffed a trainer on the cork tiles. 'Yeah, suppose so. Enough already with the Waltons crap. She was quite human, as it happens. Compared to – ' He clamped his lips shut.

'Rosie?' asked Conor quickly.

'Compared to what I was expecting,' shrugged Shane. 'And she left a tenner sticking out of my school bag.'

Conor grunted. 'In your book, I suppose that's currying favour.'

'I've no objections,' said Shane smoothly. 'Think of all the stuff you and Mum have bought me off with over the last two years.'

Conor lowered his gaze to the papers on the table.

He was mortified by a sudden desire to cuff Shane. Usually, he had to suppress an equally misplaced desire (from Shane's viewpoint) to ruffle the gleaming quills of hair as they bent over homework or poked above the duvet.

With an effort, Conor said reasonably, 'It'll be a long

time before I treat you to a pair of new trainers or a meal at the Fire Station again, so think on.'

At such empty threats, Shane's heart bled a little for his innocent fool of a father.

Chapter Six

'All I'm saying is, how well do you know him?' repeated Val, breathing wine fumes over Angela. 'Plausible bloke with good looks, distant ex-wife and apparently no decomposing bodies under the floorboards. Ah – but is that the whole story?'

Marla and Pauline looked expectantly at Angela, who was busy kicking herself and resolving never again to drink alcohol on a lunch date with her colleagues. The occasion was Marla's birthday. Five empty wine bottles stood on the table. Val and Marla, both 'social smokers', were holding forth on Issues, their greater sophistication tacitly acknowledged by virtue of the fags dangled between yellowing fingers. 'Us women never wise up,' continued Val, stabbing the air with philosophical smoke. 'We trust too early, commit too soon, practically inviting our hearts to get broken.'

'Jean-Paul Sartre, eat your heart out,' muttered Angela.

'Sorry, Ange?'

'I was just saying, I've only committed to attending his son's sports day next Saturday. He's pretending it's the son's idea to invite me, which is quite sweet.'

'This is your red-haired Irishman, right?' hiccuped Marla. She kept losing the plot.

'Of course it's her red-haired Irishman,' puffed Val. 'Go on, Ange, tell us, what's the sex like?'

'Val-er-ie!' shrieked Marla.

Through the smoke haze, Angela met Pauline's thoughtful eye.

'We – haven't – um, I mean, I haven't.'

'Blimey, what's stopping you?' snorted Val.

'Sssh!' Marla swayed and waved an abjuring finger at Val. 'Don't be tasteless, Val. Angela lost her husband within the last eighteen months.'

Val tried to access her good taste persona, but failed. 'All the more reason to get back in the swing!' she squawked. 'It's like falling off a horse or...'

'Riding a bike. Yes, yes, I know,' hissed Angela through pursed lips. 'Why does everyone make sex sound like a skill you learn at an activity centre, with an accredited course and a certificate at the end?'

'Well, it *is* an activity,' pointed out Val. 'Preferably an outdoors one taught by a hunky instructor. Maybe your bike still has stabilisers, Ange.'

'Val-er-ie!'

'Of course, there's the other possible explanation for his sexual inhibitions,' posited Val, with the inebriate's crafty insight. 'He's Irish, you're more or less Irish. Don't paddies think women have ground-up glass between their legs?'

'Oh, fuck off, Val, he's a father,' said Marla uneasily. But Angela had already thwacked down her wine glass, ready to do battle.

'What the hell are you on about, Val? You're the one stewing your brains with booze. Look at me, more or less Irish, and not even half-addled. Isn't that bucking the national stereotype?'

'Eshnick minorities,' slurred Val. 'Bloody great chips on their shoulders, the whole lot of 'em. You can't even tell Irish jokes now, when everyone knowsh the Irish make jokes about Kerrymen. Whassa difference?'

Angela gritted her teeth, her heart thumping. She found it tricky defending an identity she felt ambiguous about at the best of times. 'The difference is, you gormless bint, that you Brits have a collective responsibility to be nice to the people you treated like dirt in the name of colonial expansion. Look, there's a black bloke in the corner, having a quiet meal. Go over and make monkey noises and see if he's into self-parody.'

An embarrassed hush fell around the table. Angela cringed. Things had got out of hand. Like all the righteously defensive, she felt as if she'd taken herself too seriously, mounted a soap-box and roused her audience to nothing more fruitful than a suspicion that she was a humourless paranoiac.

A siren rose and died in the street outside the wine bar, sawing through lunchtime traffic and the silence at the table. 'Oops, they're coming for you Ange,' giggled Val. 'Someone's tipped them off about the Semtex shtashed under your keyboard. In the interest of community relations, I'd just like to say it wasn't me.' And she toppled forward onto the table, her blonde hair splayed out like starfish legs.

The extent of Val's loose-tongued drunkenness finally reminded Marla who was boss. 'I think we've had quite enough partying for one lunchtime. If you'd all care to stagger back to the office, and pretend to put in an afternoon's work...'

Pauline fell into step beside Angela on the walk back, Marla and Val stumbling ahead with linked arms.

Angela grimaced. 'I suppose I shouldn't have risen to the bait. Us plastics are a sensitive species.'

'What's a plastic?' asked Pauline, intrigued.

Angela sighed. 'A plastic paddy. That's what the home-grown Irish call the second generation – well, the second generation who apply for Irish passports and mail dog-poo to the West Midlands crime squad.'

She glanced suspiciously at Pauline, in case she was amused. Following Val's drunken assault, Angela's skin was as thin as rice paper stretched across the surface of a drum. Drunken outbursts were always a conundrum. Were they a revelation of the speaker's true opinion or just a stage on the way to the other, possibly unrepresentative stages of maudlin depression and declarations of love for the embarrassed drinking pals?

Pauline insisted at her side: 'I'm still intrigued. How does your Conor see you?'

Angela considered. 'As me, I hope. He knows I've a quixotic attitude to the auld sod, but that's my mother's fault. She's spent half her life slagging off the place to the likes of me, and the other half defending it to the likes of Val. She has a refugee's schizophrenia, a foot in both camps without feeling comfortable about calling either home. When I visited Ireland as a kid on holiday, the neighbours' kids pelted me with cow-pats for having an English accent. Back here, the likes of Val take great pleasure in reminding me I'm a mick whenever a bomb goes off. Yet if I won a Nobel prize tomorrow, I'd be feted as a true Brit. It's enough to make you dizzy.'

Pauline pondered. 'It must be the same for black kids going to Jamaica on holiday.'

'They get sunshine to make up for it.'

'Look, just forget about Val,' frowned Pauline, returning to the insult at hand. 'There's no real malice in her because there's no imagination there, either. For a start, she can't imagine what it's like to lose a husband.'

Angela studied the pavement, blushing. She longed to say something equally wise and comforting to Pauline. But she had only ever sensed Pauline's unhappiness, never been privy to an exposé of its origins. She did know that Pauline had never been married.

'I haven't been dicing with death on any more Tube platforms,' said Pauline presently.

Angela took the opening. 'Why were you – you know – so down on men that time, calling them shits?'

'I'd just been loved and left by one, of course.' She smiled sadly. 'Thing is, Val's quite right. Women rush in where any half-sober man would fear to tread. I trusted too soon and put all my eggs in one basket. I thought he loved my winsome chatter and close attentions. Turns out he thought I was a clingy old gasbag.'

A small gasp escaped Angela. 'Is that what he called you?'

'Oh no. Phil was the latest in a long line of civilised, well-behaved shits. He wrote me a letter, would you believe? A dear Joan letter. Signed his name with a curly flourish. I don't think he was sobbing with grief as he held the pen.'

'I'm sorry,' murmured Angela.

'The sex was good, I'll say that for him.'

Angela sighed inwardly. She was out of her depth again.

'At least yours can't just be in it for the sex if you haven't had any yet,' opined Pauline.

'I think we're both as nervous as each other,' confided Angela. She hesitated, then came out with the lot. 'You see, I've only had one lover – Robert. Conor has had two. His ex-wife and a fling he had after she left. His son Shane didn't hit it off with the woman, Rosie. We're a right pair of greenhorns by the permissive society's standards, which isn't as hunky-dory as it sounds. Neither of us are skilled at making the first move.'

'Forgive my cynicism,' said Pauline cynically. 'But do

you believe him? Two women in a lifetime? Eunuchs have put it about more.'

'He sounded convincing enough,' winced Angela, remembering the previous week's mortifying walk round the boating lake in Wilmesbury park.

Conor had wanted to put things straight after the lunch fiasco. Angela had assumed he meant about Shane. But putting things straight had also involved a confessional blabbing. Throwing unshredded chunks of bread at alarmed ducks, Conor had revealed the bare bones of his love life, summing it up as inglorious but not too tawdry. Just as Angela had been about to seize the moment and ask him more about Kate, they'd been buttonholed by a furious woman who'd accused Conor of trying to stone the ducks with stale wholemeal.

Angela, scuffing her toes in gravel, had felt duty-bound to offer a reciprocal account on the walk back – starting and ending with Robert. Conor hadn't been amazed, delighted or dismissive. He'd simply nodded and changed the subject to how springlike it was for the time of year.

'What do you think he was really getting at?' Angela grumbled. 'Trying to excuse or boast about his lack of forwardness? Preparing me for gauche fumblings when he does make his big move? Thing is, you'd never suspect sexual shyness to look at him. He has a tendency to verbally bulldoze his way out of awkward moments.'

'Classic defence mechanism,' said Pauline crisply. 'Anyway, while I hate to give cheesy love songs any credit, as the song says, it's in his kiss. If he was impotent or scared of women or a serial seducer, that's where you'd pick up the vibes.'

Angela walked on, considering. She hadn't kissed Conor McGinlay since their brief tussle on the sofa, cut short by Shane. Cushionus interruptus.

Frankly, she'd just made her relationship with Conor

sound like a mutual crush between sixth-formers – sweaty hand-holding, noses colliding with ears in the cinema's back row – while Pauline, habitually risking all for love, knew the real world of crumpled sheets and cruel let-downs.

She felt Pauline staring at her, and looked up to catch her smile. 'Funnily enough, a lot of Val's ramblings made sense,' said Pauline. 'Go more carefully than I've ever done. Because, alas, it's true – how well do you really know him?'

Val cornered Angela in the ladies' loo just before knocking-off time. 'Listen,' she croaked, gazing in the mirror to avoid looking at Angela. 'I was out of order with the Semtex thing.'

'And the rest,' said Angela grandly. She was going to milk this on behalf of every plastic slighted by thoughtless English folk, with their phoney sense of 'fair play' that was just an excuse to ignore the bloody partiality of their imperial past. Some days (days like this), Angela surprised herself with her dislike of the very Englishness that had shaped her own character. Maybe she was Irish, all along. Scratch a plastic, and find the real McCoy.

'I saw this thing in a Sunday supplement,' mumbled Val. 'You invest a tenner to buy your own sod of turf in an Irish bog and save it from extinction. What do you think? Would that make up for being all crass and politically incorrect?'

'Hmm,' considered Angela. 'Tell you what, just give me the tenner. I'll make sure it goes straight to the cause.'

'The bog cause?'

'No, silly, the real cause, the Provos.' She walked to the exit with a gunslinger's swagger, turning to impart a final Clint Eastwoodish soundbite: 'Remember this, Val. Our day will come.'

The call came early on Wednesday morning, shaking Angela out of her cosy pre-work routine and idle thoughts on Conor McGinlay. 'Oh my God,' wheezed Angela down the phone as she heard the news. 'Oh my God, oh my God, oh my God.'

'Get a grip!' snapped Mrs Ambrose on the other end of the line. 'The doctor's been and says she's OK, just a bit shaken up and cold from lying on the bathroom floor half the night.'

Angela shut her eyes in horror. While she'd been lying in bed, having a DIY orgasm, Sadie had been upended on her bathroom floor like a stranded beetle, the phone out of reach.

'She's getting on a bit,' said Mrs Ambrose accusingly. 'She should be in a bungalow with a warden and round-the-clock surveillance.'

Annoyance helped Angela get a grip. 'Thank you, Mrs Ambrose. I'm even now speeding round to see her.'

Angela called a taxi, fighting her propensity to tears. She felt irrationally tearful. It was just too bad of her mother to issue a health warning while Robert was still a raw memory. Was this fall – however accidental – a fated, subtle reminder of Angela's daughterly neglect?

She knew about the arthritis, of course she did. But only Sadie's version of sporadic, easily deflected pain. If Sadie had been concealing her true frailty all along, she had only herself to blame for ending up on the bathroom floor. A bathroom floor that Robert and Angela had offered to carpet a few years ago, along with the coldly tiled kitchen and hallway.

Fortified but unfooled by these delusions of her past helpfulness, Angela swept into Sadie's in combative mood. 'I haven't brought grapes,' she announced, then paused on the threshold of Sadie's living room, too shocked to speak.

Sadie lay across the settee. Purply legs protruded from

a grubby dressing-gown. Her uncombed hair lay flat and grey on her scalp, a cold sore forming in the cracked hinge of her lips. Sadie's petiteness suddenly smacked of diminishment. Angela was used to her mother moving about briskly and fully dressed, all corrugated curls and support stockings that camouflaged her varicose veins.

'I'm absolutely fine,' croaked Sadie, reading Angela's face. 'The doc says I'm as healthy as a horse.'

'Maybe he meant Shergar.' Angela moved into the room, deciding jokey briskness was the best policy. She got precious few opportunities to tell Sadie what to do.

'Had breakfast yet?' she asked, turning up the single bar on the gas fire to a blazing three.

Sadie puffed like a mad Englishman sweltering in the tropics. 'That'll singe Binky's fur and give me blotchy legs. Can you ring work and tell them I won't be in till tomorrow?'

'You should take the rest of the week off,' frowned Angela.

'No, I'll be right as rain by tomorrow. Speaking of work, hadn't you better get your skates on?'

Light dawned on Angela. 'Oh God, I haven't rung in yet. Hang on a sec.'

She dashed to the phone, followed by Sadie's quavering imperative, 'Don't skip work on my account, lovey. You don't want to get on the wrong side of your boss!'

Gritting her teeth, Angela changed direction in mid-dash and ran upstairs to get a blanket for Sadie's legs, to protect them from fire-blotch.

She grabbed the duvet off Sadie's bed and ran downstairs again. Even in so flying a visit, she'd thought Sadie's bedroom shambolic and unwelcoming-looking. It was beginning to look horribly like an old person's room when the old person had given up on dust, sheet-changing and talcum powder spillages peppered with paw-marks.

And was it her over-critical imagination, or did the whole house smell of cat — of *l'air du litter tray*, to be precise?

'Here you go, Ma.' Breathlessly, she threw the duvet over Sadie, swaddling her legs. Peering helplessly out of her cocoon, Sadie looked defeated — and manageable.

Angela made her phone calls, laying it on a bit thick for Marla's benefit to justify a whole day off. Then she scuttled into the kitchen to make breakfast, whether Sadie had already partaken or not.

She had a few moments to collect her thoughts while the kettle boiled. It was at times like this she wished she'd moved away, like Owen. Not to avoid caring for Sadie, but because she was so crap at it. Social services would've done a better job and been appreciated more. Angela's meagre efforts to cook and fuss, put the telly at the right viewing angle, and lay in supplies of *Woman's Weekly*, would be undercut from the start by Sadie's silent forbearance of Angela's low caring standards, and her spoken dismay at 'being a burden'.

Face facts, sighed Angela, facing her distorted pout in the side of the kettle. I'm not martyr material. She had never risen to the heart-swelling challenge of being depended on. Look at the time Robert had got gastro-enteritis.

Angela, to her eternal shame, had hidden downstairs with a book while Robert staggered about upstairs, mopping up vomit that had missed the toilet. He'd even had to load the washing machine with the sheets and towels he'd ruined.

He hadn't spoken to Angela for a week afterwards.

Angela tottered back into the sitting room with a mug of Bovril and buttered triangles of toast. 'Ah,' she harrumphed, surveying Sadie's wan face. 'Toast — can you manage it? With dentures, I mean?'

'Not wearing any.' Sadie wrinkled her gums ghoulishly.

'I'll just suck the butter off the soft bits and leave the crusts. Then you can run upstairs and get my teeth from the bathroom.'

'OK,' shuddered Angela, annoyed at her revulsion. Bloody hell, she'd be old and toothless herself one day. Maybe incontinent. She arranged the food on her mother's lap and plumped up the cushions behind her.

'Mum, up in your room just now, I saw the electric blanket me and Robert got you was still in its bag.'

'That's right. I like to keep it clean.'

Angela eyed her balefully. 'It's supposed to be on the bed, under the under-sheet.'

Sadie picked up a piece of toast and looked pointedly at Angela until Angela looked away. Angela did so, trying not to flinch at the terrible suction noise as toast was sort of inhaled through her mother's slackly moist lips.

'Truth is, I prefer my hot water bottle to that electric blanket yoke,' revealed Sadie, plonking down a toast crust. 'I don't like the thought of electric volts zapping up and down the mattress. Does it short-circuit in a power cut, for example? Does the mattress catch fire if you forget to switch it off? Mattresses are very flammable, full of foam.'

'I really don't know, Ma.' Perching beside Sadie, Angela struggled to hide her annoyance. She and Robert had bought the electric blanket to coddle Sadie's stiff joints. 'Lots of people use them without a problem.'

'Meaning?'

'Meaning, just give it a try. I'll put it on now for you, if you like.'

'Sit there!' Sadie pointed an imperious finger. 'Rumours of my demise have been greatly exaggerated by that tittle-tattle Ambrose. I'm neither too senile nor too immobile to put an electric blanket on my own bed!'

Angela decided to regain the initiative by adopting an

equally imperious bedside manner. 'Never mind that. Tell me straight, Mum. Did you fall over from an arthritis attack? And why couldn't you get up again? If you can't cope...'

'You might be lumbered with me.'

'Yeah, it had crossed my mind. How do you feel about voluntary euthanasia? It's all the rage for oldsters with a social conscience who don't want to burden their relatives.'

Sadie chased crumbs around the duvet with a moistened fingertip. 'You don't get rid of me that easily.'

'I thought not. So don't play silly beggars acting the martyr. Let me help you.'

Sadie said slyly, 'Are you back to your original offer of putting a carpet in the bathroom to cushion any future falls?'

'God, you're impossible!' Angela leapt up, pushing her hands through her hair to stifle the impulse to wrap them round Sadie's neck. 'You are not sending me on any more guilt trips, Ma. I've packed up my rucksack of remorse and done the round-the-world trip. What I had in mind was a panic button, or a phone extension next to your bed, so I'm never more than a few digits away.'

Sadie snorted. 'Maud Ambrose is only a wall thickness away, but I was still banging half the night before she heard me.'

'Right!' snapped Angela. 'How about teaching you and Mrs Ambrose Morse code, so you can tap out a message through the wall?'

Sadie sighed tragically. 'You can't help it, can you? At the first sign of someone besting you in an argument, you get sarcastic. I hope you haven't let Conor see that side of you. Men find it very unfeminine.'

Angela wanted to scream. 'The panic button,' she

repeated faintly. 'Do you think it's a go-er as an idea — yes or no?'

Sadie mushed her lips together. She was trying to purse them, Angela realised. 'Where would the panic button be connected to?'

'Er — next door, I suppose.'

'What if Maud was out when I needed her? And even with a phone, supposing I rang you in an emergency, and you were out gallivanting with Conor?'

'Talk about a remote chance.'

'With Rachel, then.'

'Isn't risking that remote chance better than feeling isolated?'

'I'll certainly consider it,' decided Sadie, with an hauteur that covered her panic and — to some degree — her shame. She was behaving badly, but her fall had been a demeaning shock. As for that stuff about guilt trips — what was Angela on about? After all she'd done for her. A spark of self-pity ignited briefly in Sadie, flaring under her breastbone like heartburn. Was it really too much to expect her daughter to at least offer to care for her in her dotage? Why couldn't Angela throw self-interest to the winds and suggest they live together? The offer would suffice. She would, of course, refuse it grandly.

Her eyes met Angela's. The plea was only a flicker, but nakedly obvious.

Angela cleared her throat and looked into the fire. 'There's another option. You could, of course, move in with me.'

'Wouldn't that cramp your style with Conor?' asked Sadie quickly.

'I have no style to cramp. We're just good friends.' And never likely to get beyond that stage if she became the carer of an aged, demanding mother, ever in need of clean sheets and soaked teeth. Horror loomed in Angela, followed by a wave of utter self-disgust. How could she be so selfish?

'In that case,' said Sadie, watching her daughter carefully, 'no, no! I'm only joking! You don't seriously think I'd give up my independence, do you? I wouldn't want to move into your shoebox and you'd hate living back here. I'm not ready to be wheeled round in a bath-chair just yet.'

'As if,' grinned Angela. 'And we haven't explored the third option, putting you in a home. The money from selling this place would keep you in rubber sheets for years to come.'

Sadie smiled thinly at the joke. Angela had grasped too quickly at a climb-down. It was proof positive that she did not want her mother living with her.

'When are you seeing Conor again, lovey?'

'He's invited me to Shane's sports day on Saturday. Now look, if we're going to make you comfortable...'

'Rachel said you saw a picture of the ex-wife.'

'I glimpsed a photo in passing. She's beautiful,' admitted Angela, with a generosity that hurt her heart. 'Long white neck, longer red mane than My Friend Flicka.'

'Who?' asked Sadie, who obviously hadn't read the book. 'Where did you meet this Flicka?'

'She's a girl at work,' muttered Angela, too irritated to explain that Flicka was a horse in a kids' story. 'But before you ask, no, I didn't dig up the secret of their failed marriage. Does there have to be a secret? Couples grow apart and split up, end of story.'

'It's unusual to hop on a plane and leave your only child behind,' mused Sadie. 'She must've been desperate to get away. I wonder if she sued for custody and lost?'

'I'll have to ask,' decided Angela, squaring her shoulders. Really, it was all very well for Conor to lay bare his sexual liaisons. But there were too many unanswered questions about his marriage. A sneaky idea crept into her mind. Maybe she could pump Shane, subtly, for info.

'The lad's obviously prickly because of his broken home,' pondered Sadie. 'I ask myself, how could any mother walk out on a twelve-year-old?'

'You haven't met him,' said Angela uncharitably.

'It must've been a wrench for her. I wonder if a third party was involved.'

Angela started. God, how stupid of her not to consider that! She'd just assumed that Rosie, the fling, was a direct consequence of the marriage break-up. Maybe she was also a cause.

'Yes, she could've run off with another bloke and your Conor's loath to admit it,' said Sadie, who'd been thinking along different lines.

Angela brooded, reaching out to stroke Binky as he loped into the room. As her fingers stroked fluidly, she noticed Sadie's, lying crabbed and still on the duvet. 'Taken any painkillers, Mum?'

'A couple. I think I'll have a snooze now, Angela, if you wouldn't mind buzzing off to wash the dishes or whatever. I wish you'd go back to work this afternoon. I don't like you taking time off when you're new in the job.'

'Oh, they understand, Mum,' sighed Angela, and squeezed the rough warmth of Binky's fur in lieu of reaching across to gently squeeze Sadie's gnarled hand. She was no good at that sort of thing.

Angela turned up the driveway of 23 Pacelli Road, mentally girding her loins for the afternoon ahead. A day out with Problem Child. A few hours with Conor to probe his past life without offending him. Extract the info, more like. And that was going to be fiddlier than a scientist extracting DNA from prehistoric bone marrow.

A stunning woman in tight jeans opened the front door.

'H-hello,' blinked Angela. 'I've come – I'm Angela.'

The woman didn't shake hands. She jerked a richly coiffed head of peroxide curls over her shoulder and roared in purest Estuary, 'Shane! Yer dad's lady friend is here. Get your arse into gear.'

She held the door open for Angela to come in, then sashayed across the floor, a yellow duster fluttering out of a jeans back pocket. Angela blinked. Could this vision be Mrs Turner? Bloody hell, what sort of cleaning lady was this, for God's sake? Where was the floral housecoat, the blue rinse, the endless complaints about bunions?

Angela shut the door too hard and sulked.

Mrs Turner turned round. 'Stand on that rug, will ye?' she barked. 'I've just cleaned that floor with me own spit.'

'Sorry!' Angela jumped obediently onto a little island of pastel rug. Mrs Turner grunted and sashayed upstairs, passing Shane as he loped down.

Angela was too shaken by Mrs Turner to remember immediately that Shane was her mortal enemy.

'That's Mrs Turner?' she hissed at him in a conspiratorial whisper.

He frowned at Mrs Turner's receding, denim-puckered bum. 'Was last time I checked.'

His tone reminded Angela where she was and who Shane was.

'Er – don't you call her by her first name?'

'Don't think she's got one,' snorted Shane, pushing his glasses up his nose. 'Reckon even her husband calls her Mrs Turner. When he's home from prison, that is.'

'Prison!' goggled Angela. The bloody woman certainly looked more gangster's moll than household treasure.

'I s'pose you think Dad's giving her one,' blurted Shane, with a crude rudeness designed to shock. He watched Angela carefully for her reaction. But she was too cagey for him, weaned on Sadie's wind-ups and follow-up looks.

'It's his business,' she shrugged through gritted teeth. 'Where is he, anyway?'

'Gone out.'

'Out! Where?'

'Dunno. He didn't say. International man of mystery, my dad.'

Angela held on to her temper by scrabbling fingertips. He couldn't do this to her! Drag her over from Wilmesbury, then vanish before she arrived, leaving Problem Child and Gangster's Moll as her welcoming committee.

'He must've left a note or something,' she murmured, aware she was giving Shane the opportunity to deny any such meagre signs of consideration.

'He left a message with me, didn't he?' muttered Shane. 'That he's had to go out, urgently and unexpectedly. And we should go on to the bleeding sports day, where he'll try and turn up later. If you don't want to come, you'll just make the twelve-thirty train back to Wibblesbury.'

'You'd like that, wouldn't you?' snapped Angela tiredly. 'I bet you'd give anything to skive off sports day.' She paused to deliver her final salvo. 'I know I did when I was at school.'

Shane looked at her quickly. His grey eyes gleamed briefly behind thick glasses. 'Not sporty then, were you?' he grunted.

'I'm still infamous in school history as the girl who skipped the hundred metres,' confessed Angela proudly.

'You skipped it. Jesus!' Shane exhaled flutily down his nose, whether with derision or admiration she couldn't tell.

She decided to go for broke. 'The PE teacher was a Nazi. The only reason she entered me in the hundred metres was to humiliate me. Why else would you enter a kid who ran about as fast as a tortoise with lumbago? I'd crossed her once too often with passive resistance, refusing to leap-frog over the pommel horse, slither up ropes, whack ankles with hockey sticks. Only it wasn't resistance at all. I was too scared to do any of those things, so I just froze and refused, reckoning the fall-out couldn't be any worse than breaking my neck in the attempt. But PE teachers are pea-brained, you see.' Angela tapped her head passionately. 'If they had any grey matter, they'd be teaching from proper books in proper classrooms.'

Shane's head bobbled slightly. Almost a nod of agreement, thought Angela, careful not to snatch too quickly at wimps' solidarity.

True, Shane had a physique that cried out for musclemen to kick sand in his face. On the other hand, he could be fast and wiry, ideally suited to track and field. Something in his reference to 'bleeding sports day' hinted otherwise, however.

'You two still here?' squawked the dulcet tones of Mrs Turner, reappearing at the top of the stairs. 'Can't you just bugger off and let me hoover? Honestly, what's the point, with whole bleeding armies traipsing across the floor? Fucking middle-classes with their fucking dado rails and distressed fucking wood.' She vanished again, muttering.

Now that was more like a cleaning lady, Angela

reckoned, albeit a cleaning lady out of a de Niro/Scorsese film.

'Charming woman,' she remarked to Shane as he got his coat.

'Yeah, thank God she's only filling in until the real Mrs Turner gets over flu.'

'The real Mrs Turner?'

Shane stared at Angela as if she was retarded. 'You know, her mother-in-law.'

'You have got to be flaming joking!' Angela ranted at Shane. They eyeballed each other in the khaki-coloured school corridor. Shane stood defiantly in front of a notice-board listing events for sports day. One list contained Angela's name. She'd been entered in the mothers' charity egg-and-spoon race.

'I mean, are you sick in the head or something?' she yelled at Shane, prodding his folded arms. Parents and teachers trickled past, frowning at her.

'Careful now, you'll never get on the PTA with that attitude. More like the at-risk register.'

'I am not your flaming, frigging mother!'

'Language.'

'Well, I'm not doing it, so there!'

'Ooh, the spirit of passive resistance lives. I knew you wouldn't do it, so it's no skin off my nose, like. I filled in a form for you, though, and got loads of sponsors. I'll just pay back the sponsorship money. I entered Rosie last year, and she thought it was a right laugh. Even won it. It is for charity.'

'Rosie?' Angela blinked. She gazed down at Shane, a pigeon-chested weakling in a singlet and shorts, his glasses Band-Aided to each ear to minimise nose-bruising during the long jump. Like Angela in the past, he'd whittled down the day's ordeal to one event, invariably the event reserved for the lazy, the lame and the uncoordinated who couldn't hack running in a straight line. In Shane's school, this was the long jump, a Cinderella spectacle relegated to a wind-blown sandpit in a far-flung field. Under other circumstances, Angela would've recognised a kindred spirit. Under these circumstances, she was hostile, browbeaten and spitting with rage.

'Your dad said you couldn't stand Rosie.'

'I couldn't, but she was a good sport, like.'

'Huh, falling over herself to get in Master McGinlay's good books, more like. That's not my way.'

'What was the tenner for, then?'

Angela hesitated, wrong-footed. 'Actually, that was my mother's idea. The foolish woman thought you might be grateful and even send me a thank-you note.'

'How is your ma? Didn't she fall under a bus or something last week?'

'She fell on the floor and twisted her hip. It's no laughing matter!'

'Who's laughing?'

'You were smirking.'

'Wasn't!'

'You really are a little shit.'

She turned on her heel and stormed towards the playing field, followed by the shocked expressions of a few parents she hadn't spotted, lurking within earshot behind cloakroom pegs. Fuck the lot of them! It was a long time since she'd felt such anger, a violent mish-mash of resentments directed at Sadie, Robert, Rachel, the bloke who'd tried (deliberately!) to wrong-change her in the sweet shop that morning, and bloody, frigging, flaming Conor McGinlay, who'd rudely buggered off on the very day she'd psyched herself up to ask about Kate.

Outside, the cold air slapped her with a brisk plea to cool it. She slowed down by the main playing field, staked out with ribbons to create the lanes for a four by four relay, currently in shrieking progress.

Angela skirted the excited knot of parents and siblings, her anger gradually receding. Strangely enough, she wasn't angry at Shane at all. In fact, she felt a little weepy. His horridness surely put the kibosh on any future with Conor, whatever she learnt about Kate.

Dabbing her eyes, she looked around and spotted the stony face of Shane, watching the race from the opposite side of the field. He hadn't seen her.

He stood a little apart from a group of sniggering boys, singlets clinging to their over-developed chests. They were clearly casting aspersions on Shane's athletic prowess, gawky mien and bottle-thick specs. Angela compressed her lips. The locker-room jocks! How well she remembered their female counterparts from her own days at school.

Her first instinct was to wade across the field and drag Shane to safety. But her common sense won out. He'd be appalled and he'd never live it down.

Might as well go with her second idea, which was certainly not instinctive.

Sighing deeply, Angela obeyed the crackly Tannoy summons and tip-toed towards the starting line for the charity egg-and-spoon race.

Her rivals had come prepared in sensibly tailored trousers – and even shorts, despite a cutting March wind. Equipped with a soup spoon and an egg that refused to sit on it, Angela thanked God she wore low heels, left her raincoat with an obliging teacher, and shivered on the starting line, her ankle-length green shift dress flattened against her thighs by a strong head-wind.

She glanced down the line, proffering a comradely smile. Steely eyes glanced back, then looked ahead with a take-no-prisoners determination. God, thought Angela. So much for 'It's the taking part that matters.'

As the whistle went and her legs turned helpfully to jelly, she was catapulted back to the hundred metres at school where Mrs Jeffers, a Rottweiler in a shell-suit, had stood on the touch-line, yelling encouragingly, 'Where's your competitive spirit, you stupid, spineless girl?'

Her egg wobbled off the spoon before she'd moved. She caught it with her other hand and spent valuable seconds nesting it down again, while maternal bottoms galloped past her.

'Hey, lady, your dress!' hollered a squeaky, sexless voice from the sidelines. 'Stuff it in your knickers to run faster!'

There was method in this mad suggestion. She didn't stuff it in her knickers – too many sniggering kids around and smalls too baggy and grey – but she gathered up the front of her dress and twisted it into a knot away from her knees, giving them room to propel unimpeded.

She lost the egg four more times, but romped home a far-from-disgraced third last, nose-diving towards the finishing line with as much grace as she could muster, bearing in mind that Shane was watching.

Only he wasn't. As Angela got to her feet and wiped grass off her knees, she realised that actually, few people had been watching her finest sporting hour.

The crowd had drifted away to other pockets of activity. In the distance, a shower of sand grains rose into the air. The long jump!

Reclaiming her raincoat and relinquishing the spoon, Angela hurried towards the sand-pit. Drawing closer, she saw it was an informal warm-up event for the actual long jump.

A group of boys were standing on the edge of the pit. In the centre, another boy sat astride a prone figure, making him eat dirt – or, literally, sand. Just in front of the supine victim lay a pair of glasses, half-buried in sand like the last remains of a foreign-legionnaire.

Angela's breath shortened and her chest tightened. The bullying bastards! She tried to yell, but her indignation trapped her voice in a bubble of wheezy air. She curled her fist, which tightened on a smooth, warm surface.

She looked down, surprised to find the egg still in her hand. She'd never been any cop at the shot-putt either, but here went nothing.

Drawing back her arm, Angela flung the egg with all her might, aiming for the bully astride Shane. It hit the back of his bulldog head with a satisfying thunk, exploding on impact into a runny mess.

'What the – !' The bully looked up. His cronies ran in all directions, without even bothering to see who'd chucked the egg. 'Cowardly scum!' hissed Angela, advancing on Torquemada, the ring-leader.

The boy jumped off Shane, who glanced fleetingly up at Angela, then plonked his face straight back in the sand. Angela didn't care if she was embarrassing him or not. She'd never been so grateful to be a tall woman, with hair askew, raincoat flapping wildly, dander up.

'Ever heard of the Geneva Convention, you little horror!' she screamed at the boy, one of the locker-room jocks.

'Y-you threw a rotten egg at me.' His bottom lip actually wobbled as egg yolk dripped into his ear.

'Ah, diddums. But then again, how typical. Like all cowards and bullies, you're a chicken-hearted, worthless piece of scum, aren't you?' She grabbed him by his singlet and shook him. 'Aren't you?'

'I'll get my parents onto you,' he gasped. 'That's assault.'

'You do that sunshine. And I'll raise enough of a stink to get you expelled from this school, barred from every other one and thrown into borstal for a short, sharp shock. Comprendez? Now get the hell out of my sight and don't you ever lay a finger on another kid again, unless you reckon your vital organs would look better as accessories dangling from a charm bracelet. Scram!'

He took off, boggle-eyed.

Shane mumbled into the sand.

'Eh?' Angela hauled him upright, none too gently.

'I said, thanks for nothing. I have to go to this school.'

'Can it, kiddo. I did the suffering-in-silence bit at school, when I'd have given anything for a tattooed parent wielding a bike chain to sort out the bullies for me. No point in fighting your own battles when the odds are stacked against you. I reckon that homicidal shithead got the message.'

She stood back triumphantly, folding her arms. God, it felt good to be alive.

Shane raised himself up on skinny elbows. 'I suppose you think we'll bond for life now. I'll see you in a new light and become all respectful, like, until the day we all go and live on Waltons' mountain.'

'Something like that,' said Angela cheekily.

'Dream on. You've just stood on my glasses.'

Later that evening, Conor rang to apologise. 'Something came up I couldn't get out of.' He paused. 'I hope you'll overlook my rudeness.'

'No problem,' murmured Angela, twisting the phone cord round her fingers, as if she could wind him in, rekindle that spark of intimacy on the sofa, find out where the hell he'd been.

'How's Sadie?'

'Oh, fine, thanks. Went back to work yesterday.'

'I hear you took part in the egg-and-spoon race. I wish I'd seen that.'

'I'm glad you didn't.' What else had Shane told him?

'Shane managed to break his glasses during the long jump. He's a bear with a sore head because he can't watch telly.'

'Poor kid. He did well in the event.'

'I know. He didn't come last. I don't give a stuff about having a sporty son, frankly. I'd rather he was a short-sighted bookworm with train-spotting tendencies. At least until he's got some paper qualifications.'

'I agree.'

He was silent, very silent, down the line. She tried to summon up his green eyes looking deeply into hers, the way he'd said 'Please relax' as he touched her hands, even the grunting bluffness that masked his shyness as he shoved freesias under her nose. But without seeing his face and gauging his mood, she felt him slipping away from her.

'Goodnight then, Angela. Speak to you soon.'

Her heart sank. 'Goodnight, Conor.'

Chapter Seven

The airport cafeteria was empty, except for the couple at the corner table.

Wiping the cappuccino machine with a damp cloth, cafeteria manageress Ailsa strained, unsuccessfully, to overhear the couple's conversation.

Their hands lay side by side on the small table, careful not to touch, matching luggage stacked to one side. Was it a reunion or a parting? Yes – it had to be a parting. The caff was closer to departures than arrivals.

Neither of them, thought Ailsa, looked heartbroken. Just defeated. He'd run into the caff a few minutes earlier, puffing and checking his watch. Nice-looking, in an earthy sort of way.

She'd been waiting, cool as you like, smoking wispy cigarettes. She was a stunner, all that red hair tumbling over her shoulders. Her chin was tilted at a defiant angle. It must be her leaving him, Ailsa decided, and glanced at the wall clock. Another half hour to go before her shift ended. Maybe the parting lovebirds would liven things up a bit with tears, a row, rattled saucers.

'Feeling better?' Kate murmured at Conor, as he drained his second coffee.

'You might have given me more notice! I've had to run

out on Shane and his sports day and tear across London to get here, in answer to the royal summons.'

'I know. I'm sorry. But it was worth hearing, wasn't it? I'm deadly serious, Conor. In two months, my contract will be up at work. And I want to come back. I want to be near Shane, make it up to him. You may not have noticed, but he's starting to go off the rails a bit.'

'And you would notice, three thousand miles away!' Conor flared up.

'Look,' conceded Kate, stubbing out another cigarette. 'You're the on-the-spot parent, doing a fantastic job. When I say he's going off the rails, it's nothing as dramatic as that. But each time he visits me in New York, he's a little less his old, sunny self. He's watchful and sulky. I think he's desperately unhappy, and it's our fault. I want to try and put things right.'

Conor fiddled with a teaspoon. 'For Shane's sake, right?'

'And for my own, I suppose. Making it up to Shane will chase away a few night-time demons.' She wiped her mouth delicately on a triangle of serviette. A muscle quivered on her cheek. Conor's gaze narrowed. He knew that twitch so well. 'There's no sinister third party, Conor. I haven't met anyone in New York. My therapist reckons it'll be some time before I trust men again. Perhaps never.'

Conor's face hardened.

'But Shane was telling me on the phone, *you* have a new – lady friend.'

Conor grunted, annoyed at his irrational guilt. He was divorced from this beautiful, brittle woman with the tremor in her hands and the unnatural lustre in her hazel eyes. She had summoned him to Heathrow on a stopover flight from New York to Helsinki, where her sister lived, teaching English. And he'd come running like an eager puppy. A summons from Kate? It had to be momentous. He'd been way off beam, expecting an announcement of remarriage. To hell with that. She actually wanted to return to the family fold – strictly on her own terms, of course.

Playing for time, he told her, 'Shane is not going off the rails. His grades are good, he doesn't do drugs or smoke behind the bike shed. And just because he's a slow starter with girls – for which, personally, I'm grateful – it doesn't mean he's gay, or an anorak. I was a late developer, too.'

'We both were. We helped each other develop, remember?'

Conor looked into his cup. He didn't want a common point of reference, a litany of shared memories beginning 'Do you remember the time...?' If love was a hard habit to break, infatuation had been harder. In the weeks following Kate's departure from 23 Pacelli Road, he'd cold-turkeyed on the empty mattress in their bedroom, living on toasted sandwiches and wishing he smoked, growing a beard behind closed curtains, while Mrs Turner fed, placated and lied to Shane.

'So who is your lady friend?' persisted Kate placidly. 'An improvement on the awful-sounding Rosie, one hopes. Are you planning to move her in, marry her?'

'It's in the early stages.' Possibly about to be strangled at birth.

'I've never wanted anything off you, Conor. No alimony, no settlements. I was pleased to earn my own way. It saved my sanity. But I am asking for this – to come back and live in my own home. Who helped you make it a home?'

'You helped me pick out curtains for the spare room,' nit-picked Conor.

'I'm warning you, Conor!' Her voice rose an octave

and wobbled on the point of dissolution. 'All right, so the mortgage was in your name, and you always paid it, even when I worked full-time before Shane came along. That was a mistake on my part. But I put years of my life into that rotten house, fortress McGinlay!'

She lowered her voice as the woman wiping the coffee machine looked over with interest. 'I've no desire for us to live as man and wife, Conor. That part is over. But I want to do right by Shane, and Shane wants me to come back –'

Conor jumped. 'My God, you've told him the idea has the green light? Before you even met me to discuss it!'

'I could hardly moot the idea before I'd tested Shane's reaction to it. We spoke on the phone last week, and I threw it out as a theoretical situation. He was receptive, as it happens. He didn't stop loving me just because you did.'

Her voice quivering on a sigh, she looked away, offering a perfect profile. But it wasn't as perfect as she thought. Her complexion and chin had begun to thicken and redden, in a slight but discernible coarseness.

Conor felt unbearably sad. He also felt big and rough and peasanty, insensitive to her finely tuned emotions. Just as she wanted him to feel. He clutched his chin, rasping the shave-resistant stubble. 'How could it ever work, Kate? You and me under the same roof again.'

She said quickly, 'It could. We can give Shane the stability of two parents, without expecting too much – anything, really – of each other. You'd still have your life and I'd have mine. I'll tell you how.'

As she told him how, Conor's inner thermostat went from simmer to boil. He could hardly wait until she'd finished.

'You're not bloody serious?' he thundered, then met

her eye. 'You are! You seriously think I'd desecrate my – my...'

'Your real mistress?' said Kate with precise coolness. 'The only love of your life? Yes, that's what I'm asking for, because I'm entitled. Does your new woman know all about your bricks-and-mortar and hardwood-floors fixation?'

Conor's eyes bulged. His eyebrows did a demented caterpillar dance.

Kate laughed delicately and lit another cigarette. 'Only consider my proposal,' she wound up. 'You've got two months to wrestle with the pros and cons. Will you at least do that? Consider it, hmm? You'll soon realise how sensible it is. Just think of Shane.'

Blood pounded behind his temples. He longed to hurt and reject her. He longed to ignore his much-vaunted 'responsibility' to Shane. And he longed to take that beautiful neck between his hands and squeeze tightly – or rain down hungry, bruising kisses on its creamy hollow, branding her soap-advert downiness with welts of angry lust.

But he had to hand it to Kate – she knew him so well! She knew his baser impulses were supremely self-controlled. That he trusted himself much more than he'd ever trusted her.

Glancing at her watch, she stood up to signal that the meeting was over.

Conor rose slowly, as if backing off from a guard dog.

'Everything hinges on you now, Conor. On whether you can find it in your heart to let bygones be bygones.'

He grinned mirthlessly. Slick, very slick! Pass him the sole responsibility as a test of his magnanimity. And leave just a suggestion in the air of how Shane would react, come the inevitable day when he learnt of Conor's choice.

'What happens if I won't play ball?' he asked. 'Will you still come back to England when your contract's up?'

She ruffled her hair wearily. 'I haven't thought that far ahead, because that would involve solicitors, and I'm keen to avoid upsetting Shane. I've every faith in you – in us. Goodbye, Conor.' She leant forward on tiptoe to brush his stubble with her lips. 'You can contact me back in New York, but don't leave it too long, hmm?'

'See ya Kate.' He caught her on the corner of her mouth as it slid away. He tasted nicotine and peppermint lip balm.

Ailsa watched the red-haired woman sashay across the concourse. It looked like dry eyes all round. But the bloke stood there for a while, staring after her. He was cut through the heart, no doubt about it.

Conor took the Tube back into London, shaken and perturbed. If he didn't play ball, Kate would probably make his life hell, perhaps even sue him for custody as an unfit father, citing his frequent absences and twisting his petty liaison with Rosie into a sordid affair. God, she'd been so careful to avoid other relationships! The sainted mother, driven away in pursuit of her sanity, pining for the son she'd had to leave as a lesser of two evils. Planning, always, to return as soon as she could, once the trauma of her mental collapse had passed.

Conor stood up to let a pregnant woman have his seat. When she sat down, he realised that she was just fat.

Jamming his hands in his pockets, he leant against the carriage door, reflecting that he always got the wrong end of the stick when it came to women. Starting most spectacularly with Kate, the ex-love of his life. A sensitive, gentle woman who'd survived a tyrannical bully of a father with quiet courage. Or so it had seemed.

Conor had been in danger of leaving university a virgin

when he met Kate. By that time, well into the third year
of his engineering course at City University in London, he
and his two mates, Iggy and Tommo, were united in a
frustrated quest to lose their cherries. Conor had blamed
their continuing innocence on membership of the Catholic
Society, otherwise known as CathSoc.

All three had joined up at freshers' fair. Conor was a
native Dubliner, while Iggy and Tommo were second-
generation Irish. They'd all reckoned it'd be easier to
bond with girls from a similar background.

Plus, if Conor was honest, he'd expected to lose his
cherry more of less immediately in the fervid immorality
of university life, and preferred to lose it to a girl with
some point of moral reference.

Most CathSoc members were second-generation Irish.
The blokes wore their badge of Irishness by drinking
Beamish and arguing whether Eoin Hand was a decent
manager or a total wanker. The girls had sad, mellifluous
names from Celtic mythology, long Titian hair and
cuttings from *The Irish Post* featuring their Irish dancing
triumphs.

Conor was scared of these girls for the same reasons
he'd sought cultural safety in their numbers. Nice Catholic
girls did not go in for one-night stands. He wasn't sure
he'd be able to get it up with one who did. The only boy
and the youngest in a family of four girls who'd petted
and spoilt him, he was, at twenty, still dogged by the
madonna/whore analogy. It would take Kate to impress
upon him that women were not two-dimensional beings,
neither shadows cast by a religious icon, nor the passive
non-beings in porn mags.

He, Iggy and Tommo analysed their virginity
relentlessly and crudely. One evening, after a piss-weak
beer too far in the student union bar, they made a

musketeer pact to boldly go where no man of them had gone before, that very night.

Infused more with the pioneering spirit of conquistadors than romantic sensibility, they'd set off for the student union disco, held in an unprepossessing Portakabin half a mile away.

Their dreams were not to be fulfilled. Iggy passed out while resting his head on the shelf-like embonpoint of a bored, big-breasted girl who'd agreed to a slow dance. Conor, deciding to leave within half an hour of arriving, had felt his arm clutched as he swayed towards the body-choked doorway. 'Walk out of this place with me!' hissed a female voice in his ear. 'Just to shake off that dickhead behind us!'

Conor glanced round to see Tommo bearing down with a glassy but determined smile. He didn't have time to make up his mind. His arm was wrenched and he half-fell out of the Portakabin, blinking in the sudden darkness.

Beside him, female breath exhaled harshly. 'I think that did it,' she hissed. 'Thanks.'

His eyes adjusting to the light, he caught a glint of red hair, like the flash of a tropical bird's underwing. She struck a match and soft, incandescent light illuminated the waxy perfection of her skin, the dark brows lowered in concentration as she lit her cigarette. She reminded him of a church statue of Mary, purity of expression dancing in the light of candles clustered round her feet. Only this vision was Madonna and ciggy. 'Bloody hell, you're beautiful,' said Conor with both spur-of-the-moment admiration, and a hint of reverent awe.

She laughed and looked at him properly for the first time. 'You're not so bad yourself,' she said.

After all those months spent working out chat-up lines and gleaning 'how to pull' tips from nudge-nudge-wink-wink men's mags, it seemed that girls responded to that over-rated quality of 'being yourself'. He'd made a mental note to tell Tommo and Iggy.

That night, they just had coffee and talked, back at her place. Kate, an art student, shared a dingy flat with a chain-smoking medical student. The place was a proper student den with peeling posters of Thatcher as the Antichrist, and cushions, bean bags and empty bottles covering every inch of carpet. Kate explained that her flatmate liked to recreate chaos out of any order that Kate herself imposed. She didn't mind too much, as long as the bathroom stayed clean. Conor felt embarrassed that he lived in a hall of residence, sharing a fridge and a bathroom with five other blokes who labelled their milk cartons and left damp socks to mildew over communal radiators.

Sex never entered his head that night, or successive nights. Just to touch Kate seemed an honour and a violation. When he pulled away from a goodnight kiss that night, he expected to see his fingerprints bruising her perfect skin.

Two weeks later, Tommo bounced into his room at four a.m., eating a post-coital cream cracker with Marmite. He'd done the deed.

'Julia Flynn!' he revealed. 'She'd have gone for you, Conor, if you'd stuck at it. She loves a bit of Irish inside her, ho ho. Got your leg over that posh tart yet?'

He hadn't. For all his reputation as a hard man (at least among other blokes who thought he must play rugby), he was shy and Kate was scared. Her father had made her scared of men, she apologised. He was a bully, a racist and a born-again Christian, pastor to a small bunch of rabid torch-bearers for true, Papist-free Christianity. She'd defied him by going to university in London. He'd wanted her to stay up in Northumberland, where he could keep an eye on her.

Besides, Conor and Kate were friends first, putative lovers second. Conor had never been friends with a girl before – unless he counted collecting frog spawn in jam-jars one summer with Jeanie, the friend of his sister, Grainne. At the time, Jeanie had been the same as any male friend because she hung upside-down from the monkey-bars at school with her skirt tucked into her pants, laughed loudly at her own jokes, ridiculed his frog-spawn-catching technique compared to her own. She hadn't behaved like a girl. She had behaved, Conor realised during his first months with Kate, like herself.

As Kate became herself to him, he braved the stumbling block of sex as a matter of concern between best friends. He suggested that he start off by inserting his little finger, then build up to two fingers, 'the width of your average love truncheon', according to Tommo.

But, however hard she tried, Kate tensed up when the moment came.

Patiently shelving the two-fingered entry approach, Conor had then posited 'starting with a pencil and working up to a cucumber – one of the smaller, less prickly varieties'. He showed her how to put a condom on a cucumber she had shrivelling in the bottom of her fridge.

This had left Kate unimpressed. 'I think the correlation of vegetables to sexual organs is deeply unsatisfying,' she'd said, with an art student's sense of the aesthetically valid.

She'd convinced herself she was a freak of humanity – until she read something on a problem page.

'I've got vaginismus,' she proudly informed a disheartened Conor. 'It's all because Daddy's bullied Mummy all her life, and I associate sex with the brute force of men, taking and despoiling, trampling the female will underfoot.'

'That's bollocks,' Tommo told Conor. 'I bet she still

wears jam rags so her hymen's still intact, that's all. Sex is bound to hurt a bit at first, Julia says, if you've never put a tampon up there.'

There came a night, however, when he and Kate decided to go for it. The chain-smoking medical student was away for the weekend, the telly on the blink, and London shimmered in an evening heat haze, heavy with portents and expectation.

Conor returned from the cash-and-carry on the corner, laden with condoms and a six-pack of potent beer. He and Kate sat on adjoining bean bags, gulping down beer with fear and determination. They made a pact. 'What about if we try it,' said Conor, 'and I ignore you when the screaming starts, but if you scream "Stop, stop!" more than twice, then I really will stop?'

He undressed her slowly on top of her bed, massaging her with something rich and oily from her dressing table and investing in a lot of stroking foreplay that immediately made Kate tense up because, she said, she couldn't bear to disappoint him after so much effort. 'If it took this long every time, the bloke would nod off before he got round to it,' she gasped into Conor's broad shoulder.

'Sssh,' he murmured, 'here I come, ready or not. Geronimo!'

Kate didn't scream too loudly and never more than twice. She was determined, she said afterwards, to see it out to the bitter end. Like Columbus sailing on to prove that he wouldn't fall off the edge of the world, she wanted proof of her girl friends' insistence that the eye-watering pain slid eventually into seamless ecstasy.

Ecstasy didn't come into it for either of them, but the elation of having done it was orgasmic in itself.

Afterwards, Conor lay in her arms and fell sleep from sheer relief.

Kate, fastidious as a cat, slipped out of bed without

disturbing him and took a shower, then returned to bed. When he awoke, he realised that she smelt different. The warm, musky, after-sex smell had been replaced by ashes of roses bath oil. He'd felt a twinge of disappointment.

After that, they got better at it. Kate never got out of her tree with ecstasy, but on the third occasion, she felt a definite ping, she said, a small explosion of delight that had to be the much-vaunted orgasm. They were best friends having sex. Life was good.

In December 1982, he and Kate sped northwards by train to announce their engagement to her parents.

'Best to get it over with!' Kate had said, hugging her plastic cup of coffee in the packed, sunny compartment. 'I've only said over the phone that I'm bringing a friend for the weekend. We'll lull them into a false sense of security with the pressies we've brought, then hit them for six with our news.'

Conor felt a growing doubt. 'They're not that bad, are they? I know your dad's a bit fierce and you hate his guts. But he'll come round at this news, surely? And your mum…?'

'His bark's worse than his bite!' sang Kate, almost glowing. She gripped Conor's knee, then inched her hand along his thigh and towards his balls, in full view of other travellers. Conor grinned. He came from a normal family with its normal complement of bust-ups and shameful secrets. He'd be able to handle Kate's da.

Kate must've known what was coming, though, because she told the taxi to wait while they picked their way over frozen puddles and knocked on the prissy little door of the prissy little house. Kate's mother had answered.

Kate beamed, said nothing, and prodded Conor forward.

'Mrs Stanton?' Conor held out a large, firm hand. 'I'm Conor McG... '

'Oh dear, no!' quivered tiny Mrs Stanton, fixing pale dormouse eyes on her daughter. 'What were you thinking of, our Katrina, bringing a lad? You'd better go straightaway before there's any trouble. There's a love.'

The door was suddenly flung open and a preposterously small, scrawny-necked man, a turkey cock no less, shoved Kate's mother aside.

Kate's beam almost split her face. 'Daddy! I've brought my boyfriend, Conor, from Dublin. He's a Catholic!'

'Get off my doorstep!' yelled the turkey-cock. Conor leapt off the step. But his mind, snapping in several directions at once, was already thinking, I can take you, you auld bastard. You'd better not lay a finger on Kate.

Turkey-cock slammed the front door. Unfazed, Kate lifted the letterbox. 'Yes, a Papist, and there's nothing you can do about it. We're getting married! I'm pregnant with his Papist offspring, and I'm going to have a football team for the Pope and have them all serving Mass with bells and burning handbags and candles lit to Mary and –'

A rifle muzzle poked through the letterbox. Kate withdrew just in time.

'I'm going to count to three,' snarled the malevolent voice inside.

They were back in the taxi by two-and-a-half. Kate was laughing. 'Don't worry, it was just for show. It's a blunderbuss from Cromwell's day or something. Can't fire birdseed.'

Conor was shaking with rage and shock. 'You did tell them about me! Beforehand, I mean.'

'No, I didn't. Turning up unannounced with any member of the male species who wasn't a pre-picked member of the brethren, was a red rag. I was hoping he'd die of apoplexy on the spot.'

'You said you were pregnant!'

'I'm not, so chill out. Just gilding the lily a bit. Might as well be a pregnant fornicator if I'm going all out to be the whore of Babylon.'

Conor's mind was atangle with more questions. But the least relevant one burst out. 'What's a burning handbag?'

She lit a cigarette as the taxi swung away. 'That incense thing you lot swing on the end of a rope. Exactly where I wish he was.' She jabbed her head back at the house. Her red-gold hair was braided with the dewy fretwork of damp vapour from the cold December air. Her eyes danced with Jack Frost merriment. Conor thought she looked mad. And wonderful. Only later – a whole week later – came the realisation that women could use men. He'd assumed it only worked one way. And with that realisation came the first fissure in their friendship.

Angela woke up, assailed by bird-song. She jolted upright. It was mini-market Sunday. Sadie would meet Shane. And Conor would finally meet Rachel.

Angela felt the familiar surge of insecurity.

Was it wise to have a stunning friend? Even though Rachel's affections were currently accounted for, the object of them, a businessman called Marshall, was abroad. Angela suddenly wished she was running a stall. She longed to look capable and sweetly magnanimous, marking down designer cast-offs for wary Wilmesbury matrons in the name of charity.

Although it was well out her way, she presented herself at Sadie's at ten-thirty, in time for the ten-forty-two bus that stopped outside St Anselm's.

'We could have just met there,' grumbled Sadie, locking her front door. 'I can still hobble to the bus-stop without a Zimmerframe.'

'I know,' said Angela, instantly nettled by such ingratitude. 'Shall we go? Best foot forward.' She set off at a smart pace, leaving Sadie puffing in her wake.

Conor and Shane were waiting, as instructed, in the church vestibule. Conor looked sleek and uncomfortable in his dark linen suit. Shane, complete with new glasses, was picking papier-mâché splinters off the giant thermometer that dominated the vestibule, a felt-tipped line of red nudging upwards towards the total sought for the roof repair fund.

'Half the mini-market proceeds this year are for the roof,' said Angela, stepping protectively in front of her mother. 'Hi there, Shane.'

Sadie took Shane unawares, grabbing his shoulders and shaking him gently but firmly in a top-to-toe appraisal. 'Give us a twirl, young feller, and let's see if you're as tall as your dad. Almost! Must be the growth hormones they put in beef-burgers these days.'

'Don't eat beef-burgers,' muttered a truculent Shane. He looked miserably press-ganged into the outing.

'How are you keeping, Sadie?' asked Conor, avoiding eye contact with Angela.

'Well now, I'm just fine, thank you. Not quite ready to chuck in the towel, despite well-meaning attempts to brick me into a corner with a knitting pattern and a jar of joint liniment for company.'

'Mum!' muttered Angela, looking exactly like Shane.

Sadie cocked her head mischievously. 'Seeing as we're all here and all Catholics, I thought we could say a little prayer in the church before we to market.'

Shane shrugged. 'Dad's lapsed as anything. He never makes me go.'

'Shane! That's not quite true, Sadie. I have been remiss some Sundays, due to work and whatnot.'

'Huh!' said Shane.

'Mum knows full well that I'm lapsed too,' shrugged Angela. 'But I've no objection. Probably do us all a world of good.'

She met Sadie's eye, refusing to be embarrassed by her mother's rampant display of practising Catholicism.

'Robert was a great churchgoer,' Sadie told Conor. 'He really showed my daughter up, I'm afraid. Since he left us, she's only been to his funeral and midnight mass at Christmas.'

Conor said politely, 'I've no excuse, as a former altar boy. Mind you, they say we're the first to fall by the wayside. The ones who had it shoved down our necks from the word go.'

Sadie nodded at Shane. 'In that case, he should be up for Pope. I don't believe in all this "I was force-fed" nonsense. How else do you learn the basics, except through your catechism? He's not likely to grow up and choose religion, is he, if he's never been grounded in the basics? Letting people find out for themselves – that's just a woolly-minded cop-out.'

Conor watched Sadie and Shane bob into a pew. Shane genuflected and blessed himself on automatic pilot.

Conor slumped into the pew behind, leaving room for Angela beside him.

He was assailed by inadequacy on all counts; as a father, an ex-husband and as a prospective lover of funny, sweet, good-natured Angela.

Angela knelt beside him and prayed for selfish things. For Sadie's decrepitude to stabilise, for Shane to admire her as a feisty big sister, for Conor to kiss her again.

She cast him a sidelong glance from beneath lowered lashes. He was staring at the back of Shane's head, mentally burrowing under the tufted brown hair on his son's scrawny neck. Angela couldn't be sure of anything about him – least of all, that he was thinking about her.

When Sadie signalled an end to quiet reflection by rising on creaky hips, they spilled out into brittle sunshine like prisoners released from solitary confinement.

Cars now filled every corner of the car-park. The Wilmesbury faithful and bargain-hunters streamed towards the primary school playground at the rear of the church, followed by the quartet emerging from the church porch, walking in couples.

Sadie strolled with Shane, pointing out ancient dog turds encrusting the grass verge and asking nosy questions about school. Shane replied in a flat, unemotional monotone. Angela couldn't hear his answers, but he didn't seem annoyed.

'Ange?'

She looked up in surprise. Conor had been silent so long – without quite ignoring her – that she'd fallen back on her own thoughts for some time now.

'Look, is my name still mud after last Saturday? I couldn't avoid buggering off. Some big cheese engineer flew in unexpectedly and I had to meet him at the airport.'

'Oh, well.' Relief warmed her veins at this simple explanation – though he could've told her when he rang to apologise. 'No harm done,' she said bravely. 'I got the chance to bond with Shane at the Nuremberg rally that passes for a school sports day. We both belong to the fellowship of wimps – or deep thinkers, as I prefer to call it.'

Conor grunted. 'Let me buy you something to make up for it.'

They rounded a corner and hit a sea of humanity flowing between haphazardly arranged stalls. Shane and Sadie vanished under a wave.

Conor stepped back and stubbed his toe against a trestle table he hadn't seen, heaped with old thrillers and sports annuals. The table wobbled dangerously. 'Watch it!' said a man behind teetering Mills & Boons novels.

Conor reddened and picked up a dog-eared Alistair MacLean, studying it closely.

Angela felt a wave of affection for him. For all his money and his smart house and everything, he'd never be Mr Cool. He couldn't handle the simplest social challenge – thank God.

She saw Rachel waving at them and grabbed Conor's arm. 'Time to meet and mingle, I'm afraid. Don't worry, Rache is harmless compared to my mother.'

Harmless wasn't the right epithet for Rachel, in Conor's opinion. She left a rail of floaty, diaphanous dresses to ignore his outstretched hand and kiss him warmly on the cheek. He reddened again.

'I'm Rachel, famous for leading Ange astray,' she smiled, managing to charm without sounding coquettish. 'We must all get together when the madding crowds subside, go for a drink or whatever.'

Rachel wore a creamy, hip-hugging dress of gold-embroidered lace, her only concession to March a matching shawl looped over both shoulders. The fringe canopied tastefully exposed cleavage.

Conor looked determinedly into Rachel's eyes. Angela pulled at the seams of her navy-blue jumper and asked Rachel, 'How long is Marshall away?'

'Too long,' replied Rachel mildly. 'When you've only just met someone and they zoom off into the sunset again, it's hard on the old libido. Still, he's hinted at an April weekend in Paris to make up for things.'

'Marshall is Rachel's current...' began Angela.

'Project? Experiment?' laughed Rachel. She lifted her brows at Conor. 'Angela disapproves, however silently, of changing men like wallpaper, simply because they've gone a bit tatty and blend into the background.' She held a deep green sari against a silent Conor. 'You could never be colourless, Conor. Ange, be an angel and run and get me a coffee from Mrs Thomsett's stall, will you? Conor and I want to discuss you in your absence.'

'Hah!' said Angela, with a sisterly solidarity she didn't feel. Never until this day had she realised how dangerous Rachel was. Talking about libidos, dazzling Conor with her chic sophistication. And boy, was he dazzled. He had that rabbit-trapped-in-car-headlights look.

Angela stomped off to get coffee and bumped into Sadie. 'Oh, hello. Where's the kid?'

'I've lost him,' reported Sadie, already weighed down with a pot of chutney the colour of snot and cut-price Tupperware that still reeked of school lunches.

'Lost him?' squeaked Angela. 'Was that wise?'

'It's not exactly a Moroccan bazaar, lovey. He can't come to much harm.'

Famous last words. When Angela returned to Rachel's stall with a scalding cup of coffee, she found father and son engaged in A Scene.

'Christ, what have you done now?' Conor was demanding of Shane, watched passively by Rachel. 'I give you a tenner, I tell you to spend it on what you like, and you use it as down-payment on a bloody useless heap of junk!'

'What's up?' demanded Angela unwarily.

Conor groaned. 'He's just bought a clapped-out computer that probably doesn't work, and promised the shyster selling it that I'll cough up sixty quid for it!'

'Yeah, well, if I waited for you to buy me a proper one, I'd be drawing my pension. Computers are like arseholes.'

'Eh?' goggled Conor.

'Everyone's got one.'

'I told you to wait until Christmas, when I would've bought you a decent one.'

'Arsehole or computer?'

'I'm coming to the end of a fraying rope here.'

'This computer is decent! And a bargain. It just needs a bit of tinkering.'

'Who by?' yelled Conor. 'You and I can't even set the video-plus thing.'

Angela folded her arms. Yet again, Problem Child was monopolising Conor and claiming all his attention. Perhaps Kate had left because she'd grown sick of being ignored.

'Anyway, you'll have to buy it now, cos I promised,' sulked Shane. 'An Englishman's word is his bond.'

'Lucky I'm not an Englishman,' snorted Conor. He caught Angela's eye. 'You should see it, Angela. It's scrap without the scrap metal value.'

Angela went and saw it. 'I'm surprised at you,' she told Shane. 'I thought you'd have more nous. These things went out with the ark.'

Shane looked at her warily. 'And you'd know, like?'

'Certainly I'd know. I use a state-of-the-art computer at work.'

After she'd helped Conor manhandle the computer and trailing bits into his car, she joined him on the patch of grass outside the church. Sadie and Shane had adjourned to the cake stall to guess the weight of the large pound cake on display. Shane had prophesied that any weight resulting from edible ingredients would be supplemented with ball bearings.

'You were a bit harsh on him,' said Angela.

Conor scowled. 'You've no idea what it's like, raising a stroppy teenager.'

Angela pulled up stubborn tufts of grass. 'So where does that leave us? You're always busy working or paternalising. I think the longest conversation I've had with you was on the plane.'

Conor's scowl deepened with contrition. 'Look, Angela, forget the fatherly breast-beating bit. I'm sorry. Can we start this afternoon again?'

She shrugged.

'Let's go away!' he said impulsively. 'Just the two of us. If Rachel's bloke can run to Paris in April, I can do my bit. How about Ireland?'

'You serious?' Angela peered at him. 'What about Shane?'

'He's always angling to spend a weekend with Matty Hyde. Matty has a mother who bakes things, feels sorry for Shane, and is endlessly susceptible and shockable when it comes to practical jokes. Shane loves it round there.'

'You and me – just the two of us – in Ireland.' An expedition laced with promise and danger. Forty-eight hours of enforced togetherness in a stone-clad cottage, Conor coming on to her after several pints of ice-breaking Guinness.

'Angela, what do you say?' She felt a stroking tickle on her wrist and jolted. Conor was touching her with a grass stem. 'I was thinking, the weekend after next. I can clear the decks at work and turn off my mobile, so they can't spring any last-minute surprises. Please. I owe it to you. There are things I want to talk about.'

From Conor, this was a soliloquy. She wavered.

'Gimme a kiss,' murmured Conor, transferring the grass stem to her ear-lobe.

'What, here? In the church car-park?'

'More privacy than at my place.' Or yours, he could've added, haunted by the spirit of St Robert. Uncharitable! He winced.

'I don't know.'

He kissed her. It was gentle, exploratory stuff. Angela

risked opening her eyes to make sure that Conor's were shut, his red-gold lashes perfect crescents against his cheeks. One arm held her elbow lightly, for support. His free hand tickled her hem-line and crept under it, but almost as a courtesy to her femininity, describing fond little arcs on her thigh as if she was a great big strokable kitten.

He unclasped her and brushed her nose with his sand-papery chin. 'Do you think,' he murmured, resting his chin on top of her head, 'that a kid is always better off with two parents, whatever the circumstances?'

Angela held her breath. 'What circumstances?'

'You know, if there's a legacy of a troubled marriage. Is it right to foist a nuclear family on the kid again if he's got used to the single-parent set-up?'

'Conor, I'm the last judge of that sort of thing. But – if the couple can make a go of it, why not? Everyone wins.'

He jumped up and pulled her with him. He smiled into her flushed face, his green eyes deepening against the paler, winter-shrunk green of the grass around them.

Angela suppressed an inward thrill. He was sounding her out about becoming a family with Shane. His lack of subtlety was touching in its transparency.

'Shane,' Conor began, as they cruised onto the motorway, 'Would you mind if I went off for a weekend with Angela? I thought you could stay at Matty's.'

'I'm hardly in a position to refuse anything, seeing as I'm in the dog-house.'

'Ach well, I'd still like your blessing. I'm old-fashioned that way.'

A ghost of a smile lit Shane's face. 'As long as I don't have to be Crispin the frigging page-boy at a shotgun wedding a few months later.'

Conor laughed, his rumbling bear laugh that made Shane smile, whatever his underlying mood. He looked down and fiddled with the tape-deck, so Conor wouldn't see it.

Conor gripped the steering wheel. 'I understand Mum's talked to you about the possibility she might return to England.'

'Yeah,' said Shane casually, bony knuckles tightening.

'Her suggestion is, we divide the house into two flats, her living on one floor and me on another, you moving freely between both. That would seem preferable to her living nearby, and me farming you out for visits.'

'A pass-the-parcel kind of thing?' muttered Shane. 'Yeah, sounds gik all right.'

'So you'd go for the house-sharing plan?' sighed Conor. 'She told me she'd sounded you out, and you were interested.'

Shane stared hard at him. 'D'you still love her or what?'

Conor changed lanes too abruptly. The car behind flashed its lights. 'Or what,' he chose in a flat voice.

Sadie was warming her slippered feet against the lower bar of her fire. She accepted a cup of tea from Angela. 'You look radiant, if I may say so.'

'Oh.' Angela put a hand to pink cheeks. 'All that fresh air.'

Sadie slurped her tea. 'The kid wasn't so bad. I was expecting Darren from *The Omen*.'

'Damien, Ma.'

'Whatever. Needs a good dose of mothering. Shame you're not the maternal type, but effort can make up for natural inability.'

Angela stiffened. 'Thank you, mother.'

'Oh, don't get me wrong. You're getting on with life.

Conor McGinlay came looking for you, remember, and you went out with him to try it for size. There's no disgrace in moving on, with your memories of the dead fond and intact.'

'So would you be looking for another man if you were – um – younger?'

'No,' sniffed Sadie. 'But we're discussing you. I enjoy being on my own. You don't.'

'Talking of you being alone,' said Angela swiftly, 'what about this panic button? Don't look like that, Mum! I don't want anything happening to you. And come to think of it, shouldn't we be getting you a walking stick?'

Sadie gnashed her dentures. 'I told you, I'm not ready for the bath chair and ear trumpet yet. When's your next date with Conor?'

'He's ringing me,' said Angela, sounding casual.

'Just tell her you and *I* are going off for the weekend,' suggested Rachel, dunking a chocolate finger in her tea. She could do this elegantly. Bits of biscuit never broke off and sank without trace.

Angela enjoyed a visit to Rachel's flat. Its elegant simplicity reeked of well-spent money, much like Rachel herself. Angela had recovered from her frisson of jealousy at the mini-market. Rachel, she now accepted, had gone out of her way to be nice to Conor. Nothing more.

'I'd rather be straight with Mum than act as if I've something shameful to hide,' declared Angela boldly.

'Not worth it with Catholic parents,' said Rachel briskly. 'It's like trying to explain electricity to a caveman. It's much kinder to collude in their blissful state of ignorance. My mother still thinks I go on platonic dates with my "nice young men", kissing goodbye on the doorstep after a night at the pictures. At thirty-seven! I'm sure she doesn't really think that, but as long as no one forces her to confront the unpalatable truth, she's quite happy.'

'But Ma's a paid-up member of the KGB,' grumbled Angela. 'In six months' time, she'd pounce on one of us and ask some apparently innocuous question about our weekend in Ireland. Then she'd pounce on the other one, separately, ask the same question, and compare data. Besides, as two thirty-something women, it's high time we stopped indulging her prejudices.'

'OK,' said Rachel. 'Come clean with her. Tell her you're off to trip the light fantastic with C McGinlay Esquire, recently unwedded bachelor of the parish.'

Angela hesitated, then snatched another chocolate finger. 'I'll think about it.'

'In the meantime,' said Rachel, 'I've had a brainwave about making your ma less vulnerable in her own home.'

Chapter Eight

The bloody sodding bleeper went off in her navy holdall, on the Tube to the airport.

Angela took a while to register that the insistent bleeping noise was emanating from the pocket on the front of the holdall where she'd packed her pants. She followed the worried gazes of her fellow-travellers at her Aer Lingus labels. They obviously suspected a premature bomb timer. She'd shoved everything in the holdall, even her slimline shoulder-bag. Her ticket and loose change resided in her coat pocket. The tap-dancing frogs bag, so very 'her', according to Conor, had been left at home. As a coming-of-age gift, it now struck her as suitably silly and girlish on its day, because she'd been a silly, girlish twenty-one-year-old. She hoped that girl wasn't the 'very you' pinpointed by Conor.

'Botheration!' said Angela loudly, to hide her embarrassment at the bleeping, and leant down to unzip the front pocket. Overstuffed with grey-gusseted smalls, her one and only thong leapt out and onto the shoe of an Outraged of Tunbridge Wells type, who lowered his *Daily Telegraph* and blinked in alarm at what appeared to be a dead, exotic jellyfish tentacled to his toe-cap.

'Sorry!' Angela pounced on the strip of shocking-pink satin that now matched her complexion. Ye gods! The

thong was a 'joke' anniversary present from Rachel seven
years ago. Languishing ever since under balled socks and
scattered hair-grips in a bedroom drawer, it had taken
advantage of its only outing to make its debut in the
Friday evening rush-hour.

The bleeper was still bleeping. Finally, Angela
unsnapped it from constricting knicker elastic and switched
it off. Bloody, sodding marvellous! As if making only her
second Tube journey in four years wasn't enough to strain
the nerves, now Rachel's bright idea had revealed its
glaring flaw. How were you supposed to answer a pager
summons halfway to Heathrow on a fifty-minute Tube
journey?

'Er – anyone got a mobile?' she challenged the air
around her, pink cheeks shading to scarlet.

'You a doctor?' asked a gum-chewing bloke in braces.

'Yes! I must check in!'

'Can't help,' shrugged Braces, who looked so exactly
like a mobile phone user, Angela longed to snap his
nearest brace against his nipple.

She gazed around the carriage appealingly. She met the
pebble-hard gaze of Outraged of Tunbridge Wells. He
crackled his paper upwards to shut out her face. He
wasn't fooled. A doctor with erupting, very small smalls?

Please! Angela addressed him silently. The thong was a
last-minute addition for Dutch courage. After all, I know
Conor's booked a double room at the hotel in Wexford.
I told him to go right ahead. Not that sex was mentioned.
I said it made sense economically! The pink thong sums
me up, really. All gesture and no action. Pretending I'm
a woman with racy underwear to call on, when I'm a
woman afraid to have sex with him in case I'm useless at
it, and equally afraid to deny him in case he gets bored
and moves on.

But right now – right now, Sadie was paddling the air

on a pitted lino surface, awaiting Angela's rescue plan in answer to the bleeper she'd set off. The pager had come from Wilmesbury Hospital, courtesy of Rachel's sleight of hand, and Angela had bought Sadie a mobile phone. It had only cost £9.99 and came with forty pounds' worth of free calls. The phone was small and lightweight enough to nestle in Sadie's cardigan or apron pocket, and she was under instructions to leave it under her adjoining pillow at night. Angela had keyed in the number of the pager so that, in the event of a fall, all Sadie had to do was hit 'Connect' on the mobile numberpad. This limited use suited Sadie fine. She'd assured Angela that she had no desire to play around with her new gadget or fritter away the free calls.

There was nothing else for it. Angela would have to get off at the next station and find a pay-phone. The next station was South Ealing. Its call-box was broken. Angela tottered out of the station with the rush-hour throng, her holdall bouncing off her legs. She found a call-box outside a burger joint. She'd wedged her bag in the doorway and the receiver under her chin, before she realised the phone only took phone cards. Fucking hell!

Outside the call-box, she swivelled round, scanning for the striped awning, the giant ninety-nine cone that would signal a newsagent's. She spotted one!

Sweat now running off her in channels, she ran for it, wheezing. The Pat-from-*EastEnders* lookalike behind the till was sniffy about changing a twenty for a two-quid phone card, so Angela succumbed dutifully to guilt and bought a copy of *Marie Claire* as well.

By the time she gasped her way back to the call-box, it was filled by a large West Indian man, gesticulating angrily and expansively down the phone. Angela shut her eyes. Pinwheels of red light danced behind her lids. She opened her eyes and examined her watch. She'd allowed enough time to get to the airport and meet Conor for their flight, but not ample time. And what about Sadie?

She pounded on the glass. 'I've got to use the phone! It's an emergency!'

The West Indian man, receiver buried in his muscular neck, pushed open the heavy glass door with his index finger. 'Blimey, love, you only had to say,' he observed mildly.

'Thank you, thank you, thank you!' Angela squeezed in past him, shaking fingers trying to get her card in the slot. Oh God, she prayed, please let Mum answer the mobile. But a detached voice told her the mobile she was trying to contact was switched off. Come to think of it, God was probably fed-up with her by now. She'd spent the last few days pestering him for a weekend of good weather, fresh breath and the assurance she'd be able to Do It when the crunch came, competing for the divine lughole with supplicants for world peace, famine relief and the recovery of missing children. Maybe it was Mary she should've pestered instead? Mary, a woman, would understand the weightiness of trivial fears.

She dialled again, but Sadie's ordinary phone was engaged. Good or bad sign? Sadie didn't trust the mobile, so she might've crawled to the 'proper' phone to call Maud, reached up for the receiver, and knocked it to the floor. Wouldn't that be just typical of her!

Gurning apologetically at the man waiting patiently outside, Angela phoned Maud Ambrose.

Maud answered on the fifth ring. 'Of course I'll go next door and check,' she grumbled. 'Though I saw her only five minutes ago, hanging out washing. Where can I reach you?'

'You can't,' gasped Angela. 'I'm on my way to the airport. I'll ring you from there.'

Back at the Tube station, she was stopped at the

barrier. Her ticket was one-way, and she'd broken her journey. 'Ticket machine?' she asked desperately.

'There isn't one,' cackled the Nazi on the barrier and pointed to the long, fractious queue at the window.

Angela shuffled into line, trying to stuff *Marie Claire* into the bulging holdall without detonating the coiled spring of smalls by unzipping the front pocket again. Conor was going to kill her. In fact, Conor was probably going to be leaving without her, if she didn't get on a Tube soon.

Two stops before Heathrow, on a very slow-moving train, she ordered herself to relax, though her palpitating heart begged to differ. The plane's departure time had come and gone. She had blown it. Technically, Sadie had blown it for her. Perhaps – no! Angela struggled to stifle it, but the thought escaped. Perhaps Sadie had deliberately set off the bleeper to save her daughter from the (at the very least, venial) sin of a dirty weekend? 'I knew I shouldn't have told her!' muttered Angela loudly, causing her nearest travelling companions to shift away discreetly. Guilt silenced her mutterings. What a way to think if Sadie was lying injured on the floor, wracked with pain, hip broken in three places.

This time, she found a coin phone, gleaming and functional, at the entrance to terminal one. 'She's fine,' sniffed Maud Ambrose. 'She set off the mobile by mistake, she says, moving it about in her pocket, so now she's put it on a shelf, out of harm's way.'

'What! She's not supposed to do that. She's supposed to keep it with her!'

'Fine, I'll tell her. But there must be an easier way to keep tabs on her. I've missed *Coronation Street* now.'

'I'm sorry, Mrs Ambrose. And thank you. Can I bring you back anything from Ireland?'

'A whiskey cake,' said Maud promptly. 'I love 'em. Maybe two, if you've room in your luggage?'

'No problem.'

Thank God Sadie was OK. She could well believe she'd set off the mobile by mistake.

Angela sighed. She hitched up the dead weight of holdall and trailed over to check-in. No sign of Conor. She handed in her ticket. 'I know I've missed it. Is there another flight tonight?'

'You're in luck, it's been delayed by an hour. Aisle or window seat?'

'Angela?'

She turned in confusion to face a pinched-looking Conor. He's furious, she thought. He must think I'm disorganised and rude. He must wish the plane had left on time.

'Angela, thank God! I thought you'd changed your mind about coming.'

She marvelled all through the journey that he'd been not angry but scared that she'd stood him up. He drove the hire car skilfully through plangent, steady rainfall, to their hotel in Curracloe, a good two hours' by car from Dublin airport. Or so it felt. Angela could see nothing and felt disoriented. Beyond town centres, there were no lampposts or fairy-lit urban sprawl to illuminate the dark contours of night.

'How come you never learnt to drive?' asked Conor.

'Oh, Robert gave me a couple of lessons and didn't rate my chances.'

'Spouses don't make the best instructors.'

'I hit a bus shelter. He lost his no-claims bonus.'

'Ah,' said Conor. Angela studied the map with a travel torch. Might as well try and look useful after confessing to such inadequacy. She hoped he wouldn't ask about her

last visit to Ireland, which was shrouded in the mists of
enforced forgetfulness.

She and Robert had stayed in Kinsale, but *en route* to
the gastronomical capital of Ireland, Robert had run over
a chicken, mistaking the jolting thud for a hidden pot-
hole, it had 'pissed down' as the guidebook hadn't put it
(preferring the euphemistic 'soft weather') and, to top it
all, Angela had eaten a dodgy shellfish and vomited over
the rocks in Kinsale harbour, in full view of camcording
American tourists. The row developed when she realised
that Robert was snapping her, too.

'Conor,' she asked suddenly, 'do you see me as a
plastic?'

'Bag? Gnome? A plastic what, Ange?'

'Paddy, of course. Surely Shane's been lumbered with
the name by some of your family in Dublin?'

'If he had been, he wouldn't tell me. Let's see.' He
drummed his fingers on the steering-wheel. 'Have you got
an Irish passport?'

'No, couldn't be bothered. I needed to go on a school
trip at short notice when I was sixteen, so I nipped down
the post office in Wilmesbury and filled out a form for a
twelve-month thing, complete with lions and shields and
rampant loyalty to queen and country. Are you
disappointed in me?'

'As disappointed as a man could be in a plastic who's
sold out.'

He laughed when she slumped down in her seat.
'Look, I've lived in England for donkeys' years, so my
pure-alloy Irishness must be degrading to a baser metal.
Maybe iron rather than plastic.'

'Pig-iron, if you're a paddy,' corrected Angela. She felt
reassured enough to try her hand and struggling eyesight
at map-reading again.

''Fraid we won't see the lie of the land before

morning,' said Conor, swinging between a pair of gothic stone pillars. 'But the forecast wasn't too bad. This is supposed to be a half-decent joint, so they should still run to dinner, even though it's gone nine.'

Half-decent! It was palatial compared to the B&B in Kinsale. Once the seat of a C of I bishop, Clariton House was a grey Georgian mansion where rotting wall tapestries hung on repanelled walls and modern plumbing rumbled soothingly behind antique porcelain cisterns. The sort of place she and Robert had often passed out driving, musing, 'I wonder who stays in a pile like that?' and decided complacently, 'Golf-mad Yanks who think any house over fifty years old is heaving with ghosts!'

Looking back, Angela saw their dismissiveness for what it was. A bit of harmless jealousy that their budget couldn't run to four-star Georgian piles.

'What are you thinking?' asked Conor suddenly, turning from the reception desk with a smile. Angela looked away hurriedly at a tapestry. She couldn't very well say, 'my honeymoon,' or even, 'how moreish you look in that well-cut overcoat, with your dampened-down curls and your fisherman's jumper, how very much at home you look in this imposing old house,' an odious comparison with poor, dead Robert. Upstairs, Angela hurried into their *en suite* room and made straight for the phone to hide her shyness. 'Mind if I ring Mum to check she's OK?'

'Go for it. I'll ring Shane at Matty's after you.'

Angela only half-listened to Sadie's complaints about the mobile and Maud Ambrose's 'nosiness'. She was looking down at the blue-and-white bedspread under her knees, silky and raised, its downy thickness reassuring evidence of its cost. Tonight, she'd lie under it with Conor, between fringed blue lampshades and under a ceiling studded with plaster cabbage roses. Soon, this room would resonate in memory with an outcome still unknown.

'Loo flush is temperamental,' reported Conor, returning from a gurgling bathroom. 'You have to open the cistern lid and hold the ball-cock above the waterline to let it refill. Shall I complain?'

'Well,' blushed Angela. After all, he was paying. She had offered, forcefully, to go Dutch, but he'd insisted that the whole weekend was on him. 'A wonky loo's all part of the old-world charm, I suppose. The bed dips in the middle too, but I don't mind that, either.'

He seemed relieved that she'd mentioned the bed. 'I usually sleep facing the window,' he revealed.

'Fine,' she said, and scattered her cosmetic essentials (carefully vetted) on the alternative bedside table. In its top drawer, she found a Gideon bible and a leaflet about the house, smelling of camphor. On the front was a sepia photo of the bishop and his family on the front lawn, a dour man flanked by corseted women in plume-heaped hats, parasols struck into the ground like at-ease rifles. Their eyes squinted in a golden evening of long ago. 'His wife and three daughters,' read Angela aloud. 'Look at that view!'

Sepia hills sloped away behind the colonnaded porch, intersecting pleats of burnt sienna. The sea and Curracloe beach lay in the opposite direction. 'It's much like that now,' claimed Conor. 'Wait until morning.'

It was too late for dinner, so they ordered sandwiches and tea up to the room. Cheese and chutney doorsteps arrived for Angela, cold bacon for Conor, with a steaming brown pot of tea and turf-dark stacks of moist brack, the shiny raisins reminding Angela of turf beetles. When she and Owen were kids, they'd spent summers scrambling over their grandfather's turf stacks and down his haystacks on his County Clare homestead. Angela, in truth, had spent a lot of time running away from Owen, or extracting his palpable hits – beetles rendered legless and sharp haystalks – from the back of her dress.

'What are you thinking?' asked Conor for the second time that evening.

She looked up in confusion.

His eyes were fixed on her with the green intensity of a cat's. But his smile was nervous. 'Sorry – I'm clumping my hobnails all over your innermost thoughts.'

'No, you're not – I was just thinking about when I was a kid, on my grandad's farm in the summer holidays, down in Clare.' She picked the plumpest raisin out of her brack and laid it on the plate-edge. 'He was a miserable bastard, my grandad, a tyrant. I don't know why Mum went back there, summer after summer, to blacken his range, clean his house, soak his callused feet, put up with insults by way of gratitude. Do you know, the only summer we didn't go over, my aunt came over from the States to visit him instead, and he wouldn't open the front door because she was wearing trousers! Honest to God. She had to walk to the next farm and call a taxi back to Ennis.'

'Don't tell me – like a good, martyred Irish daughter, she returned the next day in a tweed skirt, bringing a nice bit of black pudding for his brekky and a king-size humble pie for herself,' smiled Conor.

Angela grinned. 'How did you guess? He let me and Owen run amok over his crops, to be fair. Gave it in the neck to Mum, I suppose, when we were out of earshot.' Angela sat back, thinking. 'That's not me, you see, turning the other cheek. I'd have told him where to stick his attitude. What about Shane? He must have grandparents over here.'

Conor straightened. 'My ma in Dublin is all that's left.

Kate's parents in England – they don't want to see Shane.'

Angela started. 'Why not?'

Conor's brows knitted. 'It's complicated... her dad didn't approve of me, remember? When he got wind of Kate's relationship with me, he gave her the "never darken our door again" speech if she went ahead and married me.' He swallowed a gulp of cooling tea. 'That was the green light, as far as Kate was concerned. Not that I knew her dad's essential gitness made her mad keen to hang onto me. Not at first, anyway. I've no idea if her mum's just as reactionary. Her dad rules the roost and what he says goes. He's cast Kate into the outer darkness, so her child doesn't exist either. Bringing Shane up Catholic (Kate was very keen on the idea) was probably the last in a long line of straws for her old man.' He shrugged. 'We even drove up to Northumberland to announce our engagement. Old git wouldn't let us in the house.' He grinned balefully at Angela. 'And Kate wasn't wearing trousers.'

'Whew!' breathed Angela. 'So Shane's never met them?'

'Their loss,' grunted Conor, his mobile features working overtime. 'They wouldn't come to the wedding, so I had to give my parents a cover story that they saw through in ten seconds flat. Kate's charm made up for her parents' snub, but the past is always there, the uninvited guest, the bad fairy at the christening, waiting its moment to scupper the future.' He stared broodingly at the teapot and then reached for it. 'Another cuppa?'

'No, thanks.' Was he right? Was the past the final arbiter of hopes and dreams? Or was it really another country, peppered with minefields and watchtowers to stop you escaping over the border to freedom?

She used the bathroom first, brushing her teeth

rigorously and scrambling into a middle-of-the-road nightie that was sprigged with rosebuds à la *Little House on the Prairie*, but laid claim to non-salacious modernity with spaghetti straps and a short hemline. She slipped into her whitest pants, hoped chin-whiskers wouldn't sprout overnight and opened the bathroom door.

Conor lay fully dressed on top of the crumpled duvet, eyes shut, breathing down his nose. His socks were different shades of blue, and one was balding at the heel. She smiled. Conor opend his eyes.

'My God, the state of me compared to you,' he grunted, heaving himself off the bed. Angela claimed it instead, clambering under the sheet and catching her toes in the top seam. She wondered when she'd last cut her toenails, then pulled the sheets up to her chin, as Conor grabbed his bag off a chair and disappeared into the bathroom. She took his comparison of their relative states of readiness for bed as the closest she'd get to a compliment on her night attire. Would he wear pyjamas? He didn't look like a pyjamas man, but he didn't look the *au naturel* type either. She heard him fill the sink, followed by a long silence. She turned over and covered her ears with the pillow-corners. It wasn't right or fair, or a good augury for the night ahead, to tune in to a man's ablutions.

Next thing she knew, the bed was dipping next to her as he climbed in beside her. She removed her pillow-muff. By the time she turned round, he had the sheets drawn up to his own chin, which gleamed with freshly mown stubble. 'I have to shave sometimes before I go to bed,' he explained, embarrassed.

'Oh right.' She hesitated. 'Just when you go to bed with women, you mean?'

'You make it sound like I've had a haremful.'

'Sorry, didn't mean to.' Oh God, what now? They'd

lost the lazy conviviality they'd shared over sandwiches and a pot of tea.

'Is that a squashed insect on the ceiling?' asked Conor suddenly.

'Where?' She squinted upwards. The bedside lamp on his side, still on, threw long shadows across the bumpy plaster surface.

'Oh my God!' she gasped. 'It moved! It's not squashed at all.'

Conor threw back the sheets and jumped on to his pillow, so that he was just tall enough to stroke the ceiling with his fingertips. Angela inched away from his legs, curving hairily out of a pair of boxer shirts. His bare back was covered in much finer hairs, thank God.

'It's an earwig out on the razzle,' he reported. 'I think it's supposed to be tucked up at home under that loose bit of cornicing over there.'

'Kill it, Conor, I hate them!'

He jumped higher, slapping his hand against the ceiling. 'Damn, missed the bugger. I think it's fallen on your head, Ange.'

'Argh!' She dived under the sheets, shuddering. She screamed again when something tickled her neck in the darkness.

'Hah, got you!' laughed Conor, and she came up for air to find his fingers stroking the back of her neck. 'Don't worry, I whipped his ass good.'

'Really?' she trembled.

'OK. God's honest truth. It was just a trick of the light on a ceiling stain. There was no earwig. Though what the poor things ever did to you...'

'His – ancestors used to get into my pants when they were out on the line.'

'Well, can't say I blame them.'

Angela laughed. 'I walked into that one.'

His fingers moved off her neck and explored her shoulder, their progress invited by the flirtatious dip of her flesh under the concealing sheet.

'Mm,' she said, because it felt nice and she thought he should know.

He hesitated, then rolled over quickly to switch off the light. Angela sighed with satisfaction. That was much better, the hypnotic touch of flesh on flesh made mysterious by darkness. She'd never been one for doing it with the lights on, which struck her as a form of sensory deprivation. Thank goodness that Conor, complete with cleanshaven jaw and subtle hint of aftershave, felt the same way.

Slowly and irrevocably, she inched towards him.

Angela was up and dressed when he opened his eyes.

Conor stumbled out of bed, hair rumpled, skin goosepimpling.

'Did you mind me getting up first?' Angela asked. 'Bathroom's free for you.'

'Thanks.' He threw her a quick grin that diffused her nerves, and shut the bathroom door. She willed herself to relax. It was OK. He wasn't embarrassed, regretful or cautiously aware of being her first and only since Robert. Twenty minutes later, they descended to breakfast.

Angela had never known what it was like to make an entrance with a man who drew second looks. She herself was accustomed to going unnoticed. Anyway, she would've hated to stand out. Beauty was freakish, the way it set women apart from humdrum pleasantness of aspect and made them a slave to preserving it. But she'd always fancied basking in the reflected glory of a handsome escort. Robert had been like her – ordinary and patently relieved about it.

Now, as they sat down to covered dishes and napkins

so starched that they crackled, Conor said, 'You look stunning in that blue dress, Angela. It matches the view behind you.'

She whirled round to hide her blushes. Through the window, sea, sky and surrounding hills were swatches of overlaid blues. Closer to home, golfers were already wheeling their little shopping trolley things between giant urns on the front lawn.

'Isn't it beautiful?' remarked Angela non-committally about the view. She'd worn the same dress to lunch at his place. Surely he remembered?

Conor smiled, said nothing, lowered his eyes to a plate of soda bread. Her heart resumed its normal rate. She was grateful that he hadn't held her eyes and uttered that slick line, 'It's certainly a beautiful view from my perspective.'

He probably wouldn't know how to — thank God.

After breakfast, they went to the beach — pale, empty, claimed only by the wind. Angela ran straight onto it, pulling off shoes and pop sox, then flying across the hard, blond pleats of sand to run full pelt into hissing wetness at the edge. 'Jee-sus, it's cold!' she yelled over her shoulder.

Conor followed more cautiously. His loafers bit deeply into the sand. Angela cavorted like a kid, the wind flattening her dress against her thighs. He glimpsed the thin grace of her body, the V of white knickers under her dress, the dark aureoles of her cold-hardened nipples pushed out against her bra. She was alive with innocent enjoyment of a small pleasure, wholesome and sexy. His scrotum tightened and he bent down quickly to unlace his shoes.

'The wind hurts your ears!' called Angela, scampering on ahead, kicking wavelets. He paddled in her wake, leaving a careful gap. But she was oblivious, leaning down to pluck half-buried shells out of the sand, tickle slimy heaps of seaweed with a wary toe. Finally, she ran up to him with her cache of fractured, still-beautiful shells, darker inside than out, whorled edges fringed with navy and cobalt rings.

'You can pick out your favourite!' she laughed. 'Choose one for Shane.'

He chose the one he thought she liked the least.

When they'd had enough, they retreated to the beach steps. Angela flapped at her sandy feet with her hand.

'Let me,' ordered Conor, and grabbed her nearest foot in a gentle vice, wiping it carefully with a clean breakfast napkin he produced from his trouser pocket.

'You needn't.' She squirmed, embarrassed.

'Sit down and hold still, or I'll end up taking off a toe by accident.' He laughed. 'That's what I used to say to Shane when he wriggled about while I was cutting his toenails.'

He dropped one foot, grasped the other. Angela lapsed into silence. The simple act of kindness had its own sensuality; the rhythmic pressure of his big, warm hands on her slightly ticklish feet; the intimate care he took to prise every grain of sand from between her toes. At long last, she was able to stuff her none-too-attractive feet back into her pop sox and shoes. 'Is it time for elevenses?' she asked hopefully, made hungry by the tearing wind.

Conor looked at his watch. 'Quarter to ten sounds right for elevenses to me.'

It rained, on and off, for the rest of the day. They took the hire car up blackberry-hedged lanes and down sandy paths that led to deserted strands. They poked about in tumble-down cottages and rescued windblown garlands of dried flowers in a famine graveyard, fastening them against the memorial tablet with a large stone. It was a million miles from home, work – and her queasy honeymoon in Kinsale, thought Angela.

Back in the hotel room, Conor announced he was taking her out for dinner. 'I'll have to get changed,' fussed Angela, hoping her green linen dress had withstood the rigours of the holdall.

'Er – I bought you something.' Clumsily, Conor fished about in his own luggage and drew out a lop-sided parcel of tissue paper, held together with string, presenting it like a side of fresh beef.

Angela tore at the string. Out tumbled folds of cerise raw silk, sobered with a hint of black velvet. 'Is it too dressy?' asked Conor anxiously. 'I asked Rachel's advice. I bought it on her stall. She said it was your size and colouring.'

Yes, she recognised it now. Rachel had worn it to a Christmas drinks party at the hospital, to which Angela had been invited. A scallop-edged black velvet bodice tapered into a puffball of pink silk. It was beautiful, costly, technically a cast-off – which Conor wasn't to know. Angela met his anxious gaze in the mirror.

'It's gorgeous!' she exulted. 'Thank you so much.'

There was a second of mutual embarrassment before she moved towards him and kissed him lightly on the mouth. The dress rustled protestingly between them. 'I'll go and change,' she said, realising that it had been meant for tonight, and that it would look a bit odd with her raincoat thrown over the top. If she remembered rightly, Rachel had teamed it with a fake-fur black stole.

When she emerged, shyly, from the bathroom in her butterfly transformation, Conor was perched on the side of the bed, talking into the phone. He turned, still talking into the receiver. His eyes glittered with a cool appraisal that sent shivers up her spine. 'Yes,' he said into the phone. 'I'm looking at the costing specs now. What? No – not tonight. You'll have to wait till I'm back in the office on Monday. I mean it, Joe!'

He crashed the phone down, opened his arms. Angela went into them.

'Work rang me, the buggers,' he apologised into her hair.

'I didn't hear the phone ring. I was running a bath.'

'Uh-huh.' His chin nudged down a velvet strap. 'I know it's only been on you five minutes, but mind if I take this dress off again?'

'No,' she trembled.

She had to help him with the side-zip. It got stuck in fine threads of silk and a tussle developed. They fell in a heap on the bed, Conor's big, dark-red head buried in pink layers as stiff and springy as a dancer's tutu. His head disappeared under the layers altogether. Angela heard him panting as he unrolled the top of her black Dior tights. She was panting herself by now. She remembered his hands stroking her feet, firing her blood in other places. Conor suddenly paused. 'What's this?' he asked in a tone of wonder.

From between her legs came a great bark of unflattering laughter. His head reappeared. 'I didn't know you'd come straight from an audition at the Folies Bergères!'

Angela shoved him away, sat upright, pink-faced and annoyed. He'd uncovered the shocking pink thong. 'Not the classic line to come out with when you discover a sexy undergarment on the woman you're undressing.'

'Trying to undress.' He sat up, the moment of passion past. 'How did blokes manage in days gone by, with all those hooks and eyes on corsets, and twenty-six petticoats to get through? There must've been a handbook, a gentleman's guide to frustration-free stripping. Begs another key question.'

'Which is?' Angela's tone was dangerous.

'How did they cope with what a woman actually

looked like? The reality was probably a far cry from the illusion created by tightly-laced bodices. It must've been a shock for the bloke to discover love handles, orange-peel thighs, wobbly great unleashed bosoms.'

'No such hidden mysteries on me,' snapped Angela crisply.

'I'm sorry,' muttered a stricken Conor, then looked at her face and burst out laughing. 'I'm sorry, but that – thing you're wearing!'

'Thong.'

'It was unexpected. And you must've blitzed your bikini line with a Flymo to leave enough bare skin either side of the pink bit. Your poor pubes look like a freshly-plucked chicken! Sorry!' he gasped again, clamping a hand to his traitorous mouth. His eyes were deeply apologetic, but hilarity lurked behind them.

Angela turned away, so he wouldn't see her own eyes soften with tears. He touched her elbow entreatingly. 'I've blown it, haven't I? Honest to God, I deserve to lose you, Angela. Did I say pubes? Did I, really? May God forgive me – though I'd rather hear it from you.'

Angela turned to him with a sigh. His head scurried towards her lap and lay there, beseechingly. Her hand, reluctantly, scraped hair back from his forehead. His eyes closed under her touch. 'I think I love you, Angela. That's why I felt free to be myself, say the first thing that came into my head. I never meant to offend you, I swear.'

Angela's hand paused and her heart quickened. Conor peered up at her. 'Is this working?' he asked mischievously.

'You mean the 'L' word as the ultimate get-out clause?' Angela pushed his head off her lap and stormed over to the window. 'Don't play with my feelings, Conor McGinlay. Don't say things you don't mean.'

'I meant what I said!' He stared at her but didn't come

after her. 'Isn't plain speaking my trouble? I think I love you isn't the same as I love you, but it's the truth right now. And I've no idea how you feel about me.'

'You've every idea!' She turned to him hotly. 'I'm here on a dirty weekend with you! I was about to let you undress me. Unless you think I'm a sex-starved widow who's gagging for it with anybody!'

'Ach, don't be talking like that, my angelic Angela. Come over here to me and let's have a talk.'

She scowled. He was humouring her, babying her with wheedling Irishisms.

'Don't treat me like a fool!'

'Please, Angela, please. My beautiful pink-thonged Christmas fairy.'

She could resist him, but what was the point? She'd learnt a painfully hard lesson with Robert when it came to sulking. And deep down, part of her was amused at Conor's frankness, his total lack of diplomacy. If she was a what-you-see-is-what-you-get type of woman, he was a similar type of man. So now she'd pin him down, make him tell her, once and for all, what had caused his wife to up sticks and start a new life in America.

So she went and sat next to him obediently and demanded, 'I want to know what went wrong between you and Kate. I know you gave me the basics that time in McDonald's, but I want the gory, truthful details.' She folded her arms.

Conor, vanquished by his bad behaviour, sank back on the headboard with a deep sigh. 'It's quite straightforward, really. My ex-wife was, and is, an alcoholic. She was already a dipso when I met her at college, but I didn't know the signs. Anyway, she was a past master at hiding them. She had bottles stashed away in unlikely places, she chain-sucked extra-strong mints, claiming they were for nicotine breath, and she never lurched around, singing

"Rosin the Bow" after chuck-out time down the local. In short, she never behaved like your stereotypical drunk. Alcoholics rarely do.'

Angela's mind reeled. 'So – let me think. Her drinking was a consequence of growing up in a dysfunctional family? With that horrible father, to be precise?'

'Well, the old git did peddle the line that you'd only get to heaven on a temperance ticket, while all the time swigging away in his "study" where his poor eejit of a wife thought he was reinventing the wheel. Kate told me she discovered his hootch stash when she was ten, having entered the study illegally. After that, it became a game of risk for her, sampling his booze without him noticing. And then there was the buzz. Doing the exact opposite of what dear old hypocritical Daddy preached. Which is where I come in.'

His voice was emotionless, but Angela glanced at him. 'You don't think she married you just to get at her dad?'

'She did love me, but it was all mixed up with getting back at him. I sort of twigged from the beginning that he was her real passion in life, but I shied away from the implications. Once we were married, and her defiance accomplished, she got a bit bored. Drinking was still a distraction – one I was finally beginning to notice as beyond the norms of social tippling – but having a baby became her laudable attempt to find a vocation in life beyond me, work and booze. Don't forget, she was holding down a good job when Shane arrived.' He stopped. 'I don't exactly cover myself in glory in this next bit. What about that table I've booked?'

Angela bit her lip. 'I don't know if I'm in the mood.'

'Even failed husbands have to eat.'

She cast him a shrewd look. 'So you're the ultimate villain of the piece? Drove a post-natally depressed new mother back into the off-licence with a piece of swinish behaviour?' Her eyes widened as his looked away. 'Like an affair?' she croaked.

'In a manner of speaking,' he grunted, the bluff Conor of old. 'The condemned man still has the right to a hearty meal. I'll tell you the rest over dinner. Can you actually walk in that thong?'

Sadie woke up suddenly, gasping with the pain. She pressed a hand tentatively against her side, smothering the hot needles under her skin. Her face was damp with sweat, her tablets on the far side of the dressing table. It would be a long and hazardous solo expedition. Binky jumped suddenly on top of the duvet, mewling concern (she liked to imagine). 'A shame you can't be trained to fetch,' grunted Sadie, swinging one leg slowly out of bed, encased in an old leg-warmer of Angela's. As she set off for the north face of her bedroom, Binky wove in and out of her carefully paced steps, joining her in a perilous formal dance. 'Maud Ambrose was right, as usual,' muttered Sadie begrudgingly. 'Old relics living alone are better off with a dog.' She hoped Angela was having a better weekend. Best not think about the non-marital sex. The twentieth century was almost over, marriages falling apart like cleaved husks, women having sex with men to keep the man's interest. So much for women's lib!

Sadie squeezed out all other thoughts and focused on the bottle of pills. Almost there. Almost made it. Oh to be young again – fifty-five would do! She wasn't greedy. Didn't want to relive her shining, frightening youth when she arrived in London and chambermaided in a big hotel, breaking her back for a shilling, pinning her hopes of escape on the night porter at the Imperial, Fenton Feeney, asking her to dance at the St Patrick's night social. Quick, quick, quick, quick, slow, no need to look at their nimble feet, leaving eyes free to feast on each other.

Now she was old, lame, partnered by Binky. And not given to self-pity, she reminded herself sternly, reaching a clawed hand for the bottle of painkillers.

The food and ambience in Simonetti's were rich. Angela began to appreciate her dress properly. The waiter hovered respectfully, allowing his gaze to linger with professional appreciation on her velvet-upholstered bust and narrow shoulder-blades. She'd pinned up her loose, straight hair with a star-shaped clip twinkling with cheap rhinestones that shone like white diamonds in the dim-lit atmosphere. Her pasta came, ribbons of tagliatelle under a thick cream laced with wine and mushrooms. The place and its tenor were almost offensively romantic. 'You can have the veal cutlet if you want,' she told Conor belligerently.

'Spaghetti carbonara,' he told the waiter dryly, and topped up her wine.

'There's no escape, Conor McGinlay. What is it you're not proud of in the collapse of your marriage? I have to know,' she added hopefully, 'so I can absolve you.'

'Cheers,' replied Conor sardonically, toasting her. 'Where were we? Oh yes, Shane was born. A bawling bundle of non-stop demands who copped a lungful of every stray germ and had to be weaned off antibiotics to go on solids. Kate gave up work to cope, and I left her to it. As the great provider, I found ever more reasons to spend time at the office, and ultimately, abroad. Go on, then, say it.'

'Say what?'

'How could I be so selfish?'

'You're a man. Seems reason enough, judging by examples throughout history.'

The waiter appeared to scatter Parmesan. 'Are you still

wearing your thong?' Conor asked her evilly. The waiter's hand shook.

'I've come knickerless,' replied Angela, addressing the waiter directly.

When he'd scampered away, presumably *al dente*, she met Conor's solemn, self-mocking eyes. 'I've got my sensible pants on. And there seems little chance of you getting into them tonight, mister.'

'Well, OK, I deserve that. But hear me out anyway. Kate confronted me about my absentee fatherhood. I agreed to spend more time at home. So I converted the loft, soundproofed it against Shane's heartier yells, and hid up there with paperwork. Kate was hitting the bottle quite openly by then. It was a chicken and egg situation. Did I cause the drinking escalation or was I legitimately escaping from it? Time's muddied the waters on that one – at least for me. Kate started letting the house go to pot – couldn't really blame her, with Shane battering her lugholes all day and night – so I hired Mrs Turner. Taking the pressure off you, I told Kate. Getting in someone to spy on me, she retorted. Well, again, that situation just evolved. I did ask Mrs T to keep a kindly eye turned in Kate's direction when I was off the scene. Kate couldn't be trusted not to set the house alight, once she'd had a few chasers and smoked a few cigarettes. Plus, there were added concerns that she'd go flying down the stairs, baby in tow, or have a blackout at the supermarket and leave him there.'

'Didn't you get help for her?' demanded Angela accusingly. 'Poor woman had just had a baby, and was still battling the unresolved demons of her youth. While you hid in the attic!'

'I said I wasn't proud of myself. Anyway, Kate wouldn't set foot in the attic. Said my master-plan was to chain her up in it, like Mr Rochester's mad wife. Course,

I didn't have a clue who she was talking about. Thought he was an ex-colleague of hers. But I tried to deal with things, albeit it in my own, hamfisted way. I came out of my lair, got leaflets from the library about help for alcos and spread them tactfully around the house. I dangled Shane on my knee, moved into the spare room without complaining.'

'Why didn't you just discuss the drinking problem face to face? I mean, before it got to the stage of dropping leaflets and hints?'

'I'd tried.' He looked deep into his glass of mineral water. 'Kate denied there was a problem and said she'd take Shane to Northumberland if I ever raised it again.' She'd also chucked a boiling kettle at Conor, just missing him by inches, but he wasn't going to shame his marriage by sharing that intimacy. 'She meant it, so I let it drop. Couldn't risk the return of the prodigal daughter to the family fold, and Shane disappearing behind a front door that would never be opened to me again. After that, even leafleting the house was risking things.'

'Your spaghetti's getting cold,' sighed Angela, feeling almost but not quite sorry for him. She could just imagine the Conor of fourteen years ago, perfecting the art of problem avoidance while hoping to solve the problem, developing his grunting, bluff carapace as a shell to arm him rather than shrink into, when the attic wasn't available.

He ignored the spaghetti. 'Let's get this over with, and then you can dole out sixty Hail Marys as my penance or whatever. Kate tore up the leaflets and went for me bald-headed. The problem was all mine, she said, and I wasn't shifting the blame for a crap marriage onto her. She took Shane and went to stay with a girl friend. Didn't come back for eight months. I was lucky it wasn't

Northumberland, and luckier still that she rang most weeks.'

'And that's when you – had your affair?'

Conor's green eyes darkened, like lagoons in the shade. 'With Kate and Shane gone, I'd come home to silence every evening – and didn't like it. Funny how I missed the noise I'd spent months hiding from. I'd enjoyed converting the attic, so I got into DIY in a big way, therapy for blokes who can't communicate. I relaid the floors, put up shelves, built alcoves, ripped out and reinstalled the kitchen, working all my emotions into sanding and grooving and sawing. When Kate came back – on a trial basis – she was an intruder. She saw straightaway what had happened. I'd made the whole house, not just the attic, my retreat and bolt-hole. But I took advantage of the situation. Look what I've done, I said. I did it all for you! And so we staggered on from year to year, lie to lie, until she left a note one morning and disappeared to the States.'

Angela's own food was congealing. 'Why didn't she go back to work when Shane was a bit older?'

'She did, part-time. It couldn't be full-time because I was away so much. Part-time graphic designing didn't satisfy her. She was never in line for the tasty assignments or promotion. Course, she was right to blame me. I could've taken a back seat in my own career so she could kickstart hers again. But I wasn't much of a new man. And deep down, I wanted to punish her for being a secret drunk and marrying me to spite her dad.'

'What did her farewell note say?'

'That she'd had enough. And that she didn't want Shane. You keep him, the note said. Imagine if he'd read that before I found it!' Conor gave a short, bitter laugh. 'It's not Shane's fault, but he's a dead ringer for Kate's old man, right down to a few mannerisms and his tantrum-throwing technique. Poor Kate! I think she had to get away from her own son as much as me. And now the guilt's hit home. She came to see me a few weeks ago. She wants to come back.'

Angela started as if she'd been shot. 'My God, you kept that quiet! And just when I've been thinking…' She went scarlet with embarrassment.

'Yes?' He pressured her softly, his nervousness almost a plea.

'I was thinking, how far you must've come from strong, silent, emotionally repressed Conor McGinlay, to sit here like this and spill your guts. And even analyse your past behaviour in a critical light.'

'That's because of you, Angela. Believe me, when I met you on that plane, I thought myself long past meaningful conversation with a woman. And even then, I was rude and sarcastic! But you've drawn me out of myself, bit by painful bit. You asked me for the whole story, and I've given it to you. Everything I've just told you is the first time I've articulated it to a third party. Though I've had years, I suppose, to work it all out in my subconscious.'

Angela looked into her plate. 'Now Kate's coming back. Maybe you should've told me before you asked me to spend a weekend with you. Unless,' she gulped, 'this is the brush-off, the goodbye and thanks for all the fish. Sending me on my merry way with a good meal and a kickstarted libido!'

'For Christ's sake, woman, give me a chance! Listen. She wanted to come back and live at 23 Pacelli Road as a lodger – take over the attic, no less, and the whole top floor – to be with Shane, make things up to him. I would've had to convert the house, put in extra doors and partitions, an upstairs kitchen – take out other things – to turn it into two flats. Kate would've savoured that, being the cause of me mutilating my perfect home! I was prepared to go for it, too, until Shane himself put the kibosh on the plan. Said he didn't want a return to the bad old days of tiptoeing around on eggshells while Kate and I festered under the same roof. So I've made Kate an alternative offer. If she wants to move back to be near Shane, I'll help her buy a place. A nice place, not a dump. At one point, I was scared she might sue for custody. But she's the one who ran off, and anyway, Shane doesn't want to go anywhere.'

He took a deep breath and rushed on. 'She took the deal a couple of weeks ago. So I decided it was safe to plough ahead and make this weekend a reality. Before that, yes, I admit it, I would've been stringing you along on a mystery tour, where only Shane knew the destination. But me and Kate are history, joined together by Shane and separated forever by our shitty past and the way we handled it. Do you believe me?' He looked at her challengingly.

'But was there ever a point at which you could've saved your marriage?'

'Of course. Isn't there always?'

'And now? What I mean is — is there any question it might still be the right thing to do?'

'None at all. Think of my marriage as a dinghy cast adrift from the shore by two careless owners. It rounded Fastnet and went out of radio contact long ago. The coastguard have called off the search.' He scowled and opened the menu with a resounding thump. 'What's for dessert in this gaff?'

Back in the *en suite* bathroom, Angela slipped out of her dress, pants and bra, and examined her full tummy for unsightly bulging. The bathroom's subtle lighting tanned her a pale gilt colour, highlighting not crepy, dimpled flesh, but soulful hollows on her collar and pelvic bones. She looked mysterious, womanly, like an African carving.

She went into the bedroom. Conor was by the window, wearing boxers. He turned to her, a stocky bear with slightly bowed legs, a broad chest and a refined face. 'You'll catch your death,' he said, and smothered a small cough.

It was not the line Casanova would've chosen at that juncture. But she didn't love Conor because he was Mr Seduction. She loved him because she could be herself with him.

She got into bed. He joined her. At first he held back, as if afraid to shove Robert aside. She ran a finger over his mouth. Her wedding and engagement rings caught in its nervous cracks. 'No more guilt trips,' she said firmly. 'Here, tonight, this is all about us.'

When she woke in the morning, everything looked different, even her blue dress from yesterday's beach stroll, slung on the back of a chair. She was different too. Warm and replete.

Conor's hot, fuzzy back was pressed into her shoulder. Reluctantly, she rolled away and padded into the bathroom for a pee.

Shutting the door, she heard the phone ring and Conor answer it, grunting. Not bloody Joe from the office again! Angela yawned, stretched her arms, released a golden stream from tender muscles. Her stomach was all over the place this morning, thanks to last night's rich meal, topped off with fruits-of-the-forest pavlova. She'd eat like a sparrow at breakfast.

She went back into the bedroom. Conor sat on the edge of the bed, his face ashen, the receiver dangling on the floor.

Angela stopped. The phone call telling her about

Robert leapt into focus from her warmly hazy mind. Who was it this time? Sadie! Oh dear God, not Shane.

'It's Kate,' shuddered Conor. 'She's taken an overdose.'

Chapter Nine

Angela had no appetite for Sadie's birthday lunch, a tradition started by her and Robert after Fenton's death. Sadie bore the ordeal gracefully. This year, Angela had clean forgotten to book Baggio's for the Sunday, so she, Sadie and Rachel (a stand-in for Robert) had decamped to Wilmesbury's newest eatery, a garish American bistro, where waistcoated staff whizzed around on roller-skates, claiming they found it a pleasure to be at your service.

'I don't like anything on this menu,' Sadie informed their waiter, hoping to wipe the dazzling transatlantic smile off his face.

The waiter, whose name tag said 'Davey', hunkered down beside Sadie. Angela had seen him adopt the same pose with a stroppy toddler three tables away.

'If it's a question of soft food for the teeth,' crooned Davey, exposing his own gleaming set, 'I can have chef rustle up a nice runny omelette with a bit of salad. Would madam like that?'

Sadie put her menu to one side, rejecting the idea of hitting Davey over the head with it. If only she had a stale bread stick handy. 'Madam would like to see a little more imagination on the vegetarian dishes. I'm not a vegetarian, but I like a rest from meat every now and then. This menu assumes vegetarians eat truckloads of spinach with everything.'

'We do a vegetarian burger made of soya extract,' said Davey humbly.

Sadie pondered while Davey held his breath, swaying uneasily on his cracking thigh joints. Not easy to hunker down on roller-skates, reflected Angela.

'I'll have it,' said Sadie imperiously. Davey stood up with relief, but Sadie wasn't letting him away that lightly. 'Is it in a sesame seed bun? I don't like those sesame seed yokes. Can chef pick them off for me?'

Davey looked at Angela in pity. 'I'll see what I can do, madam,' he sighed, pushing off on his skates.

Angela had a thumping headache. Rachel, resplendent in mint green, looked like a crisp lettuce leaf. She patted Angela's hand sympathetically. 'So how is Conor's ex-wife after her little fiasco?'

Angela grunted, swivelling away from Sadie's beady look. 'Chucking paracetamol and whiskey down your gullet is hardly a "little fiasco". The doctor who pumped her out gave her a huge rocket, according to Conor. And, being Yanks, they've bunged her in compulsory therapy for alcohol abuse and its depressive side-effects.'

Sadie clicked her dentures speculatively. 'I feel sorry for the woman, I really do. It's the classic cry for help, I suppose, and Conor certainly went running.' Sadie paused. 'As he should have done. He still has a responsibility to his ex-wife.'

Angela grabbed her bag off the back off her chair and scrabbled about for the birthday present. She laid the small, gift-wrapped parcel by Sadie's plate.

'Here you are, it's nothing special,' she said almost shyly. 'You can take it back if you don't like it.'

In fact, she had spent several lunch hours window-shopping for it with Pauline and Val.

Sadie unwrapped the silver and amethyst Celtic brooch. 'It's lovely!' she said sincerely. 'With a lovely big clasp for my clumsy old fingers. Thank you, lovey.' She puckered up for a kiss. Angela leant gingerly over the table and grazed the papery cheek with cool lips. 'Did Owen remember this year?'

Sadie, who'd considered trying to pin the brooch to her blouse, decided against with diplomatic haste and laid it back in its cradle of purple tissue.

'I got a card. And a cheque.'

'Oh?' Angela was about to say something mean about her brother salving his conscience with a stroke of his pen, but took a sip of water instead. 'For how much, if it's not impertinent to ask?'

Sadie glanced meaningfully at Rachel, who turned tactfully away to buttonhole a waiter. 'A little something towards a new washer-dryer,' hissed Sadie. 'I mentioned in a letter a while back that it was on the blink. I think Candace must be behind it. I can't see Owen giving a second thought to a wonky washer-dryer. Doubt he's ever used one.'

'Good for Owen – and Candace,' smiled Angela, raising her glass of fizzy water.

'So,' said Sadie, noting Angela's ginger sips of water. 'Are you ever going to tell us why Conor's ex-wife made this desperate cry for help, or is it that he hasn't told you?'

Angela blinked over her glass at Sadie's pert gaze and Rachel's benign baby blues. 'Look, if it's a family thing,' began Rachel mildly, 'I can slip off and powder my nose for a few mins.'

'Don't be silly!' countered Angela edgily. 'You are family where my far-from-private private life is concerned. Fact is, Kate wanted to come back and take up residence at 23 Pacelli Road, in a platonic context, to be with

Shane. But Shane, as final arbiter of a parental patch-up, gave it the thumbs down. Conor's plan B was to help Kate buy her own flat over here, so she could still return to England and be close to Shane. Kate agreed to plan B, then went off and took an overdose. I don't think it's fair to call it a deliberate act of sabotage,' she ended defensively, as a knowing look passed between Sadie and Rachel. 'We don't know what was going through her head, what state she was in.'

'Granted,' said Rachel. 'But she got what she was after, didn't she? Her ex-hubby's flight to her bedside, slap bang in the middle of his weekend with you. At least for the time being. It *is* a temporary arrangement, isn't it, Ange?'

'For God's sake, I don't know!' Angela looked around for Davey to save her with the arrival of the first course.

'But what did he say on the phone?' probed Rachel. 'Come on, he's been gone over a fortnight! When's he coming back?'

Angela's throat went dry. 'He couldn't be specific.' No way could she tell them that Shane had gone out to New York to join his parents. That the family McGinlay were now reunited in Kate's loft apartment, with Conor and Shane dividing the cooking between them, Conor phoning when he could from his makeshift office, sounding ever more defensive, embarrassed and distant.

Not half as embarrassed as Angela, though. In their last conversation, she had blurted down a crackly line, 'I love you!' and been rewarded with a final burst of static and a dialling tone. Had he heard her before he hung up in embarrassment? Had he successfully decoded those three little words as a plea not to be abandoned in favour of an ex-wife with whom he shared a lengthy past and a child?

She turned to Rachel. 'How goes it with Marshall?' she challenged mildly.

Rachel pinkened prettily. 'We haven't exhausted our sell-by date yet! You know, dare I say it, I think he might be the man for me.'

'Honest to God?' Angela faked a bit of polite enthusiasm, ashamed of her self-absorption. Not long ago, an update on Rachel's love life would've shaken her out of even gloomy Robert-thoughts. But two nights of passion with Conor – which was all their relationship really amounted to – had been enough to throw her off-centre and off her guard.

She picked at her meal. Then it was back to Sadie's for the cake-cutting and sherry. Angela nibbled a strand of almond icing and examined the cards on the mantelpiece, while Sadie watched her carefully and Rachel kept the conversational ball rolling. But eventually, even she tired of flogging a rapidly expiring horse.

'I must be off. I've got three evening shifts on the trot coming up. Thanks for the cake, Mrs F.'

'Thank you for my lunch, Rachel.'

'Can I give you a lift home, Ange?'

Sadie stacked cake plates. 'Angela will be staying to help me clear up.'

'Huh? Oh, apparently I'm staying for a bit.' Angela exchanged a conspiratorial look with Rachel over Sadie's head. She was due either a toe up the rear end for 'sulking' doing her civic duty in the restaurant, or a bracing pep talk about not giving up on Conor/not chasing after Conor.

The front door shut. Sadie glared at her. 'Time of the month, is it?'

'No, as it happens,' scowled Angela. Despite telling Sadie firmly, at the age of fifteen, that she wished a conspiracy of feigned ignorance to prevail on this subject whenever the bathroom bin filled up with blue boxes, Sadie had persisted with motherly intrusion ever since.

Back in Angela's teens, she'd offered to soak any pants
with stained gussets and insisted that Angela spirit away
the blue boxes to the bin outside the back door, in case
Fenton or Owen glanced into the bathroom bin and
fainted.

'I'll put the kettle on,' muttered Angela as her opening
time-buying gambit.

Sadie followed her into the kitchen. 'I rang Conor in
New York last night to find out the state of play.'

Angela banged down the tea caddy. 'You did what?'

'Shane answered. They were all going out to dinner, so
he couldn't hang about. He offered to get Conor, but I
decided not to bother, in the circumstances. Face it,
lovey, Conor will have other things on his mind for a
while. But just be patient. He'll come back to you in the
end if you don't force the pace.'

Sick disappointment flooded Angela. Now they were
gallivanting off to family dinners! What man could resist
falling in love with his wife all over again as he helped her
recover from a brush with death? She could just imagine
the touching reunion that had taken place at the hospital
bed, Kate's Titian locks flowing across the pillow, Conor
covering her frail little hand in frenzied kisses: 'Oh my
God, Kate, I thought I'd lost you for ever! And with so
much left unsaid.'

This little tableau had been torturing Angela for some
time. She didn't need to hear about shared dinners! And
she'd be none the wiser if Sadie hadn't poked her snout
in. 'You're the one forcing the pace, you interfering old
trout! Now Conor will think I asked you to phone, that
I'm pestering him from afar. For once in your life, will
you kindly butt out and treat me like an adult!'

Sadie sank into a chair, her face quivering with a spasm
of pain. Physical, Angela presumed. She turned to the
sink, shoulders braced and teeth clenched, deciding to

interpret any signs of infirmity as play-acting. She began twisting a tea towel round and round the inner rim of a clean mug. 'Where did you get the phone number of Kate's flat?'

'He gave it you, didn't he, when he rang from the hospital in New York?'

'But how did you get it, Ma?'

'International directory enquiries,' admitted Sadie, with a hint of smugness. 'She was listed as K McGinlay-Stanton, so there was only one of her, even in New York.' Her instinct told her to now shut up. But force of habit, formed over years of dispensing unwanted maternal advice, got the better of her. 'I liked Conor from the start, as you know. And I still believe he'll come back to you. But it might be wise to brace yourself. There's the odd chance he could be a dodgy bet for the long-term now, with the divorce papers still warm from signing, carrying all that guilt from his marriage failure first time round. What is mean is...'

Angela turned. 'I know it's your sixty-eighth birthday, Ma, but you can decide now to forever hold your peace on the subject of me and Conor, or face celebrating your sixty-ninth alone!'

'God, you always were a touchy one!' clucked Sadie, a lemming hurtling towards the cliff-edge. 'Calm down, lovey. You're right, I shouldn't poke my nosy old beak into your messy old life. Where's that cup of tea?'

'God! Now you're patronising me! You're doing exactly what you did to me as a kid. You wind me up until I snap and then you sit back with a superior little smile and humour me — because that's what you do to people whose childish reactions have to be soothed back into — into whimpering passivity!'

'Paranoia,' muttered Sadie, needled. 'You've had a paranoid streak ever since you were a little girl.

Remember Caroline Lynch's birthday party? You came home and said everyone got a bigger slice of cake than you. It was the same with Owen. You were always watching out in case his Easter egg was bigger or he had more presents under the tree.'

She shook her head so sorrowfully that molten rage poured through Angela's veins.

'For God's sake!' she yelled at her mother. 'You can't even admit your own blatant prejudice. I'll tell you what I remember from childhood. Owen pinching me black and blue when we were both lying on the settee, recovering from the measles. And you telling me that I was making a fuss and imagining things. Christ, I even had bruises all over my defenceless little body to prove it!' Angela's voice wobbled with self-pity as unrighted wrongs overwhelmed her. 'But oh no, you took the side of your favourite, your golden only son. You weren't interested in justice. There's nothing worse to a small child than realising your parent isn't interested in fair play. From an early age, I thought boys must be more important than girls. I thought you could never love me the way you loved Owen because I was too ordinary to matter!'

Tears sloshed down her chin. She buried her chin in the tea towel and sobbed with passion for her childhood self.

Sadie was horrified. She tried to heave herself off her chair, but flailed back into it. 'You were never ordinary, Angela! How could you see yourself in that light? My God, the frozen food saga! When you came home and told me you'd packed in the job, you were going to Rachel's for the weekend, and I could lump it. What a rebel! If I seemed to take Owen's side when you two rowed – and God forgive me, maybe I did – it was because you always stamped your foot and stood up for yourself. God forgive me, I thought I was playing fair. I

188 G A B R I E L L E   M U L L A R K E Y

thought I had to put Owen's case because he wouldn't put
it himself. He was the type to let you walk all over him.'

'He was too clever to be walked all over!' hissed
Angela. 'He was a sneaky pincher, a behind-the-back toy
breaker. You just assumed that quietness equalled
goodness.'

There was a long silence. Angela turned back to the
sink and fished a packet of paper hankies out of the
cutlery drawer. She unfolded a hanky with deliberate care
and honked into it. Whatever came next had to come
from Sadie. She'd said too much already.

'You've been nursing these petty grudges all these
years,' observed Sadie sadly. 'Thinking I loved Owen
more than you. Oh Angela, lovey, how could you?'

Guilt flared briefly in Angela at Sadie's stricken tone
but, just in time, she recognised another favourite ploy of
her mother's. The emotional blackmail ploy. She wanted
Sadie to feel guilty for a change. She wanted to lash out
and give her mother's self-assurance the battering it
deserved.

'Is this about Robert in some way?' asked Sadie,
wisely, gently and infuriatingly maternally. 'Do you feel
life kicked you in the teeth yet again by taking Robert,
while Owen gets away scot-free? Let me tell you, Ange,
there's no such thing as scot-free in this life. Everyone has
their woes, sooner or later.'

'Jesus Christ, Ma, spare me the Sermon on the sodding
Mount! You want to know about me and Robert? Well,
brace yourself, hang onto your support stockings, it's
going to be a bumpy ride of unpleasant truths.'

She took a deep breath – and said nothing.

'Go on,' urged Sadie, with a vague presentiment of
doom. 'Go on, Ange.'

'All right, all right!' snapped Angela. 'Here it is.
Robert had that heart attack because we rowed about you

the night before! About whether you should come and live with us. I said let's go for it, and Robert said, very prophetically, over his dead body. I'd never seen him so worked-up. Must have sent his blood pressure through the roof. Oh, don't worry, I played my part in bringing on his coronary and I've felt suitably guilty ever since. But the reason he couldn't hack the idea was because he sussed long ago that you never really liked him.'

'I – well – that's just not true!' gasped Sadie

'Isn't it?' demanded Angela. 'Come on, Mum, cards-on-the-table time. You tolerated Robert, but you never saw him as my equal, let alone yours. He was yet another poor choice by me, along with passing up college, not having kids – the whole gamut of second-bests. I'd learnt to live with disappointing you, of course. I'd had years of practice. But you've no idea how sensitive Robert was to your low opinion of him.'

'So, you're saying – his heart attack was my fault?' gulped Sadie.

'No, no, don't be stupid!' snapped Angela, tugging helplessly at her hair. 'Don't you understand, it was *my* fault. Mine, mine, mine! But you were often a crap mother, and a crap mother-in-law. I don't see why you should get away with pretending you liked Robert, any more than you should get away with imagining how nice you were to me growing up.'

'I – well, I –' Sadie was floundering, a fish on a hot pavement. Her mouth even opened and shut in convulsive little Os. Her face had lost its colour and dignity.

Angela suddenly felt like vomiting. Almond pastry disagreed with her.

'Wait there!' she croaked and dashed upstairs to the loo. She heaved without hurling. She spent as much time up there as she could, washing her face, gathering her thoughts, casting about for a mental lasso to rein in the bolted horse. Eventually, she crept back down, feeling sick for a different reason. What sort of mood would Sadie be in? The birthday girl. Jesus! Why did she have to pick today, of all days, to row big-time with her mother?

Sadie was washing up. She raised crabbed hands from the sink, webbed grotesquely with suds, and reached for a tea towel. Her voice was quieter than a stealth bomber. 'You'd better go, Angela. I don't want to see you or talk to you for a while. I want to think things over.'

'Look, Ma, about what I said...'

'Don't make me ask you to leave.'

Angela capitulated. This was the tenor of exchanges of old. Sadie's deadly tone, gathering her strength for the storm, Angela's huddled truculence before she fled and waited for her mother to calm down. But this time, Sadie was eerily calm. This time, Angela had gone too far.

'I'll get me coat,' she tried half-jokily, but Sadie wasn't familiar with the catch-phrases of popular culture. Angela got her coat, stepped onto the porch, closed the front door slowly. 'Well, bye then. I'll ring tomorrow. You can break out the sackcloth and ashes for my next visit.'

She wanted to say more, but what? The cutlery clanged onto the draining board. Binky stalked past the front door and towards the kitchen, pausing to reproach Angela with all-knowing green eyes. Bloody cat! It was true what Sadie claimed. He had a face to fit every occasion. This face said, How could you? She's your mother! And she's got arthritis!

Conor found the postcard in the bottom of his bag, while looking for a clean shirt. It was a big night in Kate's recuperation programme. She'd survived a week of intensive therapy and her stomach was starting to lose its tender resistance to solid food. They were all going to a bistro in Greenwich Village to celebrate.

The bathroom door opened. Conor shoved the postcard back in the bag.

'Shane!' His tone was exasperated. 'Can't you ever knock before storming through a bathroom or bedroom door?'

'Ye wot? There's no privacy here, anyway. I have to share a room with you, listening to you grunt and slobber all night. I dunno why they call it snoring.'

Conor sighed. 'Who was that on the phone?'

Shane shut the door carefully behind him. 'Old Mrs Wotserface, Angela's mother. Ringing to ask how Mum is.' Shane paused, conveying added meaning with a look. The word 'ostensibly' was outside his vocabulary.

'That was nice of her. Did she want to talk to me?'

'I said we were halfway out the door. I told Mum it was work ringing for you. It's going to be awkward if Angela and her fan club make a habit of phoning here.'

'Angela won't phone,' said Conor gloomily. 'Now bog off and let me get changed.'

He looked around. The dinky little bathroom had no shelves or rails to drape clothing. Even the hand towel was spread over the top of a chest-shaped linen basket. Everything was pink and edged in fake gilt. 'A bleedin' Barbie boudoir,' in Shane's spot-on opinion.

He'd no sooner got rid of Shane than Kate's marmalade tresses snaked round the door. 'Are you decent yet? Only the cab's due in a minute and I wasn't sure if you'd shaved yet.'

'Don't worry, I tackled that first.' How easily they'd settled into old spousal routines and returned to old pet hates. She'd never liked his hirsute whiskeriness. Kate's preferred male 'type', by her own admission, was the clean-shaven dealer in off-shore portfolios who inhaled wine through a patrician nose and knew a fish fork wasn't for picking his teeth. Conor had often wondered if she'd chosen him to spite herself as much as her father; if her self-destruct sequence was always on the verge of countdown.

When he emerged from the bathroom, she was doing a twirl for Shane. The little black dress was velvet. He thought, with a pang, of peeling Angela's black velvet straps off her bony, supple shoulders. The hilarious thong. His rudeness. Angela's hurt pride and readiness to see the joke. 'You look lovely,' he told Kate honestly.

She smiled, sped over to administer a wifely fiddle to his tie-knot. 'And so do both my men.' She held out another arm to encompass Shane, who crept under it, pleased and proud of his beautiful, fragile mother.

How does she do it, marvelled Conor, as Kate's skin glowed, her hair shone, her eyes and teeth sparkled. She looks as if she's spent the last few weeks being pampered at a top health spa, not lying face down in her own stomach contents and then hauled off to a detox centre, to tell a roomful of fellow manic-depressive dipsos, 'My name's Kate, and I'm an alcoholic.'

The cab honked outside, briefly distinguishable to Conor's ear from New York's long night of lamenting sirens. He thought again of the postcard. Angela had bought it for Sadie and never written on it or posted it. In the mad departure scramble, it had ended up in his luggage.

As he held out Kate's black serape for her, he recalled their frantic leaving of Curracloe, the undignified end to what should've been a leisurely weekend of discovering each other. Then the flight back to London, knowing only that Kate was critical, leaving Angela to find her own way home on the Tube, while he dashed back to Pacelli Road, gave Shane some face-saving story about Kate and appendicitis, and packed for another flight.

As they climbed into the taxi, and Kate brushed his

knee with her elbow, he thought of his last phone call to Angela, thanking God the bad line had camouflaged his craven tone of prevarication. And then, some final words from her, wavering through the crackle, sounding like 'I love you!' But all he got was the heat of passion. Could just as easily have been 'I hate you!'

'Do you miss her?' asked Kate softly in his ear.

He jumped. It was calculated to sound sympathetic. But all it sounded was calculated, sussing out her own hold over him.

'Yes,' he said, sliding his cool hand across her own. 'I can't switch my feelings on and off, can I?'

She held his gaze steadily, allowing it to stray just for a second towards Shane, who was interrogating the cab driver. 'Do those feelings apply to me, as well?'

The bistro was heavy on ambience and scornful waiters. Shane sat very upright, grappling with a leather-bound menu and hissed at Conor, 'Shall I ask if they've a kiddies' menu?'

'Be my guest,' responded Conor mildly, his attention distracted by Kate studying a different-coloured menu. He plucked it out of her hands. 'The wine list,' he observed, and slammed it shut. 'Over my dead body. Or yours, to be exact. The mineral water probably costs more than the house plonk, but I'm prepared to pay for it by the bucket-load.'

Kate tossed her head, two hectic spots appearing on her cheeks. 'I was just looking.'

'And I'm just looking at that strawberry sundae on the next table, but I know strawberries bring me out in a rash, which tends to keep temptation at bay. And I like strawberries,' he added in case she'd missed the point.

Kate looked warningly at Shane, then dredged up a martyr-like smile. 'You're right, of course. I'd forgotten how much I need you, Conor.'

He scowled. He'd walked right into that one. Luckily, Shane still seemed engrossed in his menu.

After that, the bonhomie was laced with tension. Kate, Conor knew, was just itching for a drink. When they got back to her place, he had every intention of checking the usual places for stashed hootch.

As it was a clear, moonlit night, he suggested they take a taxi halfway back to the flat, and walk the rest of the way. 'You serious?' frowned Kate, climbing into the taxi. 'This is New York, not Ballykissangel.'

'New York, as everyone knows, is one of the safest cities in the world, since Mayor Giuliani cracked down on anti-social behaviour.'

'Softening up the locals for the rats to move in for the kill,' put in Shane helpfully. 'They outnumber New Yorkers four to one.'

But Conor was adamant. Paying off the driver, he prodded them onto the sidewalk for the second half of their journey. He had a particular reason for wanting to walk the latter half of the journey. He had something to show Kate.

As they drew near to the alleyway in question, he slowed purposefully and paused near its entrance. Then he strode down it without warning, leaving the other two puttering along in his wake.

'Conor, wait!' called Kate.

'You mad, Dad?' puffed Shane, tripping over a cardboard box in the dark.

The alleyway panned out suddenly into a square of concrete, ringed on three sides by a chain-link fence. A fire burnt dully in one corner. Round it sat a ragbag circle of people, hunched in filthy clothes, snatching back their fingers from the fire's grudging warmth to cradle liquor bottles in brown paper bags. There was no communal passing of the bottle round this campfire. It was impossible to tell either ages or sexes.

No one looked up from the ebbing heat. The winos' passing interest in the outside world didn't extend to curiosity about who or what might be watching them from the shadows.

Kate was furious. 'This is your idea of shock therapy, is it, Conor? You've got a bloody nerve.'

Conor was just as angry. 'And you're a bloody ostrich-head. Take a good look and see yourself in a few years' time.'

'A nice sight and sentiment for your son!'

'Let it be a warning to him, too. If alcoholism *is* hereditary, I intend to make sure it begins and ends with you.'

Angela picked up the phone, gnawing her bottom lip. This would have to be a whopper apology – without giving the game away. The truth loomed in her mind behind a school essay title: What Really Happened That Night Between Me and Robert.

Angela dialled, more in sorrow than in hope. It was possible that Sadie would never forgive or recover from the twin accusations of being a lousy mother and a slow-burning contributor to a fatal heart attack. Maybe she'd lose the will to live and surrender to the sword-thrusts of arthritis. Then Angela would be responsible for two untimely deaths, thanks to a tongue that was a fully loaded missile without a guidance system. Goddamit, mother, answer the phone, she thought despairingly.

Sadie let the phone ring out. She was cold. She had no energy to lean forward and switch on the fire. Binky came to complain about it, twining his wiry body around her stiff legs. The rasping caress of his body against her tights was comfort of a sort, if also a reminder that Fenton wasn't there to put his arms around her. When Binky began to purr impatiently, it sounded like a murmur of compassion, and she let the tears come then, watching them fall on her pleated skirt with almost dispassionate interest.

She rarely cried. Like a real man, Sadie prided herself on this fact.

The last time she'd cried was a few days after Christmas Day, when Angela had gone home, refreshed and all cried out, but leaving Sadie exhausted by her dry-eyed counselling role. She'd cried then out of sheer fatigue after all that cooking and listening. It had been a relief to know it was just a physical response to a punishing schedule.

But these tears splashing down on Binky's aggrieved head were big, salty pools of self-pity. She felt helpless, worthless and ashamed.

Angela had grown up resenting her as a punitive, unfair mother. While Sadie, complacent as you like, had walked in the sun of a flattering self-belief, feting herself as a strong but even-handed mother and encouraging others (especially Fenton) to share the illusion.

Had she got things so wrong? Her natural confidence rose up to rebuff Angela's claims. But just as quickly, it melted away. After all, she addressed the cold bars of the fire, look no further than Owen. A boy showered with love who scarpered to the New World at the first opportunity and put his parents and sister on the long finger, dropping occasional parcels behind the lines when guilt and anniversaries tweaked his conscience.

Oh yes, she liked to tell herself that Owen was doing well. It had been easy to fool herself that 'doing well' meant shaking the dust of home from your heels and fleeing to the other side of the world, because that was how the Irish traditionally did well.

But Wilmesbury wasn't a blighted potato field. Owen had left home to get away from his family; the parents who'd coddled and curtailed him, and the sister he'd apparently mistreated. Sadie had read somewhere that oppressors feared their victims more than the other way around.

She had lost her son by the time he was a teenager, and now she'd lost her daughter, too. Or maybe Angela had been keeping up a daughterly pretence all along, until Sadie finally goaded her into dropping it.

Robert must indeed have got himself so worked up that he'd brought on his heart attack. If she'd only tried harder to see the good points in him that Angela saw with clarity. Who was Sadie to criticise anyone, even in her heart? A cranky old woman with clicky hips, deserted or kept at a distance by children she had alienated. It was no less than she deserved.

Sadie put her head down in the fusty pleats of her skirt and cried much harder. Alarmed by the unfamiliar noise, Binky ran for cover the kitchen.

'I hate to say I told you so,' said Pauline across her keyboard.

'Then don't!' pleaded Angela, tired eyes fixed on her screen. Her other departmental colleagues were off sick or loitering in the kitchen. It had been a mistake to confide in anyone at work, even the tight-lipped Pauline. Angela had come to realise that Pauline's 'weirdness', as far as the likes of Val were concerned, was an unnatural disregard for the office traditions of sharing and spreading gossip. At least Pauline could be trusted to keep her trap shut. But she should've stopped short at confiding in Rachel. Rachel was her true friend. Besides, Pauline now persisted in seeing Angela as a kindred spirit, a failure in the relationship stakes.

'Your only hope is if Kate remarries or tops herself with a bigger OD next time. Any chance of her falling for the hunky doc who pumped her out?'

'I don't wish any ill-will towards the woman. Anyway, he told me in Ireland that he doesn't love her.' Angela jabbed her keyboard miserably.

Pauline snorted. 'She's got a bigger hold over him than love! Emotional blackmail. What if she tops herself, and leaves a note for the kid, blaming Conor? He can't take the risk. He has to humour her, bend to her will, sacrifice his heart's desire. And that makes you the fall-guy, Ange. He'll have to give you up for the greater good. Nice for him – he gets to go through life with the glow of self-sacrifice keeping his principles warm. Not so nice for you – seeing as you're the actual human sacrifice in all this.'

'Pauline, don't –' Angela's throat tightened. A treacherous tear splashed onto the delete key.

Pauline stared, not unkindly. 'Made it up with your mum yet?'

'Oh great! A fresh can of worms. No, she won't answer the phone or her doorbell. I've tried catching her at work, even waylaying her in the cemetery, but she pretends I don't exist. To be honest, my rehearsed cringing apology is unravelling at the edges. I'm beginning to feel justified in going off the deep end in the first place. I can't bear sulking. My husband was a marathon sulker,' she added as a disloyal afterthought.

Pauline was fascinated to hear more, but struggled to be tactful. 'Look, I'm having a party at my place this Saturday. More a gathering of wimmin than a party. We sit around on scatter cushions, get rat-arsed putting the world to rights and return an overwhelming vote that men are a bunch of shits. Fancy it?'

'Has your latest relationship gone down the plughole, then?' sniffed Angela tactlessly.

'I'll give you chapter and verse if you come on Saturday.'

Angela considered. 'I like the rat-arsed bit. Can I be excused from voting on men? I don't want to think about men for a whole night.'

Pauline nodded. 'I understand. Solace in the sisterhood. Bring a sleeping bag and you can crash out for the night as well.'

Pauline only half-understood. Angela didn't believe in the sisterhood of wronged wimmin. She believed they had a tendency to blame all their misfortunes on men, going back to the patriarchal reactionaries who'd written the creation story with that Adam's rib nonsense. She could just imagine the teenage Pauline haranguing a mild-mannered father with rantings about Freud and penis-envy. Still, right now, Pauline and her wronged wimmin offered an umbrella of sympathy to shelter under. Beggars couldn't be choosers. It sure beat sitting at home, being sad enough to pretend that he might ring, after all, tonight. As if! He hadn't rung now for over a week. And who else was going to phone her on a Saturday night? Not Sadie.

Conor had nearly made it to the phone when Kate appeared in the flat's hallway, pearlescent in a silk kimono wrap. 'You can't sleep either?' she yawned, padding on cat-like feet past him, and into the kitchen. 'I'm going to heat up some milk. Care to join me?'

He strode after her without answering, falling in with her pretence that he'd been on his way to the kitchen all along. How ridiculous that he needed a pretext and cover of darkness to phone Angela! It couldn't be coincidence that Kate had now materialised on three separate occasions when he'd come close to picking up the phone.

She passed him a mug of hot milk, sugaring it with her smile. They sat at the small kitchen table, echoing the few months of cosiness at the start of their marriage. 'I've been thinking about that dramatic little episode on the way home from the restaurant the other day, and I can see why you did it.'

'That's a start, I suppose.'

'You saved my life, Conor. I'll never be able to thank you,' she said softly.

Conor frowned furiously. 'The doctors saved your life, Kattie!'

'You know what I mean!' She smiled even more luxuriously. 'You haven't called me Kattie for years. Remember when you came to visit me after Shane was born, and you picked him up for the first time? "Oh Kattie!" you said over and over again, with manly tears running down your cheeks. You looked so sweet. Even sweeter than Shane.'

She lit one of her wispy cigarettes, dragging in the taste with her eyes shut. She cut down her intake when Shane was around. She'd given up altogether during pregnancy, he recalled, and made the bi-monthly gesture of chucking out half-full bottles. Fair play to her for that. Shane had been a skinny rather than an underweight baby, a wizened walnut with a critical gaze that had quickly proved myopic.

Conor drained his milk with indecent haste, plonked down the mug. 'The way things are going, me and Shane will be able to up sticks soon, and let you get back to your life.'

'Not so fast, Mac!' She wagged a playful finger, using his own nickname from days gone by. 'We still have things to discuss. Like me coming back to England, as per our original plan.'

'Your original plan, Kattie. Modified by our son to mean living near each other, sure, but not under the same roof.' He stared at her finger. She didn't wear her wedding ring any more, but a circlet of pale flesh stood out from the light tan on her fingers.

'Shane's been a different person, with you and me back together,' pressed Kate. 'It certainly gives us both food for thought — I mean, about where our responsibilities truly lie. Teenage boys don't always know what's best for them.' She stood up first, taking him by surprise. 'That milk has worked. I'm feeling sleepier already. If you've any more trouble sleeping... I know that room is cramped, with you and Shane sharing it. My door, as they say, is always open.'

She laughed softly and twinkled in the doorway like a red-haired Celtic sprite.

'Goodnight, Conor.'

'See ya, Kate.'

He couldn't ring Angela now, could he? Not with Kate's door standing open, a few yards away. He moved silently around the kitchen instead, checking the cupboard under the sink for hidden bottles. He found only a bottle of white spirit, and reflected, with a wry smile, that Kate was a long way off that stage.

God, it was so easy to pick up all these old habits: the bathroom rota, harmless squabbles over Shane's contribution to dishwashing, and the eternal vigilance of a spouse with an alcoholic partner. Only now, of course, he could be a lot more forceful and open with his disapproval. Kate's overdose had catapulted her out of the drinking closet, and she could no longer throw tantrums at being 'accused' of a nasty habit. He sometimes thought he was really getting through to her, making a difference.

On his way back to the spare room, Conor eyed the telephone on the hallway table, then Kate's open door. Are you a man or a mouse? he demanded of himself. Or maybe a New York sewer-rat, leaving Angela to wonder what the hell's going on. Affirmative action was needed. He snatched up the phone and punched in Angela's number. He let it ring out and felt irrationally hurt that she wasn't in. It was Sunday morning back in England. Where the hell could she be?

'Welcome to the house of fun!' Pauline greeted Angela at the door. Angela stumbled inside, sleeping bag under one arm, party-gift wine gripped in her free hand. Pauline lived in a basement flat in a street of terraced houses, too close to Pacelli Road for comfort and too far away from Loxton station to be the five-minute stroll Pauline had claimed. 'This way!' sang Pauline, leading her down a dark hallway to a square of light and a babble of voices escaping from under a door. 'We don't stand on ceremony, Ange, so plonk yourself down on any surface except the cat. Red or white?'

'Er – white, please,' smiled Angela. She was pushed through the door and into a throng, while Pauline vanished, complete with wine bottle and sleeping bag.

The room wasn't as brightly lit as Angela had first thought. The main light switch was off, a supplementary light issuing pinkly from a lopsided lampshade in one corner. In the grate of the small, neat fireplace, lily-shaped candles floated in cut-glass trifle bowls full of water. Leonard Cohen leaked mournfully from speakers either side of a bookcase. There were plants, framed posters of famous paintings, and a lot of wimmin.

Though, as far as Angela could tell, they were really just women. They squatted on cushions, leant on projecting shelves, talked and gesticulated in the manner of all mingling partygoers. And scattered here and there among them, like exotic starfruits in a plain old fruit salad, were men. Pauline returned to her side with a glass of red wine.

'I thought you said there'd be no men,' Angela hissed, though not accusingly.

'They're not men in the real, shitty sense of the word,' explained Pauline.

'You mean gay men? Honorary women.'

Pauline poked the nearest man with her foot. He looked up from an animated conversation on the floor, good-looking in a hollow-eyed, cadaverous way. 'You gay, Alan?'

He bridled. 'Not so you'd notice.'

Pauline buried her elbow in Angela's ribs. 'Alan lives upstairs and came down to complain about the crappy choice of music on the stereo. Decided to stay when he saw it was wall-to-wall totty and every man for himself. We'd better move away, we're cramping his style.'

Pauline found Angela a half-inch of unoccupied scatter cushion by the fireplace. 'You'll roast in that jacket, Ange. Aren't you going to take it off?'

Angela clutched her black linen jacket – a size too large – around the pink and black dress. Its pockets contained her essentials of keys, money and contact lens bottle. 'Fact is, I've come overdressed for the occasion, Pauline. When you said, party, I automatically thought party dress, as in girly frills and too much pink. I'm afraid I'm out of practice gracing the party scene.'

'Have some more wine,' urged Pauline, sensibly comfortable in her floaty ethnic skirt and long white blouse, and topped up the unwanted red plonk that Angela had barely sipped. 'I'll point out a few wounded souls to you. That's Sheila. Husband ran off with the au pair, but neglected to do her the favour of taking the kids with him. Monica nursed a live-in lover through a long illness. So when he recovered, naturally, he ran off with the next sentient woman who crossed his path.' She frowned around the room. 'A few others I don't recognise. Friends of friends.'

'And what about you?' asked Angela hastily, wondering how she'd been prefaced before her arrival. 'You said you'd give me the lowdown on your latest – um – male shit.'

Pauline slumped forward, playing with the ends of her hair. 'A bastard from yesteryear, name of Dominic. You know the press pass I got to the preview of the Monet exhibition at the National?'

'Er – no.' As the new girl, Angela was bottom of the pecking order for office freebies. She took a deep slug of vinegary wine.

'Well, Dom was there, giving me the come-on. Said his etchings were better than Monet's daubings any day of the week. We had lunch, then each other. Twice at my place, once back at his the following week. I was in seventh heaven.' She stared down at a floating candle, reminiscing.

'So, did he – um – dump you?' Angela risked eventually.

'Of course! That's twice I've let him do it to me. Why do I never see it coming? Why?'

Because you don't want to, sighed Angela inwardly, and carried on drinking. It gave her something to do with her hands.

Pauline's fawn and white cat appeared from nowhere to jump onto Angela's lap, sinking its claws into pink silk folds. Pauline nodded approvingly. 'You must be giving off good vibes for Casper to favour you. Are you fussy about cat hairs?'

'No,' sighed Angela truthfully. She was quite happy for

Casper to rip the dress to shreds. She'd worn it consciously, to banish nostalgic associations. She hadn't wanted to come across it in her wardrobe in six months' time and stare at it, rub her face against it, recall it as the dress of her night of passion. It was just a Rachel cast-off. She drank more wine.

Pauline vanished to circulate with a tray of nibbles and her sob story about Dominic.

Someone else plonked down beside Angela with a sigh of weariness. 'Jesus, my feet are killing me. Been on them all day. That's shop work for you.'

The woman rubbed plump ankles. Her shoes were high-heeled, backless and toeless, the front of each a mere strip of plum-coloured suede. They were the more obvious source of her tortured feet. 'You one of Pauline's walking wounded too?' she asked Angela.

'Definitely not,' replied Angela, affronted. 'Anyway, Pauline does talk about other things beside the iniquity of the male species. She's a good laugh.'

'Yeah, but look around you.' The woman's plump arm jangled with bracelets as her hand swept the room. 'Sooner or later, we all end up here from one of Pauline's therapy groups.'

Angela started. 'Pauline's a therapist?'

'Alternative therapist, love. Get the jargon right. She runs a workshop in the adult education centre every so often, numbers permitting.' The woman glanced at Angela curiously and with new respect. 'So you know her from the real world, then? You must have a few more screws in place than the rest of us.'

'I work with her,' said Angela uneasily. As far as Pauline was concerned, she was one of her walking wounded, as yet unrecruited into a beans-spilling, anger-letting therapy session. The woman stood up, swaying uneasily in a crushed purple skirt that reached to her painfully arched ankles. 'Well, I'm off to get more wine. Drinking to forget is the best reason I know. Trouble is, when I wake up tomorrow with a screaming hangover, I'll still remember a certain red-haired mick with an unholy brat of a son. Nice meeting you.'

The woman tottered off. Angela gazed after her in consternation, looking at her properly for the first time. That long red hair, coiled loosely on the back of her head, snaky tendrils escaping over her ears. Jesus, it was Kate! Somehow, she'd done a bunk from New York, metamorphosed at Pauline's, crept up on Angela, hoping to catch her unawares.

Angela clutched Pauline as she passed with a tray of cheese-laden crackers. 'Pauline, who's the woman in purple with the red hair?'

Pauline squinted down the room. 'Never saw her before in my life.'

'But she said she was from – never mind!' On second thoughts, better not let slip that she'd heard about the therapy group. Pauline might take it as an active recruitment signal.

Angela spent the next half-hour trying to manoeuvre herself within conversational range of the Kate apparition. She had a drinker's complexion, all right. In fact, she was a bit – well – fishmonger's wife to be the love (officially ex-love) of Conor's life. Her face was plump to the point of gaining a second chin, her blue eyes alive but watery under mascara-encrusted lashes. She worked the room, sharing hearty jokes with several women she obviously knew, but stayed close to Pauline's dining table, where the sandwiches, nibbles and wine bottles beckoned.

Angela shadowed her back to the table. The woman whirled round, thrust a plate under Angela's chin. 'Prawn sarnie?'

'Thanks.' Angela took one without thinking. Anyway,

she had to line her stomach with something substantial after three glasses of wine.

'You following me or something?' demanded the Kate lookalike.

'No! Look, the thing is.' Angela swallowed a mayonnaise-jacketed prawn. 'I was just wondering if you knew – a bloke called Conor McGinlay.'

The woman's eyes snapped open wide, then narrowed. 'Don't tell me he's had you as well? In both senses of the word?'

Angela's slack-jawed shock confirmed it. The woman shook her head delightedly. 'Oh dearie, dearie me! Pauline's right about one thing. Us women live but we never learn. Were you dismissed for upsetting the unholy brat? Or did you stumble on the shrine to St Kate?'

'The shrine?' Angela's confusion conceded the upper hand. Whoever this was, she clearly wasn't Kate. That meant she had to be the other one – what was her name?

The woman laid a plump hand on Angela's arm, steered her into a corner. 'I can see I'm going to have to fill in the blanks. Upstairs in the dream house, in the one-time boudoir of Conor and Kate McGinlay, he keeps everything on her dressing table exactly as it was on the day she departed. He replaces fresh flowers next to the bed every few days, just as she did. The drawers are full of her lace-lined undies that I bet not even Mrs Turner is allowed to touch. He sleeps with a lock of her hair under his pillow. I'm Rosalind Jennings, by the way.'

'Angela Carbery,' said Angela automatically. 'But he told me they didn't even share a bedroom after Shane!' It leapt out bitterly before she could bite it back.

'Oh, not when Shane the shithead was a baby. That kid was such a handful, you can't blame her for not wanting another brat, even by accident. But when Shane got older, and started noticing awkward anomalies, like having a mummy and daddy who didn't share a bedroom, they shacked up together in the master bedroom again. Now don't ask me if they had sex!' Rosie heaved a wayward strap back onto her shoulder. 'I reckon they must have partaken now and then over the years, for all the problems between them. They're only flesh and blood. All I know is, he fell in an absolute heap when she took off for New York. They might've had a lame marriage, but she was still his first love. For all you and I know, he tried to get her back. The man's fixated. He's no business starting out on other relationships he can't follow through.'

Through her hurt and misery, a shaft of common sense hit Angela. 'How do you know all this about Conor and his past?'

'I went out with him for four months,' shrugged Rosie. 'If I stayed overnight, we had to do it in the spare bedroom. I accepted that. A bloke's allowed to have a sentimental attachment to the ex-marital boudoir. He told me the lie of the land, putting his own spin on it, of course. Everything over between him and Kate, never were compatible for the long haul, she'd had an unhappy past and he felt guilty that he couldn't cope, blah di blah. Then I found the bedroom shrine one morning by accident when I took a wrong turn from the bathroom. I quizzed him about it and he dropped me like a hot brick. When it comes right down to it, he'll never choose anyone over her, because he'll never get her out of his system. She's a virus and he welcomes the attacks – the night sweats, the shivers, the pain-racked guilt.'

She leant forward to peer at Angela, wafting wine fumes and an under-scent of chocolate over the thin, paling woman in black. 'Look, I'm sorry if I opened my Mersey tunnel gob prematurely. You still actually involved with him?'

'No,' shuddered Angela, thinking back to Curracloe, to his kisses and whispers and lies. To his biggest lie — that he'd never articulated his failed marriage in detail to a third party. A tear fell soggily onto her prawn sandwich. 'You were right about Kate. He's just gone back to her.'

Chapter Ten

'Wait here!' Rosie told the taxi driver, and manhandled Angela out of the back seat. 'Come on, dearie, you might as well see for yourself, in case you think I'm bluffing or bad-mouthing him.'

Angela felt confused and ill. Her insides were protesting at all that red plonk and indiscriminate consumption of sandwiches. She wasn't even sure how she'd ended up in the back of a taxi with Rosalind Jennings, former inamorata of Conor McGinlay. As was she, now. They were wimmin bonded by the shattering of trust too easily pledged and love too freely given. Greenhorns or fully ripened saps, take your pick.

'God!' groaned Angela, stumbling off the pavement and into the dark embrace of dense, soft shrubbery. 'I'm not well. Where am I?'

'This way!' Rosie pinched her elbow not too gently and steered her away from the thrubbing taxi engine and the safety of its headlights. Where is she taking me? thought Angela in a mild panic. She stumbled again in the darkness as Rosie's fingers bit deeply to keep her upright. They tottered round a corner and into the quietness of a garden, a driveway.

'Behold!' snickered Rosie and thrust Angela against cold, sharp metal. Angela clutched unsteadily at curlicued spears rising from railings, paint flaking onto her hands. She knew these railings by sight but not by touch; the palings around one side of 23 Pacelli Road. Above her loomed a post, topped by a board that glimmered whitely in an opalescent night sky. It said 'For Sale'.

'I told you!' cackled Rosie. 'He's cleared off, upped sticks, headed for the New World with a pocketful of cash from the sale of this place. You were right. He has gone back to her.'

Angela grabbed the curlicues so that they hurt her palms. 'Love many, trust few, always paddle your own canoe, as my mother says,' she croaked. 'Or, never trust a man with testicles, as my friend Rachel says.'

'Too right!' Shivering suddenly, Rosie grabbed her arm again. 'Come on, our carriage awaits.'

Angela stumbled gratefully alongside her. They were heading back to Pauline's, back to her sleeping bag and the communion of wronged wimmin. She could get her exploding head down, use that big, soft cat as a pillow.

She half-fell into the taxi's back seat. The taxi driver's face swam into her line of vision, distended by her fuddled senses into something half-animal and half-human, like a creature from a painting by Hieronymus Bosch. 'Who?' he asked, turning into Robert. Robert had resented 'arty-farty stuff'. Angela's ability to recognise a few famous paintings had infuriated him with its elitism, even though she'd been introduced to most of them by biscuit tin lids.

'Where to?' repeated the taxi driver, turning to Rosie for enlightenment. 'And wherever it is, make it fast before your friend here ruins my upholstery.'

Angela shut her eyes and dozed, lulled by the taxi's smooth progress through late-night streets. When Rosie's sharp fingers began to snap at her again, she groaned in protest. 'Don't be like this, dearie! I may be a big girl but

I didn't get this way by heaving coal sacks around. Gimme some co-operation here.'

Angela tried to oblige. The sooner she got out of the taxi, the sooner she'd be sheathed in her sleeping bag. She clambered out, hugging the jacket around her ridiculous pink puffball dress. The taxi sped away. She'd have to settle up with Rosie later.

'Well, here we are.' Rosie inserted a key, pushed open a door. 'Later than I planned, thanks to the detour.'

It was only inside that Angela made a discovery. She wasn't back at Pauline's. She was in a small, windowless kitchen heaped with dirty crockery. Flowers sprang from a vase on a small kitchen table. They were long-dead, decomposing headily in the airless room, their musty petals folded over drooping heads like rotting mantillas. Angela shivered and sank into a chair.

'You'll be right as rain in a minute,' said Rosie's voice from a cupboard. 'Hair of the dog is what you and I need.'

She loomed suddenly over Angela's chair, her face blotchy from drink and the cool spring night air, a flower wilting on its engorged, purple stalk. Angela shrank back by instinct. 'I want to go back to Pauline's,' she whimpered drunkenly.

Rosie stalked to the table, shoved the vase aside. Paper-crisp petals shook onto the table with a final death rattle. Rosie banged down a half-full bottle next to a bread board. 'There's bloody gratitude for you! I direct the taxi out of my way to show you evidence he's skipping the country, and you want me to back-track all the way to Pauline's. Well, diddums.' She went to a drawer, then stuck her head in a cupboard under the sink.

When she turned round again to face Angela, a long-handled knife gleamed in one hand. Angela gasped.

'I suppose it's the shock,' mused Rosie, dumping two

lemons on the bread board with her other hand. She cleaved one cleanly with the knife. 'Gin and tonic should do the trick, going easy on the tonic. Fuckit, glasses!'

Her next trip was to the sink. She scattered dishes with crashes that jolted through Angela's skull, before extracting two greasy tumblers. 'You know, it was a shock for me, too. I mean, meeting my successor. Just when you think you're getting over being dumped, you meet the proof of how little time he needed to get over it. The bastard!' She stuck the knife in the other lemon. A bolt of pain shot through Angela.

'Ow!' Rosie held up a thumb and squinted at it. Blood gushed from a flesh wound, red and fresh. She jammed the thumb in her mouth and sucked noisily. Then, as an afterthought, she held her thumb over the rim of a glass and squeezed. 'Homemade bloody Mary,' she cackled and looked at Angela.

It was the look that did it. She's mad, panicked Angela. She thinks I ruined any chance of her getting back with Conor. She's going to make me drink her blood, then finish me off with the knife. I'll never get out of here alive. There's no window I can run to and yell for help.

'What's the matter with you?' Rosie's face darkened with a frown. Her voice rose fractiously. 'Why are you looking at me like that!'

She darted forward, the knife still in her hand, blood staining its handle.

Angela gasped as the pain ripped through her. After that, the last thing she saw was Rosie's look of shock, before she pitched forward and fell off the chair.

When she woke up, her first emotion was panic. Then came pain, sharp and orbital. Her eyes had opened onto womb-like darkness. Now, as she strained to discern the outline of her surroundings, her eyes felt like rawly peeled grapes. How long had she been out cold, with her contact lenses still welded to her eyeballs?

A spring dug into her back, clawing her spine through a couple of heaped cushions. So she must be lying on – a mattress or sofa? And someone had put cushions under her. Rosie! She sat up suddenly in the darkness and a wave of nausea swept over her. She flopped back. She was covered by a thin blanket. Underneath it, she wore only bra, knickers and tights. She didn't recall undressing! She stretched her arms out in front of her, paddled wide to both sides and finally, dropped her hands to her sides. Her wedding ring hit plastic, clanging noisily. Seconds later, a shaft of light from the hallway hit the room and Rosie loomed above her in striped pyjamas.

'You want something?' she whispered hoarsely in the gloom and righted the bucket placed strategically next to the sofa. 'Try and use it if you feel like chucking again. You didn't make it to the bathroom first time.'

There was a suppressed reproach in her voice that forced Angela to rack her scrambled brains for what had gone on earlier in the evening. Memory drip-fed titbits to her. A knife, blood, terrible pain.

Suddenly, she was alert again, springing upright on the sofa, fighting the dizziness that overcame her. 'What have you done to me?' she trembled. 'Why am I here?'

Rosie's padded bulk dropped next to her on the cushions. She grasped Angela's feebly flapping hands and pinioned them across her chest, ignoring the panic on her captive's face. 'Calm down, will you! You're here because I haven't got a spare room, and I can't let you have my bed in case you pebbledash the mattress. Not very hostessy of me I know, but there it is. You got stomach cramps and barfed up Pauline's party nibbles all over my kitchen and that posh frock of yours. What were you eating all night?'

Angela gaped at her, a terrible realisation dawning.
'Prawn sandwiches! Oh God, this happens every time I eat
shellfish. I never learn. Mind you, I wasn't paying proper
attention.' She'd been off guard at Pauline's, wolfing
down the sandwiches without thinking, distracted by
Rosie's presence and revelations. So in a way, it was
poetic justice that she'd made a fool of herself at Rosie's,
and added to the unholy stink in her kitchen. Just as she
was thinking this, Rosie patted her hand awkwardly.
'Look, I'm just across the hall if you need anything.
There's a towel next to the bucket. I sponged the worst
bits off your dress and hung it over the sink for the night.
You should be able to wear it home tomorrow without
stinking out the borough. Looks like a dry-cleaning job,
though.'

'Th-thanks. Contact lens bottle,' whimpered Angela in
a tone she hoped Rosie would interpret as a request. 'In
jacket pocket.'

Rosie leant across her and plucked the black jacket out
of the shadows behind the sofa. She draped it over
Angela's throat.

'Thanks. And Rosie?' Angela shifted experimentally,
newly aware of a fresh horror, one brought on by her
upset stomach. Humiliating confirmation crept damply
down her thigh. She gulped. 'Rosie, I hate to be even
more of a pain, but I've just started my period. It can
come early if I've just heaved my guts up. Would you –
have you got – ?'

'Christ, not a thing!' Rosie's hand tightened over her
own. 'Tell you what I have got, if it's any use to you. A
box of disposable nappies I keep for when my sister comes
round with her baby. Otherwise, you'll have to stuff
another towel down there. Sorry.'

Angela crimsoned in the darkness. She was the one
who should be apologising, first barfing, then bleeding all

over the soft furnishings of a woman she'd only met a few hours ago. But of course, it was easier for Rosie in a way. She could be magnanimous, amused even, at this close encounter with the bodily functions of her romantic successor. No doubt it would be all round Pauline's next therapy group. 'Beggars can't be choosers,' she mumbled ungratefully.

Rosie bounded off and returned with two large, white nappies flapping in her arms like trapped seagulls. 'Can you make it to the bathroom on your own OK?'

'Yes, thanks,' replied Angela, struggling uncertainly to her feet.

'I would've put the light on in here, only I thought it would blind you.'

'I prefer it this way.' Her pants were soaked. She didn't want to look at Rosie's sofa cushions until the morning.

'Need any Anadin for the pain?'

'No thanks. I feel much better after vomiting. The period pain's like being stroked with a feather compared to upset stomach pain.'

'Well, then, goodnight.' Rosie watched solicitously as Angela hobbled into the bathroom. 'Oh, and don't worry. I've no intention of sharing tonight with Pauline's lot or anyone else. G'night. Again.'

'Night,' croaked Angela, shutting the door. She collapsed on the toilet lid, fiddling shakily with the adhesive tabs on a nappy. Once swaddled, a duck's bum filling her tights, she waddled back to the sofa and rearranged the cushions, touching them gingerly for wetness. It took a long time to get semi-comfortable. Before she drifted off to sleep, the daftness of the situation sank in. Across the hall was a woman she had everything and nothing in common with. A woman who'd seen her

at her most vulnerable. A woman who'd also slept with
Conor McGinlay.

Sadie paused on the doorstep. She hoped this wasn't a
ploy by Angela, trying to outsulk her. It wasn't easy for
Sadie to make the first move twice. The first time was
that morning, when she'd phoned *Goss!* and discovered
that Angela was off sick. Sadie had been overcome with
confusion and embarrassment, but the woman she spoke
to – Paula? Pauline? – hadn't sounded the least surprised
or interested that a mother and daughter who lived in the
same town didn't keep abreast of each other's illnesses.
Maybe half of *Goss!* knew that Angela was just lazing at
home and particularly didn't want her mother to know.

Sadie jabbed the doorbell. Her readiness to forgive
Angela jibed with her concessionary arrival on Angela's
doorstep. It was Angela who should be calling on her.

The door inched open. 'Ma, come on in. I've meant to
ring you.'

Angela plodded inside, leaving Sadie to follow uneasily.
Angela seemed quite unfazed and her tone was heavy with
resignation. She shuffled into the kitchen and flicked the
kettle switch. Sadie's opening speech died on her lips.
'Ange! What are you doing in your dressing gown this
late in the afternoon? So you really are sick!'

'Thanks for the vote of confidence in my honesty.' She
moved wearily towards the teapot.

Sadie drew herself up. Sickness took precedence over
unsettled scores. 'You shouldn't be up and about at all, by
the look of you. Go and sit in the warm, and I'll make
tea. Would you like soup as well?'

Angela turned. 'Look, Mum, I've been dying to
apologise for what I said to you about Robert.'

'Water under the bridge, lovey.'

Angela's pale face scanned her mother's. 'Is it? Really?

And about the other things I said, about when I was growing up.'

'No need to say anything.'

'Shush, Ma, I've got to! You know how crap we are in this family about baring our souls and going for the group hug, so let me finish. It wasn't true. I didn't row with Robert about you on the eve of his death. As for the other stuff, I was looking for the handiest stick to beat you with, and came up with being a bad mother. I neglected to mention all the times you sat up with me when I was ill, the effort you put into making my first communion dress and loads of other things.'

Sadie had been listening – right up until the moment her gaze fell on the swing lid of the bin. Poking out of the top were flower stalks.

'Mum, you do believe me, don't you? You had nothing to do with Robert's heart attack, indirectly or otherwise.'

'I know that, lovey.' Flustered in case she'd been caught staring at the bin, Sadie looked quickly out of the window, at the row of washing on the line. She concentrated on a pink and black dress flapping in the wind.

'Nice dress. You don't wear it often enough.'

'That's because I've only had it five minutes. Conor bought it for me off Rachel's stall. It's a Rachel cast-off.'

Sadie frowned. A submerged memory shifted in murky depths, struggling to break free and float to the surface.

'And no, I'm not mad at you because you said something to remind me of Conor. Tea's ready.'

Sadie followed her into the sitting room, troubled by the fact that a key part of her speech was still unsaid. 'I don't love Owen more than you,' she insisted in a dangerously wobbly voice. 'But I've examined my conscience, and maybe I didn't play fair.'

'Oh, Mum, I'm a grown-up and got over it years ago.

You were a good mother, and only human, like the rest of us. I was just mad with you for phoning Conor.'

Sadie nodded tremulously. 'And now?'

Angela stirred tea vigorously, her lower lip jutting out like a precipice. 'The bottom line is, I love you, Mum, and don't make me say it again or elaborate because I find it bloody hard to say things like that. Park your bum and sip it slowly. It's hot.'

Sadie obeyed, meekened by Angela's brusqueness. She felt light-headed with joy and relief. Angela loved her! Verbal affirmation of soppy emotions normally had to be extracted from a Feeney with the aid of tweezers, so she must mean it.

'I phoned *Goss!* and they said you were ill.'

'Spring flu.' Angela snuffled theatrically into a hanky.

'So, nothing to do with pining for Conor?'

'Now, Ma! Don't ruin a beautiful moment between us by alluding – unsubtly – to where I went wrong with Conor and how I can still make it right. Because I can't.' She slurped her tea. 'He's sold the house and is staying in America.'

Sadie gasped. 'You've spoken to him?'

'The grapevine's bellowing the news. Suffice to say his house is on the market. I rang the estate agent's, posing as a prospective buyer. It's going for a packet.'

Sadie rattled her plate, thinking rapidly.

'Don't even think it!' interrupted Angela coolly. 'No more phoning New York behind my back.'

'But hasn't he called here?'

'No,' said Angela, and added with a sadness that belied her words, 'I don't want him to. He's caused enough damage for one lifetime. Maybe his wife understands him. She can have him.'

Sadie opened her mouth, shut it again.

'The truth is, it's not even solely his fault. I had no

business getting involved so soon after Robert. Especially in light of the row we did have the night before his death.' Angela began to fiddle frantically with a worn sofa seam.

'So there *was* still a row?' frowned Sadie, and something in Angela's averted face made her fear the worst.

'I accused him of having an affair. With that Magdalena one at Hartley's. It was all very ugly.'

Sadie clutched her tea-cup. 'An affair – your Robert?'

'Yes, my Robert. I know, it doesn't square with his image, does it? Mild-mannered man with thinning hair who hated parting with his comfiest slippers, even when the heels were worn clean away. Then we have Magdalena, Mediterranean siren with come-to-bed eyes and potential for unbridled passion. You wouldn't think Robert would be able to cope with her, would you?'

'Ange, I can't believe – are you sure?'

'No, that was the problem! Sorting out the washing, I found a restaurant receipt in his pocket for the night he was supposed to be at a travel seminar with Ian. Even then, I wouldn't have been suspicious if he hadn't been so shifty. First of all, he said he'd had dinner with Ian. But in that swank place down by the bridge? Ian would never cough up money for a place like that if it was just him and Robert. So I pointed that out, waiting to hear the fuller – and still innocent – explanation. He blushed, he gaped. And I knew! I tell you, Ma, he wasn't able to lie convincingly because he'd had no practice at it over the years. That's what made it so awful. His total inability to cover his tracks, let alone fob me off with a story I could comfortably believe in.' She pulled at her hair, a gesture of frustration from childhood. 'It made me so mad, that I wasn't worth a well-rehearsed cover story to put my mind at rest! And Magdalena hadn't been at the agency long. I'd have expected Ian to try it on with her — maybe he did. But Robert?' She pulled viciously at a green sofa thread. 'In a totally bizarre way, I was almost proud of him, that he'd found the nous from somewhere to get it on with a stunning woman.' She looked up at Sadie, pain battling mischievousness in her eyes. 'I bet it makes you see him in a new light.'

'Not a flattering one.' The toad! All these years, Sadie had seen the benefits of Robert's dull niceness — his steady, faithful, comfortable qualities. Now this!

'So you see, Mum, Conor did me a favour. He showed me a good time, then withdrew from the scene while my heart was still intact. It could've been a lot worse.'

Sadie's gaze strayed to her daughter's lank hair and puffy eyes. All Conor had done was hasten Angela's fleeing faith in human nature — male human nature.

'So you accused Robert of seeing Magdalena. Did he admit anything?'

'He couldn't. I see that now. He was scared of losing me. I almost felt sorry for him when he stood there, humouring me with, "Honestly, Angela, this clinging wife routine doesn't suit you," while his eyes went googly with terror. He stomped off to bed and that was that. I yelled up the stairs that I wasn't going to let matters rest and I planned to ring Ian first thing in the morning. Frankly, I dunno what I was planning to do. Next day, he dropped dead, and it all became academic.'

'Angela — darling. Don't let that be your lasting memory of him. You had all those good years together.'

'I know, I know.' She nodded miserably. 'It's so maddening! Whenever an incident has called Robert to mind since his death, it's always been in a negative light. If I think of the theatre, I remember that he was a philistine, or if I think of our honeymoon, I remember that photo he took of me throwing up in Kinsale. But the worst of it is the guilt. We could've made it up, spent his last night on earth pointing out that we still loved each other. Instead, I – ' Her voice cracked.

'Life wouldn't be life if the grim reaper served notice to tie up our loose ends.'

'Now, Ma, if you're going to start one of your homilies...'

'All right.' Sadie stood up, her legs shaking under her. She tried to make her voice sound extra firm. 'I'll do some shopping for you, lay in Lemsip supplies.'

'No need. I've got plenty of everything. I just... thanks for coming round.'

Sadie hesitated. She wanted to touch Angela, hug her, massage her hair with her fingers, ease away the pain of one love tarnished and the other lost. But the angular set of her shoulders reminded her of previous rejections. She wasn't brave enough to try. 'I'll take the tea things into the kitchen,' she decided briskly. 'Stay there by the fire.'

She marched out quickly with the tray, and made straight for the bin. She swung the lid gently to reveal the rubbish clinging to the black bin-liner. The flowers had been shoved in head-first. The rich scent of fresh camellias, the glow of their creamy golden heads amid tea-leaves and meal-for-one foil trays, gripped Sadie with terrible sadness. For the flowers and for their sender. If she could just edge her hand in and extract the note. She could make out its flower-embossed corner, smothered in tea-leaves like a colony of vicious ants.

'When do you think you'll be back at work?' she called to Angela, to smother any tell-tale noises and keep a trace on her daughter's whereabouts.

'A couple of days, I reckon. No need to rinse out those cups.' Angela's voice reeked of suspicion. Sadie knew that she was behaving oddly, rushing off to the kitchen not long after Angela's momentous confession.

'It's no trouble, lovey. I'll be out of your hair in a flash.'

Almost got it. just a bit further. The swing lid caught one of her more tender knuckle joints. Sadie extracted her hand with a silent yelp and the lid crashed down on the bin. She flew to the tap, running water over a cup, just as Angela appeared in the doorway.

'Are you up to something, Ma? You're taking the news very well. I thought you'd be bursting with "I told you so," and "I always thought his eyes were too close together."'

'Come off it, lovey.' Sadie turned from the sink, genuinely hurt. 'It took me a while, but I learnt to back off and let you and Owen live your own lives. And I did like Robert, even though you seem to have thought I didn't. I liked him for his goodness and his decency. He had old-fashioned virtues that are missing in men today. I *still* like him. My only beef with him now is that he might have hurt you.'

Angela nodded tiredly. 'Fair dues, Ma. I'm not letting you win either way, going on like this. Don't feel you have to rush off. Would you like to stay for dinner?'

'Not tonight, thanks all the same.' The square of sodden cardboard was burning a hole in her skirt pocket. She longed to decipher it on the bus. 'You get yourself off to bed for an early night. I'll call tomorrow for an update.'

Folding a tea towel to avoid Angela's eye, her gaze strayed out of the window again, towards the dress on the line. The stiff pleats rustled in the wind, and in Sadie's memory. Deep pink and darkest velvet rose with sharp-edged clarity out of the murky depths. Above the bodice swam a creamy neck. A stiletto heel arched daintily, its owner climbing into a car. The car door swung shut.

Smoothly, the car moved out of sight, carrying Sadie's memory with it.

'Mum, did you hear me? If you don't go now, you'll wait another forty minutes for a bus. Look, stay to dinner and I'll call you a taxi. I'll call you a taxi anyway. You shouldn't have to bother with buses in the first place.'

'No, no, I've got to get away. Thanks for reminding me about the time. Now look after yourself, Ange!'

Angela was half-strangled in one of he mother's more emotional embraces before she had time to react. But she allowed it, trying not to stiffen or squirm. Her mother was permitted this indulgence. After all, Angela had said the 'L' word (which the poor woman had waited a lifetime to hear) and then crowned it with a juicy story of Robert's did he/didn't he adultery. No wonder Sadie was emotional.

Waving her mother off, she closed the front door, weariness washing over her. She'd have to snap out of this! To hell with Conor McGinlay. People in the third world were starving, as long as you had your health... Mentally repeating every truism she could think of, Angela shuffled back into the sitting room and turned up the fire, drawing an armchair closer to it. She'd have to go back to work before the end of the week. Pauline still had her sleeping bag. That night already seemed a lifetime ago.

The heat made her drowsy. Around her, the house came alive with sound. She was at the centre of it, seeing and hearing, but trapped in her chair, dozing.

Robert came in, slamming the door behind him. He looked shame-faced and sulky, but still defiant. 'This whole thing is too stupid for words!'

Angela leapt off her chair to face him. 'So why didn't you tell me straight off that you had dinner with Magdalena?'

'It slipped my mind. It was only a welcome-to-the-team meal out. It was after the travel seminar, which didn't last as long we expected. So Ian suggested we take Magdalena out to dinner.'

'Before, you said it was just you and Ian at the seminar.'

'Er – Magdalena turned up off her own bat. She heard about it somewhere.'

'So how come Ian booked a table for you two at the most expensive restaurant in town and then cleared off? Anyway, you need to give at least a month's notice to get a table at Tosca's.'

'They had a cancellation. It was the last place Ian tried on his mobile.' Robert warmed belatedly to his story. But he'd had a good half hour to come up with this, thinking in the bathroom, since she'd first flourished the restaurant receipt. 'I remember Ian's groan of anguish that the only restaurant with a vacancy that night was the priciest one, and he couldn't even go. He – he had to pick his mum up from bingo. He forgot about that until the last minute.'

'You didn't get home till nearly one!'

'You know how these swank restaurants like to make a meal of it, ha ha.'

'Liar, liar! Your Y-fronts are on fire! There was no bloody seminar. Just a candlelit dinner with Miss Big Tits butter-wouldn't-melt-in-her-gob! And God knows what else for afters.' Angela looked around for something to throw at him. Something chunkier than a cushion but less lethal than an ornament.

'Look, Ange, it's all true, I swear.'

'Fine. I'll just ask Magdalena myself next time I meet her. Or maybe Ian and his mum would be better bets.' Angela peered at the sweaty till receipt still clutched in her hand. 'Choc and orange sundae. You hate that combination. You see, Rob, the more people you drag into a lie, the more people you have to keep tabs on, in case they let the truth slip out.'

Robert's soft jawline suddenly hardened. He picked up the remote control and flicked on the TV.

'Robert!'

'I'm not listening!' He turned up the volume. Onscreen, the Mitchell brothers were knocking seven bells out of someone on *EastEnders*. But Angela could roar louder.

'You're so fucking childish sometimes! Why can't you be a man and own up to things when you're caught out?'

He turned the telly down a smidgen and narrowed his beautiful brown eyes at her, wary and frightened as a trapped animal's. 'Now who could've given you cause to question my manhood? Wouldn't happen to be your old bag of a mother?'

'We are discussing you!' She flourished the receipt as exhibit A. 'And your fancy woman.' She couldn't believe she was using words like that!

'Did Sadie put you up to this? "Go on, love, thumb-screw it out of him. You found a restaurant receipt? My God, I bet he's bonking the Dagenham Girl Pipers!" He made a rattling noise with the loose change in his pocket, in cruel and spot-on imitation of Sadie's dancing bottom plate when she got agitated.

'She doesn't know about this and never will. It's our shame to live with.'

'Maybe she's on her way over this minute. By broomstick.'

Angela turned her back and strode to the window. She hated rowing with Robert. They'd had mercifully few major rows over the years. They always digressed – no matter what the origin or provocation – into Robert's verbal assault on Sadie.

His dutiful son-in-law act hid a seething resentment

that surfaced all too quickly when he lost his temper for other reasons. It upset Angela and would've appalled Sadie.

'I know what Sadie thinks of me, and at times like this, I wonder if she's swayed you over to her side. She thinks I'm weak, unsuccessful, lacking moral fibre. So of course I'd hop into bed with a woman after sharing a side-salad with her. Have you looked at Magdalena properly? Why would she hop into bed with me?'

His logic was comforting. Angela turned to him, almost relieved to side-step the issue of the receipt by soothing his ruffled feathers over Sadie.

'Mum's critical of everyone. Look how I've disappointed her, leaving my job without even being pregnant as a cover story.'

'But mostly, you've disappointed her by marrying me, Mr Average. She sized me up long ago and found me wanting. She needles me all the time, pretending it's a cosy bit of family ribbing. I've tried with her, Ange — because she's your mother.'

'I know you have. Maybe — you know — you've tried too hard.'

The wrong thing to say. 'What do you mean by that?'

'I just mean, you should always be yourself with her. I told you that from day one. Don't even give her the satisfaction of trying to impress her. You kind of invite her to despise you.'

'And this,' said Robert slowly, 'is the woman you were thinking of inviting to live with us. Thank God I knocked that idea on the head. For a start, we wouldn't be able to have private slanging matches like this, would we? We'd have to go out for a drive so you could accuse me of bonking Magdalena.'

'But Robert.'

'The subject is closed! I told you the truth. It's up to

you whether you choose to believe me or not. I accept no responsibility for your paranoid suspicions. That's my final word.' He sat down and turned up the telly.

Rebellion bubbled in Angela. Robert only occasionally invoked the 'final word' clause of their marriage contract, an unwritten clause that Angela usually acquiesced to because it was invoked so sparingly and always when she'd pushed him further than she'd accept being pushed herself. But this was different. She wasn't being paranoid. She'd seen the panic in his eyes, the deep blush of guilt on his face when she'd pointed out the strange anomaly of stingy old Ian booking his underlings into a pricey restaurant, then happily buggering off. It was a shot in the dark, and it had struck home.

She switched off the telly and stood in front of it. 'You're perfectly entitled to take Magdalena out for a meal. And I'm entitled to wonder why you've been so shifty about it. You're jumping around like a scalded cat, protesting your innocence too much. I didn't come down in the last shower, Robert, and you're a crap liar, for which I' – here her voice broke, – 'for which I've always been thankful. I never wanted to marry a double-talking smooth bastard.'

He turned to her earnestly. 'And you didn't. You married plain old Robert Carbery, who couldn't cheat on you if Miss World came through that door wearing a G-string.'

His look went right through her. 'Oh, Robert, don't let's fight!' She flew to him, leaping on top of him in the chair and crushing the life out of him. Privately, she remained unsure that he'd done no more than swap fortune cookies with Magdalena. But as long as she was unsure, she had to believe him.

'It's OK,' he mumbled into her hair. 'Apology accepted.'

She stiffened and drew away. 'I don't remember apologising for anything.'

He threw up his hands. 'So we're back to square one.' He shoved her away, depositing her in a heap on the floor, and stood up. 'Honestly, Angela, this clinging little wife routine doesn't suit you. This is what comes of giving up work and festering at home all day, imagining all sorts about the people who are out there in the big, bad world. Well, for your information, I can't avoid women on the bus or Magdalena at work. I suggest you get a life before it's too late, and give your overworked imagination a rest.'

Tears stung her eyes. He'd never criticised her before for giving up work. In fact, he'd often commented on how much he enjoyed returning to a cosy, lit house and a hot meal – especially in winter.

'I'm off to bed,' he said gruffly and stomped from the room. She ran after him, and caught his arm. He shook it off, taking the stairs two at a time. She clutched the banister and yelled at his departing back, 'I'm calling Ian first thing in the morning to check on this dinner he had to cry off from at the last minute. So you'd better get to work at the crack of dawn and brief him on his story for the clinging little wife!'

She thought about adjourning regally to the spare room. But the bed needed making up, and it was colder than a fridge.

In the end, she went to bed an hour later and inched carefully in beside him, careful not to make bodily contact of any kind. He had to make the first move.

His hands snapped round her waist straightaway, drawing her rigid back into his chest. She didn't resist, but made no other move, willing him to try harder.

'Forgive and forget, Ange? I don't really hate Sadie.

When you get mad at me, I see her in the background, cheering you on.'

She hesitated. He wanted her to forgive and forget everything about the night's proceedings, presumably. And this attempt at an apology (which hadn't included the word 'sorry') only encompassed his rudeness about Sadie. It wasn't that difficult pleading *mea culpa* for harsh words about Sadie. He did it all the time.

'What about slagging me off for giving up work?' she mumbled, deciding on a piecemeal approach to extracting humility (and hopefully, the truth about the other thing) from him.

'Yeah, yeah, course I'm sorry for that, whatever it is I said.' He kissed the back of her head. She ground her teeth. He had a foolproof way of giving that meant she received nothing. Now she'd look ungracious and childish if she didn't let bygones be bygones. It was his hand creeping under her T-shirt that did it. Of all the nerve! He not only expected unconditional absolution for sins not even confessed, he also expected to seal their entente with a bit of nookie!

'Don't!' She slapped his hand away ferociously.

He spun away, turning his back on her, dragging the duvet with him.

She curled into a ball of misery on the edge of the mattress. The next thing she heard was his soft snoring. Typical man! Faced by the conundrum of an unhappy woman, he'd given up working her out and gone to sleep.

In the morning, they didn't speak at the breakfast table. His head was slightly bowed over his toast, presenting her with a poignant view of his thinning crown.

She cleared her throat. 'You can rest easy. I'm not going to chase up Ian over that dinner.'

His head snapped up. 'So you believe it was all above-the-board?'

Why hadn't she said yes? It would have cost her nothing to send a condemned man to his death with a hearty breakfast and a lightened load.

But she'd just shrugged, offering him a cool cheek to graze with his lips. Their last physical contact. Even then, his mouth had felt wispy, insubstantial, like a frond of ghostly ectoplasm.

She was trying to make a pineapple-upside-down-cake peace offering when the call came. It was just after midday. The phone made her jump and she cut her finger on the half-opened lid of the pineapple tin, moving slowly towards the ringing phone, trailing a shred of unravelling kitchen towel.

At first, she couldn't understand a babbling, incoherent Ian. She'd thought it had something to do with the dinner receipt and the row. That Ian was telling her off for impugning the behaviour of his beloved Magdalena. 'Come now!' he screamed. 'I'm at the hospital, but they won't tell me anything. It looks bad.'

At the hospital, Ian told her that Magdalena had tried to revive Robert back at the agency. But even from the other side of the room, ringing for the ambulance, Ian had seen Robert's face and lips turn blue. When Ian told her about Magdalena's kiss of life, Angela had started giggling hysterically. So her accusation of snogging Magdalena was true in at least one way!

She'd sought out Magdalena in the relatives' waiting room, tried to drag her down to the chapel of rest for 'moral support', but really to show her the end result of her adulterous handiwork. But Magdalena had resisted heroically, clinging on to Ian and staving off Robert's madwoman widow until Sadie sailed into the room, prised Angela's hands off Magdalena and said she would escort her to the chapel of rest.

At least she'd only had to look at his face, the white

pallor of death overlaying the blue, like a ripened Stilton. The rest of him had lain under a sheet emblazoned with the hospital initials. She'd concentrated very hard on the W.G.H., stamped blackly on pale blue cotton. She'd wondered if a casual observer would mistake the sheet for monogrammed linen.

The coffin was brought into the house the following day by the undertakers.

Time passed in frame-by-frame sequence as they drew the living room curtains, draped the mantelpiece in purple crepe paper and set out the closed casket on runners next to the telly. When they left, and it was just her, Sadie and Robert's mother, she'd stared fearfully at the closed lid.

She imagined it padded inside with pastel silk. Robert wearing some New Age smock chosen at the undertaker's discretion (she'd declined to surrender his best suit for the occasion; she couldn't bear to part with it), his lids closed over brown eyes that would never sparkle on the world again, cotton wool padding out his sagging cheeks with a 'peaceful' idiot smile and his hands folded across his chest, the back of one still fresh with scratch-marks. She'd scratched him accidentally the previous week, during a bit of horseplay on the sofa in *Coronation Street*'s ad break.

But even as she looked, the lid began to creak open. The bitten half-moons of his nails appeared, pushing up the heavy oak.

She gasped and looked in terror at his mother and Sadie. But they'd noticed nothing. Sadie went on saying the rosary with half-closed eyes, his mother crying noisily into a bloomers-sized hanky.

Angela turned her eyes back to the lid, shaking with terror. His wedding ring glimmered from the coffin's maw as his hand went on pushing up the lid. She screamed.

She woke in a terrible sweat next to the hissing gas fire.

It was dark outside. She was bathed in the fire's orange glow as well as its heat. She sat up, wrapping her dressing gown lapels round her neck. Bloody hell, what a nightmare! All brought on by discussing their last row with Sadie.

Angela yawned, stretched, shuffled into the kitchen. She avoided, at all costs, looking at the flower stalks sticking out of the bin.

Chapter Eleven

At the back of the bus, Sadie spread the battered little card over one knee. Most of the message was illegible. It started out boldly with, 'Dear Angela, please for…' then vanished frustratingly under a melange of damp stains and runny ink. The mind boggled. Please forgive me, but Kate's need is greater…? Please forget me and get on with your own life? In the bottom right-hand corner, the letter 'C' had clashed with a globule of pesto sauce, elongating into a Book of Kells 'L', the sauce posing fancifully as a fire-breathing snake wrapped round the base of the character.

But Sadie remained convinced it was a C. The flowers had still been fresh, so couldn't have been long in the bin. A delivery that very morning perhaps? Whatever the content of its message, the card and flowers had provoked a violent act of closure from Angela. But you never knew with Angela. Conor might've written, Please forage about in the wardrobe for your best glad rags, and meet me for dinner next week. She was the type to hack off her nose to spite her face, wallow in self-pity and contempt for human nature, and ignore olive branches and second chances as they followed her down the street, screaming for attention. Angela expected the worst, so that if it materialised into the merely bad, she'd be able to cope.

Yes, but wait! Look what had happened after years of marriage to her soulmate. He'd very possibly done the dirty on her! No wonder she found it hard to heed the pleas or excuses of a bloke she'd only known five months!

Blinking out of the bus window, Sadie hastily pocketed the card. She heaved herself up and tottered to the front. 'Sorry, I've just missed my stop. Can you drop me anywhere here?'

The bus-driver declined to pull in, but stopped suddenly in the middle of the road. The rubber doors hissed and folded back. Sadie clambered down with as much haste and dignity as she could muster. It was a secret dread of hers that one day soon, a boy-racer bus driver would squeal away while her trailing foot still rested on the bottom step.

Her destination was only a ten-minute walk away, though her visit was impulsive, and it'd be just her luck to find her quarry out.

She began a rather tired walk down the respectable, spring-green avenue.

Flat 5A had deep bay windows and '1803' carved into rosy brickwork over the mullioned front door. In the last five years, this area had become a sought-after location for the London over-spill. The flat was worth at least six times its original value at the time Rachel had bought it.

Rachel opened the front door, bearing a precarious pile of toast on a plate. Sadie's relief that she was in clashed with dread at the impending confrontation.

'Mrs F, come in! I'm in a bit of a rush. Got a date waiting for me in town and I'm already late. Treat 'em mean and keep 'em keen!'

Sadie followed her silently into the sunny, thickly carpeted interior. Rachel was dressed for going out. To match her pale gold hair, she wore a pale gold dress patterned with an intricate red zigzag design, like the flag of some emergent nation. She seemed to have an inexhaustible supply of beautiful dresses.

Sadie eased downwards into one of Rachel's comfortably deep armchairs. She had no intention of hurrying or apologising for the interruption. 'I suppose we'll see that dress on the mini-market stall next year.'

Rachel looked down at herself, slightly puzzled. She'd detected Sadie's unwillingness to be no trouble at all. 'I don't know if…'

'Was it really necessary to flog Conor that pink and black dress, knowing he'd present it to Angela? Did you get a perverse pleasure out of humiliating her that way?'

Rachel blushed prettily as if she'd just been paid a compliment. Hers was not a face to fold into ugly creases of fear or anger. 'You'd better explain that one to me, Sadie.'

'I saw you!' hissed Sadie, leaning forward. 'That night, in town. I saw you getting into a taxi with Robert. At the time, God forgive me, I thought it was a man who looked like Robert. I only got a side-on view. And all I saw of you was a tall woman with pale hair. But after what Angela's just told me, it all fell into place. You had an affair with Robert, didn't you?'

Please deny it, an inner voice begged. Please give me a cock-and-bull plausible story that I don't have to swallow but I can take away and ponder at length.

Instead, panic and confirmation filled Rachel's face. 'Angela knows?' she squeaked.

Sadie's heart crumbled. 'She suspects Robert of infidelity. She's targeted that poor woman who works at Hartley's.'

'We were so discreet,' mumbled Rachel. 'What were you doing in town that night?'

Sadie replied in a flat, iron-hard voice, 'I'd done the evening shift at the newsagent's. My boss Gupta gave me a lift home and detoured through the town to point out an empty shop-front he had his eye on.'

'It was just the once,' said Rachel quickly. 'No affair and nothing planned in the first place. It just – happened. I went to book a holiday at Hartley's that afternoon. Robert saved me from the sweaty clutches of Ian Bradley. He offered to look up a few prices for me and have them ready for me next time I came in. So I offered to collect them at the end of the day, and give him a lift home as well.'

'But you turned up in a taxi. Wearing that dress.'

'My date had blown me out for the evening, but I'd already booked a table at Tosca's. So I decided to take Robert, as a thank-you for his Sir Galahad impression. Thought if I phoned him first, he'd find excuses to put me off, but if I turned up dressed to go, he'd feel inclined to cave in.'

'How well you knew him,' observed Sadie dryly.

'Well, be fair, Mrs F. I'd known him even longer than he'd known Angela. I mean, Angela met him on the evening of that wedding. I'd met him in the afternoon, before Ange turned up to spend the weekend with me.'

Sadie sat stone-faced.

Rachel sighed. 'Anyway, he said he'd ring Ange first to tell her he'd be late. I said, "Ask Ange to come too, they can easily set an extra place, and we'll make it a real night out." He disappeared into the back office without answering. I had no reason to suspect he'd cooked up some fairy story. He told me later that he'd pretended to be at some industry do with Ian.'

'The pair of you did have it planned between you, so!'

'No, no. Silly old Robert made it more complicated than it need ever have been.' Rachel clucked almost affectionately. 'God, if he'd just been honest like I expected him to, and told Ange that his dinner date was with me, that I came into Hartley's to book a holiday and that I needed cheering up after a man let me down, do you think I'd have touched him with a barge pole later on in the evening? Look, I never expected to get the hots for a man I'd known for years. I thought dinner *à deux* without sexual overtones would be just the pick-me-up I needed after my date blew me out.'

'A novel experience for you?' snorted Sadie.

'The other thing happened by accident,' continued Rachel, as if Sadie hadn't spoken. 'I accidentally touched his leg under the table, and he thought it was deliberate. Not that he made a move on me. But he looked at me in a new, expectant way, just for a millisecond. Or maybe I imagined it.' She shook her head. 'I began to tease him – naughty, I know. When the taxi dropped me at my place, I asked him in for a night-cap – just to see what he'd do.'

'Spare me the gory details!' Sadie stood up, too agitated to sit. 'Why, for God's sake, did you have to play with fire with your best friend's husband? I don't suppose Robert knew what hit him.'

'I didn't have to twist his arm! We'd both had a fair bit to drink by then. He was mortified and wringing his hands before I'd even called another taxi to take him home. Said it would kill Ange to find out, if she didn't kill him first.'

'Funny you should say that,' said Sadie coolly. 'Angela accused him of adultery the night before his massive heart attack. I think it's fair to say the two events were linked. Ever since, my daughter's been tortured with guilt. For all she knows, her accusation might not even be true. They had a huge row, and she blames herself for packing him off into the afterlife with a flea in his ear. While you get away scot-free, ye strumpet!' Sadie's vernacular resorted to its Irish origins when she was deeply stirred. Her bottom plate jumped in sympathy.

Rachel smoothed a fold of her dress over one tanned knee. 'Come now, Mrs F, you've never believed that folk get away scot-free in this world. "Everyone has their woes sooner or later" is one of your favourite maxims, no doubt stitched into a sampler and hanging over your bed next to a rather lurid Sacred Heart.'

'Don't you talk down to me!' screeched Sadie, as she saw before her Rachel's patrician Englishness asserting itself, to distance her terrible act from any impact it might have on backward micks. 'Don't make out I'm overreacting after what you've done to my Angela and her marriage! You should be down on your knees begging forgiveness. Walking barefoot round Lough Derg until your feet are shredded and bloody! And you make sure you stay away from my Angela for the rest of her life. Ye slut!'

'Do calm down, Mrs F.' Rachel was coolness itself, but Sadie noticed, just in time, a telltale bead of sweat gathering on her hairline. 'I don't mind you putting all the blame on me, because Robert's not here to yell at. But just remember, it takes two to tango. And you must feel vindicated in all this. You never liked him. You never thought him top-drawer husband material. Not if you're entirely honest about it.'

'You're arguing like a Jesuit,' snarled Sadie, secretly appalled that her tolerance of Robert had been seen through so thoroughly by Angela, Rachel and – worst of all – Robert himself.

'I think you started blaming me for things way back. You think it's my fault that Angela met Robert at all, because it was at a wedding I'd invited her to. And if she hadn't met him, you and Fenton might've persuaded her to go to college.'

'He encouraged her to give up work and vegetate at

home for four years,' mused Sadie, lulled by the seductive truth of Rachel's words.

'I happen to know that was entirely Ange's decision!' said Rachel sharply. She sighed. 'Look at me, Mrs F. What do you see?'

Sadie looked at her grudgingly. 'A viper in the bosom.'

'Oh today, I'm a viper. On a good day, I'm a clothes horse. Perfect Rachel with her perfect life. I wonder if you and Angela have ever seen past that.'

Here it comes, scowled Sadie. The fabricated claim of a loveless childhood with lots of material possessions but not the one thing she really craved. Only it wouldn't wash. Sadie had never felt comfortable around Matt and high-falutin' Ginny Cockburn, but she knew that they loved Rachel. 'Meaning?' she snapped.

'If you look perfect on the outside, people don't want to hear or believe that you've got problems on the inside. It's just selfish to whinge when the gods have given you so much, and your problems can't be as bad as theirs. Angela's my best friend. I've confided loads to her. But I still cried in secret when I heard girls at school sniggering about my over-developed chest, calling me the local bike, just because I had the equipment if I fancied making use of it. I was the first in my class to need a bra, and I was punished for it. Then there were the bullies who decided Rachel Cockburn needed taking down a peg because she wasn't ugly and spotty. If problems didn't exist for me — as far as other people could tell — they made it their business to invent some.'

'So folk were jealous of your beauty and gave you a hard time, not bothering to consider that you had feelings too. Very sad, Rachel. But a poor excuse for doing the dirty with Robert.'

'You still don't see!' Rachel slapped her brown leg angrily. 'I had a moment of weakness. I'm tortured by it every time Angela plonks herself down in that very chair and pours out her heart and soul. God only knows why she didn't tell me about her row with Robert on the night before he died, but thank God I've been spared that.' She paused. As far as Sadie was concerned, she was pausing for effect. 'Why do you think I didn't marry Kevin?'

'I don't know,' confessed Sadie, unwittingly intrigued by this outburst. 'Because you like to play the field, I'd always assumed.'

'That's the way perfect Rachel would have it.' She rose and gazed dispassionately into a mirror. 'The real reason is that Kevin saw right through me, teased me about my hang-ups, tried to get me to tell all about the school bullies and cry it out of my system on his manly shoulder. If I'd married Kevin, I'd have had to be real all the time.'

'But see here.' Sadie sat down again, shocked by her compassion for the hussy adulteress. 'Everyone needs someone they can be completely at ease with. It's too tiring, keeping up an image all the time.'

'It suits me. I *am* my image now. Marshall's a married man, you know. They all are since Kevin. And they have to be married men with no desire to leave their wives. They just have to want a change from reality, an hour or so with the image their wives used to keep up, before marital boredom and babies set in.'

'That makes you a – a prostitute,' said Sadie firmly. 'Even you deserve better. Think of your immortal soul, lovey.'

'I'm a bad Catholic, Mrs F. I've never been convinced of its existence. The body as perishable wrapping for the priceless treasure inside? It just sounded like another swipe by the ugly brigade at anyone whose wrapping wasn't plain brown paper. Can I give you a lift home? I really am late for my date with Marshall now.'

Sadie gaped at her momentarily. She'd come here, fired

with righteous anger. Now she was confused – and a little scared – by the hollowness at the centre of perfect Rachel. Sadie could almost hear the wind whistling over a sea of inner vastness that was either too shallow to plumb or too deep to fathom.

But she and even Angela had been happy enough to foster Rachel's image. Rachel was such a good listener and dispenser of advice. They'd refined her image, projected their feelings onto her – even predicted her responses to bolster their own conclusions. They'd used her in the same the way that Sadie used Binky.

They'd shied away from the chance of getting close enough to realise, as Kevin had, that Rachel was just as capable of unhappiness and cankered feeling as everyone else.

But getting close to Rachel would've tainted her observer's role, brought the counsellor and clothes-horse down to the level of the rest of humanity.

Perhaps if she and Ange had tried harder – harder even than Kevin – to access the real Rachel under the protective layers, some moral imperative would've stopped her from sleeping with Robert. 'No,' said Sadie finally, thinking aloud. 'I can't accept that we're to blame. Everyone's responsible for their own actions.'

'Well, of course,' agreed Rachel, peering at her closely. 'It's called free will. Are you serious about banishing me for ever from Angela's sight? Won't she wonder why I've pulled the plug on our lifelong friendship?'

Sadie hadn't thought of that, and admitted as much. 'But she can't stay in the dark for ever. I'll have to weigh up which pain would be harder to bear, knowing about you or living the rest of her life wondering about Robert.' Sadie glanced at Rachel sharply. 'But stay away from anyone she meets in the future.'

'Is it all off with Conor?' asked Rachel politely. 'I promise you, I only sold that dress to him because he took a shine to it. And he was completely impervious to my standard flirtation. He saw the real me all right, and backed off. I think he heard me hissing with a forked tongue when I spoke.'

'I don't know the state of play between him and Angela,' said Sadie briskly. 'Angela's wary of him because he's a complicated package of a man. Whereas with Robert, they both knew she could've done better, so she felt secure in his gratitude. Which makes his betrayal all the more shattering.'

Sadie shut her trap belatedly and made for the door. She must get out of the habit of treating Rachel as a confidant. It wouldn't be easy after all these years, and Angela would carry on doing it. Unless and until Sadie put a stop to it. God help her, it was a poisoned chalice all right. Angela had lost her husband. She probably wouldn't thank a righteously angry mother for taking away her best friend as well, never mind exposing her dirty secret.

'For what it's worth, I'm sorry,' said Rachel on the doorstep. 'I'm sorry Angela has to cope with guilt over Robert's death. That's why I've been dying for her to find happiness with someone new.'

Sadie hovered on the step to deliver one parting shot. 'I'll give you back that pager yoke. I've already made Angela take back the mobile.'

'Who is it?' yelled Angela, sloshing tea dregs into the sink. She'd just completed her first day back at work and was too bone-tired to walk to the door and find out for herself. If it was Jehovah's witnesses, they'd soon tire of trying to offer salvation through the letterbox.

'It's me, Ange,' a strangely listless-sounding Rachel

called instead. She made no comment about the fact that the doorbell still wasn't fixed.

Angela tugged open the door, sighing. 'Evening, Rache. Look if this is another pep-talk about my love life, can it wait till I'm up to dealing with it? You can imagine what Mum's been like.'

'It can't wait, no,' said Rachel, with unusual crispness. She moved past Angela into the hallway, unwinding her soft woollen scarf with fumbling fingers. They weren't just fumbling, Angela noticed. They were shaking. And her hair, usually immaculate, had a slightly greasy sheen. It had to be Marshall.

Angela's mind raced with possibilities. The likeliest was that he'd called time on the relationship – perhaps the first man to do so in a long while – and Rachel had reached that age and stage where it was no longer water off a perfectly exfoliated back. At once, Angela was all concern. Rachel was owed a long, girly listen-to about her life. 'Plonk yourself down, Rache. Tea or something stronger?'

'Whiskey, and pour one for yourself,' advised Rachel, following her into the kitchen. 'I don't want to sit. I want to get this over with.'

Angela paused. 'I sort of guessed Marshall was married. Has his wife found out?'

'No. Sadie found out.' Rachel looked down at her shapely nails. 'So I thought *you'd* better find out before she decides to spread the word on my behalf. It's about me and another married man, actually.'

'But what's Ma got to do with it?' Angela had forgotten all about the whiskey.

Rachel looked up at her, blue eyes couched in shadows. 'I'd prefer it if you guessed.'

'Guess what? Come off it, Rachel. I never was a code-cracker.'

'Fuck it, anyway,' said Rachel with feeling and took a deep breath. 'I had a one-night stand with Robert. I was the one who had dinner with him. If I had any idea that you suspected him all along, I'd have come clean before now and spared you the guilt of an unproven accusation and a pointless grudge match against that woman in the travel agent's. May I sit down?' Suddenly, Rachel was standing on ceremony, stressing the formality of her announcement and the chasm she'd just opened up between them.

Angela sat down instead. She simply gaped at her best friend, whose beauty was now distorted by the ugliness of deception, her scalloped nails the claws of a mistress hooking spoken-for men. 'You utter fucking bitch,' she managed at last in a tone of wonder. 'How many other women's lives have you wrecked?'

'Oh, so you're suddenly sorry for Marshall's wife, I take it? But if I'd just confessed to a split-up with him, you'd have been all sympathy, without a thought for the relieved wifey who'd got him back.'

'You absolute bitch,' repeated Angela in a daze. 'All those months of fucking guilt. I was hardly able to think straight. Every memory of him was poisoned by suspicion. And you... hang on! Jesus, Mary and Joseph and a cast of thousands, how did Ma find out?'

Rachel told her, grateful for a chance to side-step the issue of her utter fucking bitchiness. Angela wanted to flay her best friend's perfect features. But she was stopped by the realisation that Rachel would let her. Rachel would take her punishment on the chin and not fight back. She had no heart for self-justification because she had no sense of guilt, only a disinterested awareness of upsetting less dispassionate people with her behaviour. She had no heart at all.

'You,' said Angela, trembling, 'are a vapid, empty

excuse for a human being. At least poor Robert would've felt guilt afterwards. Oh my God. Oh, dear God!'

The tears spilt out of Angela's eyes in a purgative torrent. She put her hands over her face, perversely ashamed of her loss of control in front of Rachel.

Rachel flapped a clean paper hanky, glimpsed by Angela through wet fingers as she sobbed. She ignored the hanky, so Rachel put a hand on her heaving shoulder and left it there, a light, consoling touch, almost coolly impersonal and awaiting its next instruction from Angela's body language.

Angela's shoulder pitched and tossed under the hand's dry-leaf weight. To think that she was weak enough to let Rachel comfort her, to let Rachel slip back into the role of patiently abiding counsellor when she herself had triggered the breakdown!

'Fuck off out of it, Rachel!'

'I can't just leave you like this, Ange.'

'It's a bit late for your touching concern.'

'Look, Robert was in bits over it. I invited him to dinner, got him very drunk and came on to him like the Tasmanian she-devil. I practically trussed and bound and raped the bloke, to be honest. My date had blown me out and I was feeling vengeful towards men in general, while needing a bit of sexual reassurance.'

Angela wiped her face with the back of her hand. 'Then why,' she snivelled, 'didn't you hitch your skirt for passing lorry-drivers, like every other local tart? Or try a dildo?'

'I don't know, I really don't. Except, I didn't plan it. And Robert certainly never had it in mind.'

Angela grabbed the hanky off the kitchen table and blew her nose. 'The bloody swine! Telling me I was paranoid, going off on a tangent about Mum. He needn't think he'll get away with this, just because he's snuffed it!

I'll dig him up and have him cremated! He was always scared of naked flames. Wouldn't go near a barbecue or a bonfire in case a sausage exploded.' She choked on a harsh laugh that turned into a sob.

'I'll make you a sandwich,' offered Rachel. 'I'd be grateful for something to do, and if I know you, you won't bother to eat tonight otherwise.'

'Oh you *do* know me, that's the problem. You and him both. You risked jumping into the sack together because thick old Ange was so easy to fool.'

'It was never like that.'

Angela stood up, suddenly bereft of fight. She stumbled out of the kitchen and up the stairs to the womb-like sanctuary of her duvet, wrapping it round her and fattening its fourteen-tog cotton with her tears. If there was ever a time when she needed Conor McGinlay, this was it. Not so much to comfort her (after all, the whole fiasco didn't show either her marriage or her husband in a light that flattered her wifely qualities), as to remind her that she'd moved on, regained control of her life.

But as Rachel's confession had made clear, her comeback from Robert's death had been as brittle as the icing on Miss Havisham's wedding cake, nibbled away by the sharp teeth of self-deception until it finally crumbled to dust when the shutters were flung open on the truth. She'd never forgiven Robert for hiding something or herself for doubting him. How did you come back from that contradiction?

Still crying, she drifted off to sleep.

When she awoke, a cold toasted cheese sandwich stood on the bedside table, next to a cup of scummy tea. Her stomach rumbled its protest over her emotional objection to sustenance. A healthy appetite was hardly part of the pining process. After a moment's hesitation, she wolfed down the cold, greasy sandwich and lukewarm tea, perfectly spiked with just the right amount of sugar. Well, Rachel wouldn't neglect an intimate kindness like that, would she? The tears came again but this time, her mind worked in tandem with her swirling emotions.

Hobbling downstairs in the duvet with the dirty crockery, she switched on the kitchen light. Rachel, sitting at the kitchen table, lifted her hands against the blinding light.

'Why the fuck are *you* still here?'

'Don't laugh if I tell you,' replied Rachel in a furry voice.

Angela glared. 'It wasn't top of my agenda.'

Rachel shoved the whiskey bottle into the centre of the table. 'I was hoping, if I drank enough of this stuff, I could make myself cry.'

'So I'd feel sorry for you instead of wishing you dead?'

'No,' hiccuped Rachel regretfully. 'So I could feel as bad as I'm supposed to about betraying my best friend. But I can't. See, the mascara's still perfectly dry. You're right, I am a vapid human being. I couldn't even cry on cue if a funeral demanded it.'

'And that,' growled Angela, 'is supposed to excuse your total lack of morals? The old argument that predators can't help their characters?'

'Not at all,' sighed Rachel, her puffy face testament to her whiskey consumption. 'It's supposed to make you realise how lucky you are, Ange. Better to have loved and lost than never to have felt more than a collection of nerve-ends stimulated in the groin area, my only approximation to love.'

'Oh, get out!' roared Angela. 'I'm sick to death of your rational analysis of your alley-cat behaviour. And I don't care if you're so drunk, you crash the car on the way home, though you'd better hope I don't ring the plods and tip them off.'

'Consider me gone,' said Rachel with grave dignity and only swayed a little bit as she walked to the front door.

Chapter Twelve

Angela lay face down on her beach towel, heat buzzing in her ears. Above the rim of her sunglasses, balanced painfully on her blistered nose, she had an uninterrupted view of the beach. The pale yellow sand was mostly unpopulated and as flat as plaited rope, a heat haze thickening its surface and vapourising under orange and blue beach umbrellas. Angela squinted up at their own umbrella. The sun had edged round it, pouncing eagerly on her exposed back. She stood up to reposition her towel. 'The beach is the same colour as Rachel's hair,' she said deliberately invoking The Name to gauge Sadie's reaction.

'Hmm,' said Sadie non-committally, reading *Woman's Weekly* from her deck-chair, huddled against the umbrella pole. 'You want to be careful, Ange, or your shoulders will go the same way as your nose. Need more lotion?'

'So we can't mention her name? I was thinking, at least she had the guts to tell me face to face.'

'Only to get in her version before I dished the dirt,' snorted Sadie. 'The sun's softening your brain, lovey.'

'To err is human, to forgive divine, as you die-hard Christians never seem to say when put to the test,' sniped Angela controversially. Seeing her mother's face sag, she backtracked quickly. 'You're right of course, Ma, there are no extenuating circumstances.'

She flopped back on her towel in the shade. 'I hope I've got a job to go back to. This is my second week away in five months. Marla's none too impressed. I've had to volunteer to work lunch-hours into the millennium.'

'You're on a mission of mercy, taking your creaky-jointed mother to warmer climes,' flapped Sadie with her magazine. 'You know, like them artists who thought a nice, sunny holiday would cure their TB.' Best not to point out that it was in fact Angela's third holiday in five months, if she included the weekend in Curracloe.

Angela eyed her mother with new respect. It was Sadie who'd picked out the holiday in a brochure and avoided booking it at Hartley's.

Kalithea was fairly quiet in May. An island off Rhodes, its tourist trade was largely restricted to day-trippers who poured off a steamer and bought sponges in the quayside shops before grabbing a quick lunch in a waterfront cafe and reboarding the steamer. The action centred round the jetty, where smacks with painted prows bobbed on their moorings. Behind the vine-clad tavernas lay steep streets winding upwards between white, cubed houses towards a clifftop monastery.

Sadie and Angela had an apartment – three cool, whitewashed rooms – over one of the quieter harbourside tavernas.

Since their arrival two days earlier, they'd developed a routine. Mornings on the beach, lunch at the same taverna (Yanni gave them big helpings and a discount), then up to their rooms for a two-hour siesta, and down in the cool of the evening to take a leisurely stroll and eat dinner. Sadie was lapping it up. She'd been abroad before, on family holidays to the Costa del Sol when Angela and Owen were small. But here, she was in her element. For

one who feared enforced inactivity, the luxury of
unplanned hours filled her with a rich drowsiness, much as
the sunshine leaked into her joints, softening spiked ridges
of pain.

Angela, watching her mother blossom, felt the familiar
onset of guilt. She should've taken her away long before
now. Sadie, watching Angela prone in the shade, rejoiced
in her brainwave of this holiday. Now, if only everything
else went to plan!

Angela peered down the beach again. At its southern
tip, the white early afternoon steamer scraped between
the rocks towards its berth and began unloading its twice-
daily cache of crumpled visitors. A few, like Angela and
Sadie, had come to stay. The others were content to snap
photos of basking cats before fleeing to air-conditioned
hotels back on Rhodes.

The dedicated sun-worshippers turned at once to the
stone steps leading down to the beach. Angela peered past
them, searching for the flaking green railing of their
apartment balcony. She could just make it out if she
narrowed her eyes, and even discern the damp towels and
hand-washed shorts hung out to dry.

A couple advanced down the beach. The woman wore
a white halter-neck top, showing a bronzed midriff. Her
sun-whitened hair was whipped up like candyfloss. The
man wavered in the heat beside her, dressed too sensibly
in long trousers and a dark shirt that was bound to be a
sun-trap. He had reddish hair.

Angela smiled sadly and shut her eyes. She thought
about the moment she'd realised that she probably loved
Conor McGinlay right back.

It was on the drive back from Simonetti's in Curracloe.
She was watching him covertly from sleepy eyes, admiring
him like a sculpture, the way his arm muscles bunched
changing gear, and his hair curled so delicately around the

outer shell of his ear. Suddenly, he'd turned and smiled, catching her in the act of covert admiration. It was the smile he'd tried to dazzle the traffic warden with, outside the offices of *Goss!* But this time, its sweetness was instinctive, not manufactured. Her insides had contracted, her heart pounded in her ears. It was the feeling – part chemical, part physical and wholly indefinable – that she'd felt within minutes of meeting Robert. It was love. Probably.

She opened her eyes and saw that the couple weren't walking together, as she'd thought. Perspective had lent a false impression. The man was some way ahead of the woman, unconnected with her. He was Conor.

Angela shot upright on her towel, hauled up her costume straps and reached for the long T-shirt dress crumpled on the sand next to her. 'You!' she said furiously, scattering sand as she pulled it over her head. 'You set this up, Ma!'

'Did I?' Limp with relief that he'd come after all, Sadie turned a page.

'I told you not to ring him!'

'But you didn't tell *him* not to ring *me*.' Sadie was enjoying her upper hand. 'Now he's here, you'd better deal with it, don't you think?'

Conor ducked under the umbrella, scowling mightily with fear of rejection. 'Hello all. Come here often?'

Angela drank him in. She was getting used to interpreting his repertoire of defensive facial expressions, even after an absence of weeks. His presence was deliciously undeniable against a backdrop of sea, sea breeze and vibrant blueness. He was much browner than she was. His skin knew how to tan. 'What happened to your nose?' he asked abruptly, clearly thinking along the same lines.

Angela touched her pulsating beakiness, mortified.

'Tactful as ever. You can't have come all the way from New York to trade insults.'

'Haven't come from New York at all, you presumptuous gobbeloon of a woman. I'm back in Loxton, as I planned to be all along, and as I explained I would be in the note with my flowers. Didn't you get them?'

'Back to sell your house and collect the loot!' huffed Angela, stuffing things into her tap-dancing frogs bag. She was too excited to think positively. It was best to assume he'd come in person to deliver a shattering, final blow to her last vestige of hope. She felt Sadie's beady eye upon her and looked up, frowning.

'Yeah, Sadie told me you'd somehow found out about the house sale from a workmate who lives nearby,' growled Conor. 'Look, let's all go and eat.' He kicked the umbrella pole gently.

'You two go off and eat,' corrected Sadie in exasperation. 'Let's not pretend you don't have things to thrash out. I'll stay here with my fruit and bottled water. Where's Shane?'

'Taken a donkey ride up to the monastery,' grunted Conor, catlike eyes fixed on Angela.

She started. She hadn't taken Shane into the equation. 'It's Whitsun half-term,' shrugged Conor. 'I've done enough leaving him with Mrs Turner. Well?' His direct look challenged her. 'Shall we go?'

'Yes, yes, might as well hear what you've got to say this time.' She heaved a martyred sigh and shoved her feet into canvas flatties. 'If you need me, Ma, I'll be at the Fig-Leaf, two up from Yanni's place.'

Sadie waved her away, fearful and exhilarated. Oh please God, let her not blow it this time! Angela had gone out of her way to ignore him, and he'd still followed her here, taken the risk of looking a fool for love. The least she could do was listen to him. Sadie had listened when he'd phoned her from New York, and she'd believed every word.

Angela found a table in the shade. All of her felt red and raw next to Conor's brown smoothness. Prickly heat was already swelling on her collarbone. Under the table, cats twined round their ankles in the hope of scraps. She plunged her gibbon-like proboscis into a menu. 'Now then, Angela.' Gently and firmly, he plucked the menu from her hand. 'This isn't going to be like Simonetti's all over again, is it, with you being all aggressive and interrogating me?'

'I don't know, Conor, because you had things to confess that night. And it seems you've high-tailed it over here with a new batch of confessions.'

'You left me no choice, except to make the grand gesture. S'pose I could've waited till nightfall and shinned up your balcony with a rose between my teeth.'

'Oh great. That means Mum's told you where we're staying.'

Conor eyed her balefully. 'How long are you going to maintain this sniffy attitude? I'm supposed to believe that not one bone in your sexy body is secretly pleased to see me come running, cap in hand?'

'More like all guns blazing! I'm portrayed as the baddy in all this because I elected to get on with my life when you swanned off to New York, seeing fit to phone me a handful of times and then not at all.'

The waiter arrived. Angela asked for a Greek salad, unable to face grappling with a hearty meal. Conor messed around, asking in measured tones if the souvlaki was well done and the olives pitted, as if the preparation of his lunch was the only thing on his emptied, vacationing mind. This was a ploy, Angela knew, to seize the initiative by playing on her nerves.

'Look,' he said as the waiter left, 'it got nigh

impossible to ring you from Kate's and hold a private conversation, and as I ended up virtually working from her place…'

'Ever heard of a pay phone? Not that I cared.'

'Then I thought, sod Kate, and phoned you one Saturday night – only to find you weren't in.'

'Well, excuse me for having the temerity to get on with my life.'

'So I sent flowers,' he continued doggedly. 'I told you on the card that I'd be back within the next few weeks. I thought that would put your mind at rest.'

Angela could think of no logical reason for him to assume otherwise. 'Huh! The fact is, I didn't believe you'd be back for good. Especially when I found out you were selling up. Remember Rosie?'

Her name had an instant effect. He drew back from his earnest position of elbows on the table, eyes locked with hers. She distinctly heard his armoured shell click into place. A small arrow of panic pierced her superior coolness.

'I bumped into her at a party in Loxton. She was the one who told me you were selling up. *You* never mentioned it in your phone calls or floral tribute.'

'I didn't tell you because I knew you'd read between the lines of a few words scribbled on a card, and come up with a load of negative nonsense. I had to explain it all, face to face. I've sold up to give Kate her half and discharge my final responsibility towards her as my ex-wife. You could've trusted me for once, Angela.'

The tragedy in his voice upped her panic. She'd committed some irreversible *faux pas*, like the princess who has everything but still can't resist peeking in the forbidden room at the top of the tower. 'I don't understand,' she began crossly.

'I don't love Kate! I told you that in Ireland. For a

while there, I thought I'd have to shelve my own needs and look after her, because she's too unhappy to look after herself. I knew she was manipulating me, but I thought – wrongly – I could rise above it and care for her anyway. Only trouble is, I'm not St Francis of Assisi.'

Angela snapped a bread stick between shaking fingers. 'Hardly.'

'Every time I showed some independence, I knew she'd do some kooky, attention-seeking thing to pull me back into line. So I called her bluff. I told her I'd flog my precious house and give her half the money from the sale, and she could settle in Loxton or wherever she fancied. But I didn't love her, and I didn't want to live with her, in any capacity. And furthermore, Shane knows I don't love her. That was my trump card. She couldn't use Shane as her hold over me, because he knows the score. And anyway, by selling 23 Pacelli Road, I was giving her something she'd always wanted. The proof l care more about her than my silly house. I care what happens to her in the long-run. I'll do all I can for her. If nothing else, she needs the money for future medical bills, if she stays on the booze and in the States.'

Angela's prickly heat swelled. 'But Rosie said – she said you were fixated.'

'That's rich, coming from another prize head-case. I really do pick them.'

Angela traced her finger round a stain on the chequered oilcloth. Desperate to reclaim his good opinion, to pierce that armoured shell, she babbled her account of meeting Rosie at Pauline's – and hearing about the bedroom shrine, the lock of hair under his pillow.

'And you believed her?' Conor shook with hollow laughter. 'Didn't you stop to wonder how Rosie had such an intimate knowledge of my bedroom, when she'd never spent a night in it? Shane caught her in there one morning, going through Kate's stuff. She must've spun you her fantastic yarn as some sort of revenge. The woman's off-balance.'

'I see that now,' muttered Angela, deciding to keep quiet about her night in Rosie's flat. Off-balance or not, she'd been kind in her own way. Oh, why the hell were people so complicated? Compared to her, anyway.

'*Did* you try to get Kate back when she walked out on you?'

'Yes – once she let me know where she was. Rosie was right about one thing. I was still infatuated with Kate, long after the love died a natural death. I didn't want to give up on my marriage, after promising in public that I'd make it work for life. The sense of failure was driving me mad! Every time we spoke on the phone for about three months after she left, I'd drop "When are you coming back?" abruptly into the conversation, hoping to catch her off-guard. At first she got angry, then she started ignoring the question, and I gradually stopped asking it. I was getting used to life without her. And even liking it. There are compensations to losing your wife when your wife's an alcoholic whose drink dependency makes you feel so ruddy inadequate in the first place.' He looked at Angela. 'As far as I'm concerned, the ball's in your court now, Ange. I told you in Ireland that I loved you.'

Her heart soared, but she was still too unsure of herself to get carried away. 'That you *thought* you loved me. The hedge-betting of a sensible man, not a fool. And besides –' She hesitated, loath to mention Rosie again, but needing to get things off her chest, 'Rosie knew... things. In Curracloe, you told me you'd never articulated your past to a third party.'

'And I hadn't! Did she know Kate was a drinker?'

'Well, no, she never said...'

'All Rosie got were the bare bones of my marriage,

which she fleshed out with her imagination. If I'd told her
the whole story, she'd have realised that Kate and I were
finished for good. But I didn't give Rosie the whole story.
We never got that far in our relationship. And it would've
raised her expectations, unfairly.'

'Oh!'

'So come on, Angela. The boat leaves again in an hour
or so. Did I mention that Shane and I are staying back in
Rhodes? Say the word and I'll stay. Or tell me it's a waste
of time and there's too much baggage between us, and I'll
shove off for ever.'

'Wait!' she croaked in panic. 'That's not fair,
delivering ultimatums.'

'I think it's perfectly fair. I came all the way out here
to tell you how I feel about you. Affirmative action –
which isn't easy for me to take. Now put yourself on the
line. Tell me you love me too.'

Angela's panic mounted and with it, a dizzying sense of
speaking now or for ever holding her peace. She didn't
want him to get back on that steamer, simple as that. The
waiter plonked their meals in front of them. Conor picked
up his fork.

'Think about it over the meal.'

'I love you!' shouted Angela, startling the waiter and
the cats under the table. 'I love you and I don't want you
to get on the steamer. Is that enough?'

Conor McGinlay's nut-brown face split into a slow,
steady grin. 'It's a start.'

'Fancy Dad telling a whopper like that!' crowed Shane,
slathering honey over a wedge of fluffy white bread.
'Didn't know the old man had it in him. Getting back on
the steamer in an hour, indeed!'

Angela stared at the buttery knife left in the honey-pot.
Like Sadie, Shane had blossomed in the ripening heat.

His muddy hair looked thicker and glinted with gold highlights. His scrawny frame was browning nicely. They were having breakfast as a foursome in Angela's and Sadie's apartment.

Conor and Shane had pre-booked an apartment in a nearby street for the week. Conor had never had any intention of clearing off on the steamer. He'd used the threat of his departure to put teeth in his ultimatum. As he'd teased her over dessert in the Fig-Leaf: 'You didn't really think I'd shell out for a holiday and then flounce back to Rhodes to spend the rest of the week there in a deadly huff, without getting my money's worth here?'

Not that Shane and Sadie were privy to the reason for his lie – though Angela was pretty sure Sadie could work it out. One thing *was* clear to both mother and son. Angela and Conor were back 'on'.

'Shane,' said Conor through a mouthful of grapes. 'Tell Ange and Mrs F about the new house.'

'Oh yeah, like, it's a dump,' said Shane enthusiastically. 'Coming down with mildew, earwigs in the woodwork… Loads of potential, though,' he ended in a mumble, under the heat of Conor's glare. 'So Dad says anyway.'

'It's closer to Wilmesbury,' explained Conor, turning to include Sadie. 'Needs a lot doing to it, but that's right up my street. I was thinking, Mrs F, of converting the downstairs level for easy mobility, in case, you know, you ever wanted to visit and stay on for a bit.'

Sadie tried not to look too thrilled. 'It's very kind of you to think of me, Conor.'

'You two getting married and living with me in this show house, then?' demanded Shane. 'What?' he asked of his father's despairing expression. 'It wouldn't exactly be a shock, would it? And I'm only asking what everyone else is thinking.' He flung down his half-chewed bread. 'I'm honest, me.'

'Too honest for your own good,' concluded Conor, using paternal fierceness to avoid looking at Angela. She'd been strangely quiet since their arrival for breakfast. He hoped to God she wasn't going cool on her declaration of love.

She stood up abruptly, her gaze straying to the balcony where another perfect blue day beckoned. 'I think I'll go and finish my postcards out on the balcony. I'll be home before anyone receives them at this rate.'

Conor's wondering look strayed after her. Sadie stood up with almost sprightly ease and nodded at Shane. 'Conor, why don't you take your son off to the supermarket? I bet you haven't stocked up your apartment yet.'

While Sadie piled crockery, Conor's look stayed stubbornly fixed on Angela, who now leant on the balcony rail, apparently oblivious to the domestic bustle behind her.

'I thought we'd be eating out all the time,' Conor muttered belatedly to Sadie, with a mulish dislike of being humoured that made him look, suddenly, like Shane.

'You'll still need the basics. Be off with you now, the pair of you!' She looked steadily at Conor until his mouth quirked and his instinct told him that Sadie was trying to help – again.

'All right, you win. Come on, Shane.'

Shane's interest was guarded. 'Can I get Pop Tarts?'

'I'll let you know when I see them.'

They clattered out, Conor determined to make an exit that signalled his grasp of the subtleties of a mother–daughter hotline. Whatever was bugging Angela, maybe Sadie's instinct was right, and it was best left to maternal probing.

Sadie dragged a chair onto the balcony. Angela was slumped on a white iron garden chair that dwarfed the wobbly Formica table beside her. She'd spread her postcards into a peacock's fantail of rainbow colours on the table-top. She'd already told Sadie who she was sending them to. One for the girls at work, one for Magdalena at Hartley's and a couple of others she'd probably keep as souvenirs. Sadie looked down at the postcards. They were still blank. Angela stared out over the rooftops of Kalithea, chewing her pen. For once, reflected Sadie, she seemed genuinely preoccupied rather than ignoring her over-solicitous mother in the hope she'd go away.

'What's got into you, lovey? Conor's worried sick that you're having second thoughts.'

'Huh!' Angela looked round. 'No way. I'll have to talk to him about his fragile male ego. To be honest, I was wondering whether or not to send Rachel a postcard.'

'Oh,' sniffed Sadie. 'Well, of course, forgiving Rachel would be an act of Christian charity.'

'I've already forgiven her,' said Angela, to Sadie's amazement. 'The truth is, since I found out, I feel kind of at peace. I find, after thinking a lot about it, I don't hate her or Robert. She liberated me from torturous suspicion. And I can see she's an unhappy woman.'

'As far as I can see, the best thing is to cut her out of your life.'

Angla said slowly, 'No, I've turned my back on people who need me once too often. Maybe – maybe if I can rediscover the Rachel I knew and liked at school, before she got all hard about life, I can make up for – neglecting someone else. A stranger, someone I can't stop thinking about this morning.'

'Who?' asked Sadie, intrigued.

So, shutting her eyes briefly, Angela decided to go for confessional broke. She prepared to tell Sadie the ultimate thing, the thing she kept buried under all the other guilt, in a lead-lined box. She began to tell her about the girl on the Underground.

'She was the real reason I gave up working in London on *Woman Today*. It had nothing to do with being tired of London *per se*, or anything to do with Robert, just in case you thought he was a factor.'

'I never did,' put in Sadie defensively.

'Well, anyway, I was travelling home after working late one night. It had gone nine o'clock. There was no one else in the Tube compartment apart from this girl – well, girl hovering on being a woman. Pretty but plastered in make-up. She had a small suitcase. The man got on at Tufnell Park. He made straight for her, screaming, "You're coming with me, you bitch!" I could smell the drink off him from a foot away. I'll never forget the naked terror on her face. Or when she looked across at me and mouthed two words, "Help me!"'

Angela paused and avoided Sadie's eye, and her depth of attention.

'He held her by the hair until the next Tube stop,' she resumed. 'I caught his eye by chance and he yelled, "What're you looking at?" and I feared for my miserable, cowardly life. The Tube stopped and he grabbed her case and dragged her off by her roots while she screamed with the pain. I sat there, frozen, full of relief. Hurrah! Saved by the next stop! There were a few people on the platform, but they did nothing either; just another couple of crazies to side-step on the Underground. He dragged her off by her hair, and I just sat there.'

Sadie waited, but this was the end of a sparsely told story, minus the gorier details imprinted on memory. 'It wasn't just you,' she said gently. 'There must have been a few strapping blokes who could've gone to her aid.'

'But she spoke to *me*. And I looked away. I scuttled home to Robert and we rang the police to report an assault. A policeman with bum fluff came round and took a statement, said they'd pass it on to the Met. But it was too late by then. He'd probably done her in, or she'd taken an overdose. I know I'd have topped myself if I'd been in her shoes, and another woman looked the other way, left some brute to batter me into submission.'

'How could you have confronted him? He'd probably have attacked you, too.'

'I could've pulled the emergency cord! I could've – oh, I dunno. Anything but look the other way. What's that saying? All it needs for evil to triumph is for good men to do nothing. I had to give up my job,' she hurried on, forestalling her mother's next soothing platitude. 'The journey forced me to relive it every day, see her haunted face pleading with me every day. I couldn't cope.'

And then some. The Tube journey from work to Victoria had become unbearable, peppered with sweats, cramps, panic attacks. Her self-disgust was laced with different kinds of fear that she'd come face to face with either the man or girl-woman again. Her GP had told her she'd crack up if she didn't get counselling and change work locations. Afraid of being labelled an eggshell personality and, much worse, a bad Samaritan, she'd given in her notice, hinting only to Lazlo of a mini-breakdown caused by a personal nemesis.

'I meant to get a job locally,' she resumed. 'But it became easier and easier to hide away at home, and more and more difficult to face the world, which meant that counselling didn't get a look-in either. Because you're right, Ma, it wasn't just me. I kept asking myself, what sort of people are we all? Collective scum? The world looks such an ordinary place, but its very ordinariness is full of shadows. It's always the harmless-looking bloke who turns out to be the rapist or serial killer. The outwardly doting parent who shuts the garage door, turns on the car engine – and takes the kids along for the ride. The house was my refuge from all that tainted horridness.'

'Look, lovey. You acted – or failed to act – on the spur of the moment and lived to regret it. Then you sat at home, brooding over naturally depressing things, letting them swell out of all proportion to reality.'

'Robert said I'd used all my luxurious brooding time to build a case of adultery against him.'

Sadie looked uncomfortable. 'Well now, you said yourself, you've moved on from that. Rachel's confession means you don't have to wonder any more. One day soon, you'll be able to look back on the good times of your marriage, without a – a one-night stand getting in the way. My point is, there are as many examples of the kindness of strangers as there are of man's inhumanity to man.'

'Do you think so?' asked Angela thoughtfully. She'd already resolved to tell Conor – one day soon – about Robert and Rachel and, eventually, about the Underground girl. She'd suspected for a long time that Conor saw Robert as a husband beyond reproach, simply by virtue of having died young, and been retrospectively canonised by her. But she couldn't start her new life clinging to a lie about the old. And putting Conor right didn't mean assassinating Robert's character. It had been one lapse in a lifetime.

Sadie bent forward suddenly and wrapped her old, gnarled hands around her daughter's. Angela recoiled out of sheer habit, but in the next instant, relaxed and returned the pressure. Her mother's hands had a sure grip and resonated with the heat that they'd lapped up from the sun, lying in her lap as she sat on the balcony. The intensity of her touch, strong and yet almost impersonal, was a marvellous thing. Only a short time ago, before she was sure of Conor's love and had found the courage to declare her own, Angela couldn't have imagined sharing such an intimacy with her mother. She felt the pebbly little scree in her heart, marking the spot where her last secret had lain buried, skitter away and let in the sun.

'You and Conor can have a marvellous life together,' said Sadie. 'Ultimately, what happened to that poor woman was her own responsibility. Maybe someone did help her, outside the Tube station. We just don't know.'

'I suppose it's that collective responsibility thing,' sighed Angela. Robert had said the same sensible, placating things. 'You can't always walk by on the other side and leave it to someone else.' She was thinking, too, of Conor's responsibility to Kate. He wasn't abandoning her to fend for herself, like a domestic cat dumped in the wild. She could cope with the fact that he still cared about his ex-wife. It made him a better man to be all hers.

'I know you shouldn't always walk by, lovey. But you can't go on punishing yourself for past mistakes either.' Sadie smiled sadly. 'I speak from experience.'

They exchanged a look that bonded them in pure, unsullied mutual understanding. This moment may never come again, thought Angela, holding her mother's hands on the sunny balcony. Its rarity value makes it so special. I'll go back to being difficult, unpredictable Angela, and she'll go back to 'advising' me and driving me up the wall.

Sure enough, seconds later, the spell was broken by the slam of the apartment door and Shane yelling, 'Hi honeys, we're home.'

Sadie roused herself. 'I want to go and buy my own postcards.' She rose stiffly and looked down at Angela. 'I think you'll find someone's male ego needs reassuring. I'll rope in you-know-who for another expedition to the shops.'

'He won't like it,' smiled Angela. 'Shane's not daft.'

But he went out again with surprising compliance, promised all manner of bribes by Sadie.

'She's playing a blinder,' announced Conor, joining Angela on the balcony and stretching his arms. 'How much longer with the old quill and parchment?'

Angela looked down at the untouched cards. 'Nearly cracked it.'

He sat down abruptly on the chair vacated by Sadie. 'You're very strong and silent this morning, Angela. I hope you're not reneging on your feelings less than twenty-four hours after declaring them. Is it this?' He swept a brawny arm across the panoramic view from the balcony. 'You're afraid this setting might have duped you into a romantic outburst that won't stand the test of rainy Mondays back in Wilmesbury?'

'No, Conor, I'm not!' she said firmly, and surprised him by springing out of her chair and onto his lap. 'I have no second thoughts about anything.'

'So what did Sadie hang around to have words about?'

'Mysterious mother–daughter stuff.' She tapped his nose for nosiness.

'Yeah, so I gathered, but anything I should know about? She's just shoved off with Shane to give us a chance to have another heart-to-heart. Forewarned is forearmed and all that.'

'Suffice it to say that my little confab with Ma has no bearing on what I told you in the restaurant. It's not all that hush-hush either, and I'll tell you when I've finished smoothing your ruffled feathers.' She landed a quick kiss on his nose. 'But you'll have to get used to me being strong and silent some mornings. I'm just not the world's best morning person. Think you can live with it?'

His face softening with relief, he tightened his arms around her. 'I suppose I could give it a try. Give us a kiss first to see if it's worth it.'

His mouth swooped down on hers without warning, his sun-thickened stubble tickling her. Grinning, she kissed him back with hope, fervour and anticipation.

'*Shall* we get married?' he asked eventually, almost lazily. 'I assume you realise I'd bought the new house for us, the odd family as opposed to the odd couple. You, me, the child from hell and the mother the twentieth century forgot. What do you think?'

'I don't know,' replied Angela breathlessly. 'Kiss me again, McGinlay, to help me make up my mind.'

He obliged her. He was spreading the vista of a shared future before her. For now, she was content to lay her head on his broad shoulder, and contemplate the vision that shimmered and danced, close enough to touch, in the morning unfolding around them.